# Twylite

# Twylite

*Rhonda M. Lawson*

www.urbanbooks.net

Urban Books, LLC
97 N18th Street
Wyandanch, NY 11798

ISBN 13: 978-1-60162-408-6
ISBN 10: 1-60162-408-5

First Trade Paperback Printing April 2014
Printed in the United States of America

10 9 8 7 6 5 4 3 2 1

*This is a work of fiction. Any references or similarities to actual events, real people, living or dead, or to real locales are intended to give the novel a sense of reality. Any similarity in other names, characters, places, and incidents is entirely coincidental.*

Distributed by Kensington Publishing Corp.
Submit Wholesale Orders to:
Kensington Publishing Corp.
C/O Penguin Group (USA) Inc.
Attention: Order Processing
405 Murray Hill Parkway
East Rutherford, NJ 07073-2316
Phone: 1-800-526-0275
Fax: 1-800-227-9604

# Dedication

To the women and men who suffer silently for fear of showing weakness. We are strong today because of your strength. Never let anyone forbid you from shining your light on the world!

Please know that the author is writing from the perspective of front-line service in the war against sexual violence. I had the distinct privilege of working with Rhonda when she served as a sexual assault victim advocate for the soldiers of the 2d Infantry Division in Korea. She handled some of our most challenging and heart breaking situations with great compassion, tremendous competence and unflagging courage. Her narrative is compelling because she has been there.

—Dan Silvia, Sexual Assault Response Coordinator:
Camp Casey, Korea

# Acknowledgments

Writing *Twylite* has been a true labor of love. I worked as a sexual assault victim's advocate for a year, and it was one of the most challenging things I had ever done. From offering strength even when you feel weak, to the struggle to not give advice even when you know in your heart that it is needed, but not wanted, to the silent groans when someone sees you approaching, VAs can often be underappreciated and misunderstood.

It was my goal with this book to bring to light an issue that not many people talk about. When we hear about rapes in the news, many of us shake our heads, mumbling how much a shame it is. Yet, how often do we think of the young woman, or in some cases young man, who must live with the aftereffects of the crime? What's more, what do the people who are charged with helping them through the process go through?

Writing this book brought back the memories of the young ladies I tried to help when I was a victim's advocate. As I crafted Twylite's story, I thought about those ladies and the challenges they faced. They each had different experiences, but the inner turmoil they went through was similar. And, although *Twylite* isn't based on any of those ladies, I hope they know that I heard them, and understood their pain.

To help me tell this story, I brought back two of my most popular characters. Many of you may remember Isis from my second novel, *A Dead Rose*. Having gone through her own troubles with men, she was the perfect person to really see through Twylite's pain and help her find herself. Alexis, whom you got to know through *Cheatin' in the Next Room, Putting It Back Together*, and *Some Wounds Never Heal,* had also had her negative experiences with relationships, and provided the perfect glue to bring both Isis and Twylite full circle.

There was no way I could have written this book by myself. A special thanks goes to my Sigma brother, De Moe, a police officer from Chicago, who read some of my chapters and was never shy about letting me know when I was off base. A thank-you also goes to my friend and former battle-buddy Rick Lewis, a police officer in Georgia, who sent me his much-needed input as well. I would also like to thank Dan Silvia, my advisor when I was a victim's advocate in Korea. As I wrote this book, I could hear his voice in my ear as he helped me to work through my cases.

I would be remiss if I didn't send special thanks to my literary family. Lisa Dumas Harris, thanks for dragging me off to Starbucks to get a kick start on finishing this book! William Frederick Cooper, you pop up every now and then in my life, but you always have a positive word to say. Thank you for that. Fred Williams and Toschia, thanks for your encouragement and friendship. I wish I could be there with you to make Divine Literary Publishing the success that I know it will be. My editor, Carla Dean, thanks for helping to bring my written words more depth. My agent, Portia Cannon, thank you for keeping me grounded when I was ready to fly through the roof. It takes a special blessing to have the level head that you possess, and I appreciate all you've done for me.

Other thanks go to my Facebook group, "Friends of Author Rhonda M. Lawson." Thank you for all of the provoking conversation, and for your help in writing my book. You may not have known you were helping, but you definitely were! To New Movement Bookclub in Richmond Hill, GA, you ladies and gentlemen are awesome! You can analyze a book six ways from Sunday, and I love it! Brian W. Smith, my friend, fellow Kennedy Cougar, and brother of the written word, all I can say is thanks. You know what for. To the authors I have yet to meet but have loved your work, thanks for setting the example for what real writing is all about. It's not a side hustle, it's not a hobby. This is our lives! There are so many other people I can name, but I know I can't, so I'm going to thank you all and wish God's blessing on all of you!

Lastly, I can't end this without thanking my biggest fans—my family. My wonderful parents, my loving sister, promoter aunt, my cousins, and uncles, you all have played an integral part in my career. Thank you for keeping me motivated! To my sisters of the Order of the Eastern Star, I am so glad to be connected with you and I may not say it enough, but I love you dearly. To my Sorors of Zeta Phi Beta Sorority, Inc., thanks for keeping the fire burning! And, most importantly, to my readers. Without you, there is no reason for me to write. Thank you for telling me when you loved my work, and gently critiquing me when you didn't! You are the reason I strive to get better with every book, and I hope I didn't let you down this time!

So, until the next story, which is coming soon, I wish you peace, blessings, and literary happiness. Stay in touch through Facebook "Friends of Author Rhonda M. Lawson," Twitter @MsLawson, my Web site, www.rmlawson.com, or just shoot me an e-mail at rhondamlawson@hotmail.com. I love hearing from you!

# Prologue

The darkness made the trees look like threatening giants standing guard over her, ensuring she wouldn't or couldn't run. Twylite's head bopped mindlessly to Trey Songz's "Bottoms Up" as she scanned her surroundings while thinking of a way to escape this mess she'd gotten herself into.

She couldn't for the life of her find the logic in getting into Peanut's car. Her first mind had told her to keep walking when she saw his forest green BMW pull next to her. She was just trying to get home. Her English paper was due Monday, and she was supposed to be going to choir rehearsal tonight for the first time in weeks.

Common sense had told her that nothing good could come of this meeting. After all, she'd broken up with him more than two weeks ago. It wasn't an amicable breakup, and it ended with a barrage of curses being thrown at her, topped with a promise that she would be nothing but a book-smart ghetto bitch without him. She shot back that his old ass needed to find a woman his own age and leave her alone. She would be just fine without him.

Now here he was, popping out of the blue without so much as a text in the last two weeks. Here he was smiling in her face like nothing had ever happened, beckoning Twylite to get into his car.

And she did it.

Despite the voice in the back of her mind screaming, *no,* she did it.

She had to admit that he did look good. His looks and car had always made Twylite the envy of her all-girls school. Tonight, his hair looked as if it had been freshly faded. That, along with the diamond rock in his ear, made his dark skin look smooth and sexy. He wore a light sweater and a pair of baggy jeans, a sensible outfit for the cooling weather. It was August, but it was still fairly warm. Even now, it wasn't cold, but the breeze had caused the sun to give way to what her mother liked to call "jacket weather."

"How you been?" he asked as he drove down Chef Menteur Highway toward the bridge. He glanced at her quickly, and smiled as he turned his attention back to the road.

"I'm good," she mumbled, staring out of the window.

He pushed a little harder. "Did I tell you how good you look in dat uniform?"

She looked down at the pleated blue, white, and gold checked skirt, the main staple in her Saint Francis Academy uniform, and mumbled, "Thanks."

She wondered if the education she received at the historic New Orleans high school was worth the reputation every girl who went there received. Everyone thought the SFA girls were just a bunch of wild girls incapable of being tamed by the nuns who taught them. Twylite was no angel, but she knew she'd never done anything to earn such a badge, so she refused to wear it. While other girls enjoyed hanging out in their uniforms, she always went straight home and changed, which was what she should have been doing now instead of mentally struggling through this situation.

What did Peanut want? She knew he hadn't picked her up just for a little small talk. He wasn't even saying anything, which made Twylite even more nervous. He kept giving her these sideways glances. Something was definitely on his mind, but she couldn't figure out what.

Red flags waved violently as Peanut pulled into a wooded area. *Stupid!* She'd been so consumed with her own thoughts that she hadn't paid any attention to where he'd taken her. Now here she was, stuck in the woods trying not to look scared out of her mind.

She looked over at Peanut, who had shifted his position so he leaned against the driver's door while staring at her. One of his feet rested on the gear shift, which sat between them. Why did he keep looking at her like that? His eyes displayed a curious mixture of anger and tenderness. He sat quietly.

Watching her.

Could he smell her fear?

"Why you bring me here?" Twylite asked, shifting her own position so she could look him in the eyes. She refused to let her nerves betray her. She would never again let him have power over her.

He didn't reply, just stared at her.

His silence fueled her anger. "Did you hear me, boy?" she demanded. "I don't have time for this, now. I got a paper to write. I got stuff I gotta do."

"Girl, calm your ass down," Peanut said, seemingly unfazed by her display. "You'll be home soon enough. Lemme just talk to you for a minute."

"Then talk."

He rolled his eyes and pursed his lips. "This is what I be talkin' 'bout. Dat damned mouth of yours is gonna get your li'l ass in trouble one day."

Twylite's face softened. Her irritation only made matters worse. "Peanut, please, can you take me home?"

"You ready to be my woman again?"

She should have known that was what this ride was all about. "Peanut, ain't nothin' changed in the last two weeks. I meant what I said."

"Stop tryin'a be hard, Twy," he said with a dry laugh. He leaned forward and ran his fingernails softly across her breasts. The motion used to send tingles through her spine, but now all it did was make her shudder with revulsion. "You made your point. I was wrong, now let's get on with our business."

She brushed his hand away and glared at him. "You never did take me seriously, did you? I said I ain't changin' my mind."

"Who you talkin' to like dat?" he asked, wincing at her boldness. He leaned forward again. This time, he grabbed her left breast. "I told you about dat mouth before."

Twylite tried to lean away from him but the passenger door blocked her escape. A quick glance out of the window told her that no one would come to her rescue, and her wooden guards were still on duty. She looked back at Peanut, and begged him to let her go. His clutch tightened, drawing tears to the corners of her eyes. She tried with everything she could not to let them fall.

"You act like you forgot everything I did for you," Peanut snarled. He let go of her breast and shoved his hand under her white button-down blouse. He moved closer to her, kneeling on the console between them. When he bumped his head from sitting too high, he held her down and moved onto the seat with her. In one move, he reached down and moved her seat back so he lay on top of her.

"Peanut, what are you doing?" Twylite screamed, using what little leverage she had to beat on his chest. She knew he wouldn't move, but she had to try. Part of her mind wanted to believe that he wouldn't take her sex by force. He was only trying to scare her. He cared too much for her to hurt her, didn't he?

His left hand joined his right under Twylite's shirt and gave her a painful massage. His full weight was now on top of her. There was no way she could move, let alone run. "I made you what you are. It wasn't for me, you would be just another plain-ass bitch in the ghetto. A cute-ass uniform with nappy-ass hair. You wouldn't know your pussy from a hole in a wall if it wasn't for me, and now your stuck-up ass thinks you can leave without so much as a thank-you?"

Now, he was beginning to scare her.

"Kiss me," he told her, his hands violently rubbing her breasts.

She turned her head, afraid to see the fire in his eyes. This was a mess she wouldn't be able to talk her way out of. And judging from the grip he had on her, she wouldn't be able to fight, either.

"Peanut, please let me go," she whimpered, tears beginning their descent across her cheek.

"Please?" he sneered. "Where dat shit come from? You had all that mouth earlier and now you wanna say 'please'?"

"I'm sorry," she whispered, her head still turned. She never thought she would think it, but she really wanted her daddy right now. He would kill Peanut for the way he was treating her.

"The fuck you sorry for? You meant dat shit. Now if you don't kiss me I'ma give your ass something to cry about!"

She tried to wriggle free once she felt his crotch rub up against hers. She couldn't believe that very action used to turn her on. Now it only felt like denim scratching against her privates, protected only by a cotton barrier.

She turned her face toward him in the vain hope that a kiss would make him soften his grip on her. He didn't even wait for her to pucker; he just dived in, kissing her like he was sucking on a T-bone. Her face felt wet with his saliva.

"Stop, Peanut," she cried. "I'll do whatever you want. Just please let me go."

"I told you what I want." He stuck his tongue in her ear, prompting her to jerk away. He looked surprised. "The fuck you pullin' away for? Your ass used to beg me to do dat. You really do think you're too good for me now, huh?"

Twylite longed to wipe off her wet face and rid her ear canal of the pool she felt inside of it, but she still couldn't move. All she could do was slightly shrug her shoulders and sigh. "I don't think that. I just need to concentrate on school. I'm going to college next year."

"What dat gotta do wit' me?"

"Peanut!"

He let one of her breasts go and reached down under her skirt, softly rubbing the crotch of her panties. "You savin' this young pussy for one of those college boys?"

"No, Peanut, it's not like that," Twylite pled.

"Then what is it?" he demanded, his finger wiggling around the cotton shield.

She opened her mouth, and then closed it just as quickly. This just wasn't the right time to tell him he was controlling, and that her mother had finally convinced her that he was too old for her. That she was tired of him yelling at her, of him snatching her around. Her daddy had seen him snatch her the last time and swore he would kill Peanut if it ever happened again. He would have shot him then had his gun been in reach.

"You can't say shit now, huh?" Peanut mocked, his index and middle fingers jamming themselves inside of her. "All dat mouth earlier, and now you can't say shit."

Anger began to rise inside of Twylite's stomach with each thrust. She didn't know if she was angrier at Peanut for what he was doing, or at herself for showing him fear and yielding her power. She couldn't believe she had even loved him. How could she love someone who could treat her this way? Was she just blinded by his money, car, and status?

"Get off of me!" she yelled, the anger boiling over. Rage had overtaken her. She wasn't about to let this thug of a man manhandle her anymore. It had finally hit her that he was only acting like this because she'd let him for so long. Well, not this time. She snatched her free arm from under Peanut's body and did her best to smack some sense into his head. "Bastard, I said let me go."

The initial shock from Twylite's slap momentarily froze Peanut in his tracks. But the shock quickly wore off and gave way to rage. He snatched his hand from between her legs, his nails scraping some of her sensitive skin. Before she could move, he grabbed her by the throat.

"Bitch, you lost your mind?" he growled, squeezing her breast with one hand and her throat with the other. His smile grew as a tear streamed down Twylite's cheek and touched his fingers. "Don't fuckin' cry now. You wanna be woman enough to hit a man, you best be woman enough to take this ass whuppin'."

"You gonna hit me?" Twylite croaked, refusing to back down. She tried using her free hand to pry his fingers open, but she only succeeded in scratching them. Still, she refused to show any more fear. She couldn't let him win this time. "Just 'cause I don't want your ass?"

Peanut's smile widened. "Yeah, dere go dat mouth."

He finally let go of her breast and grabbed her braids, pulling her head toward the passenger door. "So you just all that now, huh? Shoutin' at me, hittin' on me. I don't know why you think it's just gonna be that easy to walk away from me. I done told your ass, I made you, bitch. You leave when I dismiss you, no sooner, no goddamn later."

"So I'm your slave now?"

Instead of answering, Peanut eyed her as he unlocked and opened the passenger door. He finally let go of her throat, but before she could breathe a sigh of relief, he grabbed her by the shirt and dragged her out of the car. He pushed her down and stood over her. "Get up!"

"You just pushed me down, Peanut," Twylite croaked, still panting as she breathed the warm August air. Her white shirt was now crumpled and stained with mud and leaves. She rose to her knees, still weak from the pain her former boyfriend had subjected her to.

"I said get your ass up." He paced back and forth, his anger obviously getting the best of him. "Young-ass bitch think she can just talk to me any kinda way. I run these goddamn streets. You do what I fuckin' say. Now get your dumb ass up."

Twylite rose slowly and faced Peanut. Her body ached. She was sure she looked like living hell. Something in the back of her mind told her this might be a long night. Her parents were sure to be looking for her. She hadn't heard her cell phone ring, but who would hear Rihanna's "Rude Boy" on her ring tone over the noisy rap music blaring from Peanut's speakers? She could still hear Nicki Minaj rapping about making someone's bed rock although Peanut had slammed the car door shut when he pushed her down.

Maybe if she could just reason with him, he'd calm down and realize the error of his ways. "Peanut, baby, you need to calm down. I can't talk to you when you get like this."

He shot her an evil glare as he continued to pace. "Oh, so now I'm baby, huh? Not even ten minutes ago, I was all kinds of bastards."

He'd finally stopped pacing. Twylite wondered if he'd begun to calm down as she watched him fold his arms and look into the starry sky. She decided to push a little to make sure.

"Peanut, I love you," she said slowly. "I really do. But I really have to concentrate on school. My momma's talkin' about not lettin' me get a car after graduation if my grades aren't where they're supposed to be. She said she didn't spend all that money for me to go to Saint Francis's just to mess around with you."

It was only a half truth, but desperate times called for desperate measures. She needed to get him to soften up just enough for her to get home without the situation getting worse. She had no idea how she would explain her dirty clothes, but she'd worry about that later. Right now, it was time to put a plan into action.

She leaned against the car and looked down at her feet. "Baby, I really wanna be with you. I just can't."

"Be with me then," he said softly, walking toward her. He wrapped his arms around her waist and pulled her toward him. She knew what would come next, but before she could roll her eyes in disgust, he kissed her again. His kisses were far from tender; they felt desperate, as if he was trying to force her to be in the mood. She'd have to pretend to be. It was her only hope to get out of this without more injury.

She moaned, feigning pleasure, and unbuttoned her top button. He took it as an invitation and tore her shirt apart, hungrily plunging his face into his bosom. Her mother was going to kill her.

*Think, Twy!*

She could kick him and run, but where the hell would she go out in these woods? She didn't even recognize the area. Maybe she could try getting away from him long enough to jump in the car and leave him there. After all, he had left the keys in the starter.

"Slow down, baby," she whispered. "This shirt is jacked up now."

Peanut's kisses were relentless. He began unbuttoning his jeans. "I'll buy you another one."

He reached under her skirt and tried to tear off her panties, but the cotton material refused to give. Instead, he tried snatching them down, but scratched her hip.

"Ouch!" she screamed. This was not what she'd bargained for. "Peanut, stop."

"What?" he asked, looking confused. "It was just a scratch."

"Peanut, take me home," she grumbled, pulling together what was left of her shirt. This wasn't the plan, but a little attitude always worked, and she wouldn't have to give up any sex. "This shit ain't workin'."

"What?"

She tried opening the passenger door, but Peanut slammed it shut again.

"Where you think you're goin'?" The glare had returned to his eyes.

She looked at him as if he'd lost his mind. "Where you think? You're taking me home. I come out in the middle of nowhere with you, knowing my momma and daddy are gonna whip my ass when I get home, and all you did tonight was fuck me up. You fuckin' choked me, pushed me down, and scratched me up. What more do you want? I tried to push that aside and let us be together, but this shit ain't workin'."

She tried to reach for the door handle again, but Peanut didn't budge. She groaned. "Come on, now. Take me home."

"I ain't takin' you no-muthafuckin'-where," he growled. "You gonna stay here and finish what you started. You trying to use pussy control over Peanut? I'm the one taught you how to use your pussy in the first place, and now you gonna try to use it against me?"

Before Twylite could reply, he grabbed her hair and forced her back to the ground. With a death grip on her braids, he used his free hand to push down his jeans and boxer briefs. "Now, you got all dat mouth? Use it then."

She lifted her tear-filled face to him and pleaded for him to stop, but he jerked her hair toward him, bringing her face to face with his manhood. "Bitch, you don't get to suckin', I'm gonna mess dat pretty face up."

"Peanut, stop," she begged, but before she could get out another word, she felt lightning strike her left cheek. It hurt so badly that she could coax no sound from her mouth. All she knew was that she didn't want a repeat performance. Without another word, she leaned in and did as she was told.

His orgasm took forever to come, but when it did, he held her hair tighter, forcing her to swallow his seed. Once he finished, he pulled her up and bent her over the hood of the car. Her tears seemed to mean nothing to him. He went deaf to her screams.

"Please, Peanut," she begged again. "This hood is hot."

"You don't like this?" he asked, snatching down her panties. He scratched her again, but Twylite didn't seem to feel it. She refused to believe she was being violated in such a way. All these months of giving it to him whenever he wanted it, and it had to end like this.

He finally let go of her hair once he forced himself inside of her. He grabbed her wrists and pulled back on them, allowing him to go harder and deeper. Was he laughing at her screams?

"Tell me you like this shit," he demanded, continuing to pull her wrists back. When she didn't reply, he repeated his command more forcefully, pushing himself as far as he could inside of her. "You used to beg for this. Come on, lemme hear it again."

"Give it to me," Twylite whimpered. Her request sounded nothing like passion, but it still seemed to turn on her boyfriend-turned-assailant.

"Say it like you mean it, baby!" he said. "Louder."

"Give it to me!" she shouted, more out of pain than pleasure. Actually, this was absolute torture. *How can someone who claims to love you turn around and treat you this way?*

He let go of one of her arms and bent her leg so it lay on the hood. This allowed him to go even deeper, continuing the torture. Twylite knew that begging wouldn't stop him, and she had no strength to play tough. All she could do was bury her face in the bend of her free elbow. If her body couldn't escape, maybe her mind could.

# Chapter One

Twylite stared at Dr. Duplessis's office door, wondering whether she should knock or run. Dr. Duplessis had been her doctor for the last six years, and was like a big sister. They could talk about anything, and sometimes Twylite would hang out at her office even when she didn't have an appointment.

She wasn't sure if she wanted anyone to know what had just happened to her, but Dr. Duplessis seemed to be the safest bet. The doctor wouldn't judge her. Although she would be disappointed in her, she wouldn't yell at her like her momma and daddy would. Speaking of her parents, how was she going to call them? Her backpack was still in Peanut's car.

How could he rape her and then leave her like that? Had it not been for the cab in the Winn-Dixie parking lot a mile away, she didn't know how she would have gotten to the doctor's office. Aside from a couple of dollars for the city bus, she had absolutely no money. It had to be only the grace of God that allowed the cabbie to drive halfway across the city without asking for anything in return. Then again, only a heartless monster would look at a teenage girl wearing shredded clothing and not take her to get help. At least she wanted to think that.

Now here she was, so close, yet so far. She stood at the door, afraid to knock. Afraid to face the truth. Afraid to recount what had happened nearly an hour and a half ago. She pulled at her torn shirt, trying her best to keep herself covered.

"Stop being stupid and just open the door," she told herself quietly. "Get some damned help!"

She shook her head. It was almost eight o'clock. There was no chance that Dr. Duplessis could still be at work that time of night. Maybe she'd just go home and face the music.

Voices.

They came from the other side of the door.

The doctor was there after all.

Suddenly, panic struck. Her mind was being made up for her way too fast. She still hadn't convinced herself that she was ready to talk to anyone, but soon someone would take one look at her and ask what happened. She wanted to run, but her weakness wouldn't allow it. Instead, it turned her feet into lead, keeping her planted in that hallway, leaning and sobbing against the wall.

The voices had reached the hallway. Two women were laughing, but within seconds the laughing stopped.

"Twylite?" a voice asked.

She knew it was the doctor, but she couldn't answer. She tried, but only louder sobs surfaced.

Someone touched her shoulders, but she snatched away as if the lady's fingers were made of white-hot steel.

"Baby? You okay?" an older woman's voice asked.

Twylite was sure that voice came from Dr. Duplessis's nurse, Ms. Kay, but she couldn't bring herself to look up. Neither woman said anything for a minute. She guessed they were standing there, watching her, wondering what they should say.

"Twylite, sweetie," Dr. Duplessis beckoned, gently pulling her by the shoulders. Twylite snatched away again, but the doctor was undeterred. She guided her into the office anyway. "Come sit down and talk to me."

Twylite did as she was told, but kept her head down and face covered, afraid of what she would reveal if she looked Dr. Duplessis in the eyes. She hadn't even looked in the mirror. It wasn't hard to know that her once-pretty face was now beaten, burned, and tearstained. Why look at something like that?

Dr. Duplessis guided her to the sofa in her waiting room. Twylite's hands remained over her face. She knew she couldn't hide her wounds forever, but she would delay the inevitable for as long as she could.

"Ms. Kay, can you get her a cold drink or something?" Dr. Duplessis asked. "Twylite, you want something to drink?"

She shook her head no and continued sobbing.

"Baby, what happened to your clothes?" Ms. Kay asked. "What happened to you?"

Twylite sighed and uncovered her face. The moment had come. Both women gasped and covered their mouths when they took in the horror that had overtaken the young girl's beauty.

"Twylite, baby, who did this to you?" Dr. Duplessis asked, nearly shouting her words. "I should have known something was going on. You standing in the hall crying with your clothes all torn and dirty. Have you been to a hospital?"

Ms. Kay turned to her, concern etched into her eyebrows. Dr. Duplessis rolled her eyes and shook her head.

"What am I saying?" she asked, smacking her forehead. "Of course you have. That's why you're here. I'm a doctor. You're in my office."

"Doctor," Ms. Kay stated, grabbing her shoulders gently. "Calm down. You ain't gonna be a bit of help to anybody, you keep acting like this."

The older nurse turned to Twylite, who had begun crying again. "Where are your parents?"

Twylite shrugged. "I guess they're at home. I can't call them because Pea . . ." She stopped just short of saying

Peanut's name. Would he come after her if he knew she'd told people what he did? What if her momma gave her the beat down of her life for even putting herself into this position by getting into his car?

"Why can't you call them, baby?" Ms. Kay asked. She looked at her carefully, the concern growing deeper in her brow. "Everything all right at home?

"Oh, yes," Twylite said quickly. She hadn't meant to insinuate that her parents had anything to do with this. The tears trailed down her face once again as she turned to Dr. Duplessis. "Can you please call them for me?"

Without a word, the doctor rose and walked to the phone on the receptionist's desk. Quiet overcame them as she went through the Rolodex on the desk. Once she located the number, she quickly dialed and picked up the receiver.

"Mr. Knight?" she asked, her voice scratchy. She turned away and cleared her throat before announcing, "Your daughter Twylite is in my office."

She placed her head down as she listened. Twylite was sure he was yelling into the phone, demanding that he be told what was going on.

"Sir, I haven't done anything with her just yet, as she hasn't told me what happened, but I do believe you should get over here as soon as possible. And, Mr. Knight, can you call the police? From the looks of things, this is a very serious matter."

Twylite felt her heart would beat right through her chest when she heard Dr. Duplessis mention the police. Soon, everyone would know that she was stupid enough to get herself raped by her older ex-boyfriend. Her parents, a deacon and deaconess at Greater Zion Baptist Church, would have to face the embarrassment of explaining this to Pastor Coleman, and having a bunch of nosey members disguised as well-meaning sisters and brothers ask them if poor little Twylite was doing okay. She could just hear it now:

*"I saw Twylite the other day. Her face didn't look too good. How she holdin' up?"*

*"Did they catch that boy who did that to her?"*

*"You should make sure she ain't pregnant. You'd hate for her to have to raise a baby born outta this situation."*

"Mr. Knight, she looks pretty bad," Dr. Duplessis continued. "I normally wouldn't do this without you being here, but I would really like to do a SAFE kit as soon as possible on her. If I can get your permission to examine her without a parent escort, I can have Ms. Kay accompany me. That way when the police get here, we can turn the evidence over to them right away."

"She's holding up under the circumstances," she said after a few seconds. "She's pretty shaken up. Um, Mr. Knight, I'd like to go ahead and get started on her. I'll fill you in on everything else when you get here. Don't forget to bring her a change of clothes."

Once she finally got Mr. Knight off the phone, she turned to Twylite and took a deep breath. "Twylite, I'm going to give you an exam. I don't know what happened, but I have a feeling. I'll wait for your parents to get here to ask you what happened. I don't want you to have to relive this any more than you need to."

"Doctor, are you going to be okay to do the exam?" Ms. Kay asked. She sat next to Twylite, rubbing her shoulders to console the tears away, but her eyes bore into her boss.

"I'm fine. What's important is making sure Twylite is okay." She turned toward the teenager sitting in a ball on the sofa next to her nurse. "Twylite, can I do an examination on you?"

Twylite looked up, fear decorating her eyes. "What kind of exam?"

"I don't know what exactly happened, but I think you were raped. This exam is called a sexual assault forensics exam. It will help us to collect evidence if you want to press charges."

"Press charges?" Twylite repeated, her eyes widening. It was already starting.

"You do want whoever did this to you to be punished, don't you?" Ms. Kay asked, patting her shoulder reassuringly.

Twylite hesitated, wrestling with whether she was ready to send Peanut to jail. Yes, he'd raped her, but deep down he had to be sorry, right? But then again, how could anyone rape the woman he loved and leave her on the side of the road like that?

Dr. Duplessis shook her head. Twylite could see the doctor's hands tense into fists, and then loosen. Anyone else probably would have missed the slight action, but Twylite had known her too long. She was pissed, but struggled not to show it.

"Twy, I know you're not considering letting this man continue to walk the streets after what happened," the doctor said, her voice shaky. "I love you like my little sister, and I refuse to let you do that."

Twylite sighed, knowing Dr. Duplessis was right. Besides, what harm could come out of getting the exam? At least she could get cleaned up. "What happens in the exam?"

Dr. Duplessis smiled slightly, relaxing her shoulders. She nodded at Ms. Kay, who tapped the girl's thigh and helped her up.

"Come on in the examining room and I'll explain it to you," Ms. Kay said as she led the girl toward the back.

# Chapter Two

Once alone, Alexis paced back and forth in the waiting room, finally letting the tears fall. She could no longer hold them back, so she was relieved when Twylite finally agreed to the exam.

She'd known Twylite Knight since she was eleven years old. Her parents were one of the few families who followed Alexis when she decided to open her own practice after Hurricane Katrina. Over the years, she and Twylite had grown close. She was even considering giving the girl a job as a part-time receptionist.

Never had she expected what she'd seen tonight. Up until now, the only thing Alexis had seen on Twylite's face was a smile wider than the Greater New Orleans Bridge.

It had to be that boy she was sneaking around with. She'd seen him a couple of times when he dropped Twylite off at the hospital. He always seemed a little too clingy for her taste. And she wasn't sure how old he was, but he looked too old for an impressionable teenager like Twylite.

Even his mannerisms indicated that he'd seen a lot more in life than Twylite had. She got excited about things that he felt were no big deal. Many times she would complain that they never did the things that many of her girlfriends did, like going to movies, dances, or even Burger King to hang, like he was above such things. Where she seemed happy and excited, he was stoic. Yet, when she would leave him, he would pull her by the waist and kiss her like she was a grown woman.

*"I don't like dat boy,"* Mrs. Knight commented to Alexis. *"I know she done slept wit' him. Let my chile come up wit' a STD one time, and I'ma shoot his dick off myself!"*

*Alexis thought it strange that Mrs. Knight didn't seem as concerned about Twylite getting pregnant, but she tried not to let on. Instead, she just nodded and lifted her eyebrows in agreement. But she nearly choked on her Diet Pepsi when she heard Mrs. Knight's next statement.*

*"Maybe you could talk to her, Docta Duplessis, 'cause she sho as hell ain't listenin' to me and her daddy,"* she said, a glimmer of hope in her eyes. She tried to hide it by looking away, but Alexis saw it. This woman was serious.

*"Me? I . . . I'm just her doctor,"* Alexis stammered, holding on to her desk for balance. *"Why would she listen to me?"*

*"She'll listen to you,"* Mrs. Knight said, staring at Alexis's shoes. She shifted nervously, as if asking another woman—a younger woman, at that—to do her job was the worst embarrassment she'd ever experienced. *"Y'all talk all da time."*

*"Yeah, but I don't get in her business,"* Alexis replied, drumming her pen on her desk. *"I let her say whatever's on her mind, and then she goes about her business. I try not to cross that line."*

*The worried mother nodded, choosing not to push the issue any further. After a couple more minutes of small talk, she excused herself and disappeared within the madness of downtown New Orleans.*

That was three weeks ago. Guilt kicked her in the ass as she thought back to that evening. She wondered if she had done as Mrs. Knight asked would she be standing in her office at nine o'clock at night about to perform a sexual assault forensics exam on one of her oldest patients.

"If 'if' was a spliff we'd all be messed up," she mumbled, wiping away the last of her tears. She wasn't sure where she'd heard that phrase, but for some reason it seemed to fit this situation.

It was time to get back into doctor mode. The Knights would storm into her office any minute, and she didn't want to be in the waiting room when they did. If she was, she'd never get the exam started because she'd be too busy trying to answer questions she didn't have the answers to. Twylite was the most important person in this situation. Alexis would have to deal with her guilt later.

She reached behind the receptionist's desk and fished out a notepad. After scribbling a note for the Knights, she reached for the phone and dialed home.

"Hello?" asked a gruff male voice.

Alexis smiled slightly, knowing she'd woken her husband Jamar from a deep sleep. "You asleep already?"

He yawned. "Yeah, I had a long day. You on the way home? I'll tell you all about it."

"I wish, baby, but I got a rape victim in tonight, so I'm about to do an exam." She didn't want to tell him it was Twylite. Although he'd never met her, she talked about the bright, aspiring singer all the time, so much so that he felt like he knew her. Saying her name would only prompt more questions, and she was running out of time. "I'll be late, so go back to sleep and I'll tell you about it in the morning."

He yawned again. "All right, babe. Ring me when you're on the way. I'm about to hit this pillow again."

"Okay. I love you."

"Love you too."

Alexis smiled, glad that after all the frogs she'd kissed over the years she'd finally found her prince. It felt good knowing that she'd have arms to lie in once she got through all the drama she was sure was on the way.

"Doctor."

Ms. Kay's soft voice broke her thoughts, but that was a good thing. It was time for doctor mode. She turned and faced her nurse.

"She's ready."


Not long after Alexis disappeared into the examining room, Adele and Earl Knight burst into the doctor's office, torment and worry animating their every step. Who could blame them? Their only daughter had been through God knows what, and there was nothing they could do to take away the pain. Even if they could, what could they do? No one was even sure what happened.

Adele Knight looked around the waiting room, adjusting her sweater. It was warm in the office, much warmer than it had been outside. Yet, she couldn't bring herself to take off the sweater. Getting comfortable would seem too social, and this was definitely not a social visit.

She stared toward the closed door that blocked what was going on in the examination room. The tears she thought had run their course in the car returned in force. "I guess they're still in there."

Earl Knight walked to the receptionist's desk and picked up the handwritten note Alexis had left propped against a vase. "I guess so."

Adele continued staring at the door as if trying to burn a hole through the solid wood. She then suddenly snapped her head toward the front door. "What's taking those damned police so long?"

"Baby, we only called dem about ten minutes ago," Earl tried to reason. "Give dem a chance to get here."

"Dey shoulda been here. Damned police precincts all over this town. I told dem Twylite had been raped. Dey shoulda been here."

"Baby, we don't know dat fa sho," Earl said.

"What else could it be, Earl?" Adele began pacing the same route Alexis had paced earlier. Only her pace doubled that of the doctor's. "She been gone half the night, and her damned docta calls us? What else could it be?"

As the words came out of her mouth, Adele wished she could take them back. Earl had taken a seat on the sofa, and held his head in his hands. His foot absently kicked the old schoolbag where Adele had packed Twylite's clothes. She knew he was scared. Yet, he took his role as the man of the house seriously. He had to be the strong one. He had to be the one to take care of his women. He needed to be the protector. Now his only daughter was being examined for only God knew what, and his wife was distraught. She knew he felt like he had failed somewhere.

She covered her face with her palms and inhaled deeply. The smell of the perfume she'd spritzed on her wrists at Lakeside Mall earlier still graced her skin. Why hadn't she bought that perfume? She couldn't even remember the name at this point. It just wasn't important right now. Adjusting her sweater once again, she took a seat next to her husband and leaned her head against his muscular shoulder.

He responded by placing his arm around her shoulders and squeezing her tricep. The gesture wasn't very strong, but Adele knew it was all he could offer under the circumstances. Silence hung over them like a wet rug. It was almost deafening. The couple continued to stare at the closed door for what seemed like hours.

In reality, they'd only waited about ten minutes before a click caused their eyes to dart toward the examination room. The door opened. Seconds later, Ms. Kay stepped out, her face pensive once she saw the Knights huddled together in the waiting room.

"Mr. and Mrs. Knight," she greeted them quietly, with a quick head nod. "We're done with the examination. Thank you for letting us get started."

"We just want Twylite to get the help she needs," Earl said, taking his arm from around Adele's shoulders and grabbing her hand. "Did she tell you what happened?"

Before Ms. Kay could answer, two of New Orleans's finest walked into the office. "We're looking for an Adele Knight?" announced the taller one. He was an African American, who, despite his towering height, looked to Adele to be young enough to be her son.

She stood, her husband following suit. "Dat's me. What took y'all so long?"

"We got here as soon as we could," explained the shorter one. Adele thought he looked to be the older one, so to her he had to be the one in charge. He was also African American, but looked to be straight out of the Seventh Ward—heavy set, light skinned, and smooth talking. Although it had been years since the Creoles separated themselves from the common darker-skinned black folks in New Orleans by moving to the Seventh Ward, the area spanning from Esplanade Avenue to Bayou Saint John, it was still an easy assumption that many light-skinned blacks either lived or grew up there.

"Since we didn't know what we were responding to, I'm sorry to say we, uh, couldn't get here faster," the shorter policeman continued.

Earl's jaw tightened, but to Adele's relief, he didn't raise his voice. "My wife told you on the phone dat we think our daughter was raped."

The older policeman sighed. "Can we all sit down?"

Ms. Kay stepped forward. "Mr. Knight, are those Twylite's clothes by your feet? Can I get them? Dr. Duplessis talked her into telling us what happened, but I'ma need to warn her that the police are here. I hope the poor girl don't get scared and clam up."

"Was it a rape?" the younger policeman asked. "If it was, we're required to contact a sexual assault victim's advocate. I took the liberty of calling the rape crisis center just in case."

"What's sexual assault—" Adele asked.

"Excuse me," Ms. Kay whispered, walking forward and grabbing the bag herself. Once she retrieved it, she retreated to the examination room and closed the door behind her.

"First of all, we should introduce ourselves," the older policeman said. "My name is Officer Mosley, and this is Officer Yarbrough. Like I said, we got here as fast as we could. I didn't want to waste too much time, so I had Officer Yarbrough call the crisis center to send somebody over."

"But we don't know if there was a rape yet," Earl broke in.

Adele looked up at her husband, feeling sorry for his wishful thinking. He still refused to picture his baby as the victim of a crime of passion. How he would react when the truth that she was sure would come out finally surfaced remained to be seen.

She exhaled heavily and asked, "Who did you say is coming over?"

"A sexual assault victim's advocate," Officer Yarbrough explained, empathy seeming to replace some of the tension that filled his voice when he first walked into the office. "This person is pretty much there to give the victim support throughout the investigation process."

"But dat's what we're here for," Earl protested.

Yarbrough nodded sympathetically. "Sometimes victims, especially teenagers, feel better talking to people other than the folks closest to them."

An uncomfortable silence filled the room, broken only by a click coming from the examination room. Adele could no longer contain herself when she saw the bruises and burns that followed Dr. Duplessis out into the waiting area. She ran to her daughter, wailing so loudly she could have woken the dead in the next parish. She cupped Twylite's face gingerly in her hands.

"I'm okay, Momma," Twylite whispered. She tried to smile, but Adele could see right through it. This wasn't the same girl who'd left their home for school that morning.

"You sho?" Earl asked, standing right behind Adele. She moved to the side so he could hug his daughter.

Twylite nodded. "Yes, Daddy. I'm sorry."

"Whatcha sorry 'bout?" he asked.

"This was my fault," she replied, her eyes downcast. "If I woulda listened to you, this woulda never happened."

Another uncomfortable silence, broken only by Adele and Twylite's sniffles. Everyone looked at each other.

"Excuse me."

The group turned toward the office entrance at an attractive African American woman wearing what seemed like needle-thin cornrows that reached halfway down her back. She wore a pink warm-up suit and carried a shoulder bag crammed with books and papers. She shifted a bit under all the attention she received.

"Um, my name is Isis Reynolds, from the Survivors Advocacy Network," she announced. "I'm the victim's advocate."

"The victim," Earl mumbled.

"I'm sorry," Isis retracted, shaking her head. "Victim is such a terrible word. I prefer to use the word 'survivor,' but when I refer to my title, I have to use the 'V' word."

She tried to smile, but no one seemed to follow suit. Dr. Duplessis finally cleared her throat.

"Ms. Reynolds, have a seat," she offered. "We'll get a couple of extra chairs so we can get started. Twylite was just about to tell her parents what happened, but I don't think she was expecting this much of an audience."

The doctor gave the teen a sympathetic look before gesturing for Ms. Kay to help her to get chairs from her office. Once they left the room, Officer Mosley offered Isis his seat on the sofa, while Officer Yarbrough offered Twylite the armchair he sat in. Adele and Earl stood behind her protectively, while the two policemen took seats on the loveseat across the room.

Isis pulled a file out of her bag and looked up at the Knights as Dr. Duplessis and Ms. Kay returned to the waiting room armed with two folding chairs. She waited until they took their seats near the receptionist's counter before speaking. "Sir, ma'am, I know you're upset. I'm guessing you're the parents, and I know you want what's best for your daughter, but would you mind sitting on the sofa with me? It might make a more comfortable environment if everyone sat down."

Adele looked at her husband, and then down at Twylite. Her daughter looked back at her, her eyes still wet with tears.

"Please?" Twylite asked. "This will be hard enough."

Adele pursed her lips and looked back at Earl, who gestured toward the sofa. She silently nodded and complied.

Once everyone was seated, Isis cleared her throat and nervously ran her hand over her braids, swinging them over her right shoulder. "Please don't mind me. I am only here to ensure that"—she looked down at her file—"Twylite gets the support that she needs. The police are going to have to ask some tough questions."

She looked directly at Twylite as she continued. "Ple understand that they are only doing their jobs. T might even sound like they don't believe you, but it's job to get to the truth. If it's what you want, they v after the person who did this to you. How much them will make the process much faster."

Twylite bit her lip and looked away. She looked around the room nervously, and Adele was afraid she would back out of telling them what happened. But when the girl's eyes landed on her doctor, she seemed to sit up a little straighter. She nodded, and then turned her attention to the police officers sitting across from her. "I'm ready."

By the time she finished telling her story, Twylite was exhausted. She'd had to stop at least three times to keep from crying, but her battle was futile when she saw the tears flowing from the eyes of her mother and Dr. Duplessis. Her father tried to stay calm, but the lump in his throat could be seen from across town. She knew he was ready to go out and kill Peanut.

But the worst of it all were the questions those police-men piled on her:

"How long did you know this Peanut?"

"Do you know his real name?"

"Why did you get in his car?"

"Why didn't you run when you had the chance?"

"Why did you wait so long to call the police?"

Their questions made her feel stupid. As if she could feel any more stupid for putting herself in the situation in the first place. She felt like they were trying to paint her as some freak who got off on having sex in the woods. Like she liked it rough.

Who did they think she was? There were plenty of girls at Saint Francis's and even a lot of the public schools who wouldn't mind doing the things Peanut made her do, but definitely wasn't one of them. Although to let them, she was the queen of the whores. All they saw was tting picked up from school in a green BMW every nd they automatically thought she was sleeping with a drug dealer. It wasn't even like that. He an older guy who worked for his money.

She almost smiled when she told the policemen how she met Peanut.

*She'd been visiting her girlfriend Pam when she saw this young-looking mailman walk up to the house. At least he looked young to her. Pam's regular mailman looked old enough to be her grandfather. She and Pam both smiled hard as he dropped the envelopes into the mailbox. He smiled back.*

*"You gonna make sure ya momma get this mail?" he asked, displaying a gold tooth and otherwise gleaming white teeth. As the two girls giggled, he smiled again and headed back on his route.*

*"You have a blessed day," Twylite yelled after him.*

*He stopped and walked back to the house. He leaned on the gate and shot her another of his winning smiles. "What's your name, sweetness?"*

*"Twylite."*

*He scrunched his eyebrows. "Dat's your real name?"*

*"Yep."*

*"Come here, lemme talk to you for a minute, Miss Twylite."*

That short conversation led to more than a year of dinner dates, late-night phone calls, movie trips, and lots of sex. He had been the one to break her virginity, although it would be months before she told her mother.

Actually, she'd never told her; Adele had just found out. She said she could tell because Twylite's attitude was different. Her walk was different. And she could tell because Peanut had gotten even more controlling. Mrs. Knight could hear Twylite on the phone explaining her whereabouts, and justifying her absences when she and Peanut weren't together. Twylite's entire conversation always centered around Peanut.

It was no surprise to Twylite when her mother demanded that she break up with him. Yet she couldn't do it. Yes, he was a bit controlling, but she loved the gifts he gave her. She loved the status of being driven around in a luxury car. She loved never having to ask her parents for money, although she'd never held a job like some of her friends did. She dreamt of marrying Peanut after high school. She would still go to college, but her name would be Mrs. Twylite Cooper. They would move close to the University of New Orleans campus, and she would get home soon enough to study and make dinner while Peanut finished his mail routes.

She had her plans all figured out, but she didn't have enough heart to stand up to her parents. It wasn't long before she began sneaking around with Peanut. Pam would always be her alibi for why she was out a little later, or gone on the weekends.

Unfortunately, her weekend jaunts had taken a toll on her grades. Her straight As had become Bs, and had soon morphed into Cs. The Knights had a fit! This time, Twylite tried her best to stand up to them. Peanut's constant lectures about how she was a grown woman who needed to stop sneaking around like a little girl were finally starting to make sense, and she told them so.

What she didn't plan on was the lightning she felt strike her right cheek.

*"Oh, so you think you're grown now!"* Adele shouted. *"If you were so grown, you woulda came and talked to me like a woman. You been lying to me and your daddy for months, jeopardizing your fuckin' college career for dat nigga?"*

*Twylite couldn't even muster a reply. She just stood her ground, rubbing the sting from her cheek.*

*"Sleeping with a grown man and letting him control ya every move is not being a woman," her father told her. "You gotta understand I know what kinda man dat boy is. I used to be him before I met ya momma.*

You think you da only one? You just his young girl he tryin'a mold. Dat little bit a money he givin' you ain't shit compared to what he gives his real woman."

Twylite was horrified at her father's words. How could he say something like that? Peanut would never disrespect her like that.

"Daddy, that's not true," she pleaded.

"Oh yeah?" he challenged. "When is the last time you sang?"

She pursed her lips and looked away. It had been weeks since she'd been to choir rehearsal, and her director was adamant that no one sang on Sunday if they didn't show up for Friday night rehearsal. She hadn't even sung with the school choir because Peanut told her they didn't have time for that. It hadn't mattered to her because she was spending time with her man.

"He always talkin' 'bout what he teachin' you, right?" her father pushed.

That was true, too. He'd taught her how to please him in bed. He'd taught her, or so he said, how to be a woman. He encouraged her to finish college, but he said she would never learn as much about life as he could teach her.

"And when is the last time dat li'l nigga spent some time with you on a Saturday?" her father demanded.

Wow, she never thought he noticed all of that. Peanut had always told her he had to work on his route on Saturdays, and then he would go home and go to sleep. She didn't expect to see him on Sundays because the Knights had mandated Sunday as family day. It was just them and the Lord.

"I want you to leave dat boy alone," her mother said. "He ain't worth your life. You got too much goin' for you. Dat boy is just gonna drive you in the ground."

*It took her all night to think about what her parents had said, but that very next morning before catching the bus for school, she called Peanut and broke it off with him. She just couldn't take the fighting anymore. And, besides, what was she really fighting for?*

She had to admit that the last couple of weeks had gotten better. Her grades had improved because she stopped falling asleep in class. She'd begun going back to choir rehearsal at church, and had even been chosen to solo on a new song they'd been rehearsing. She had hoped to sing the song on the fourth Sunday, but it didn't look like that was going to happen. There was no way in the world she would stand in front of the congregation with her face looking the way it did.

"Twylite?"

Isis's voice woke Twylite from her painful walk down memory lane. She was so deep in thought that she never felt her mother's arms snake around her shoulders. When she looked around, the police stood across from her, scribbling notes into their pads, and Dr. Duplessis spoke quietly to Ms. Kay. Isis had scooted closer to Twylite. The lady clasped her hands together tightly as if afraid to touch her.

Twylite looked around the room. "Where's my daddy?"

"He went to bring the car around," her mother replied. "You ready to go home?"

Before Twylite could answer, Isis quickly asked, "Mrs. Knight, would you mind if I talked with Twylite alone for just a minute? I promise not to take too long."

Twylite could hear her mother's mind click as she thought about whether to let this woman talk to her. She wasn't sure what Isis wanted to talk to her about privately, but she seemed nice enough. And if it was true that she would be there for her throughout this entire process, then now seemed like as good a time as any to get to know her. She looked up at her mother and nodded her head.

"I'll walk her to the door, ma'am," Isis assured her.

Twylite could feel her mother's arms retreat from around her shoulders as she straightened. "I'll wait with your daddy downstairs."

"You two can talk here," Dr. Duplessis offered as Mrs. Knight left the reception area. She looked at Twylite and nodded. "We'll be in the back putting your prescriptions together."

"Thanks, Dr. Duplessis," Twylite whispered.

The doctor turned to leave, with her nurse following close behind. The policemen, following everyone else's cue, also bade their good-byes.

"We'll be in touch as soon as we apprehend Mr. Cooper," Officer Mosley assured Twylite, touching her lightly on the shoulder.

She flinched from the touch. "You gonna go get him tonight?"

"Absolutely," Yarbrough said. "After what he did to you, that's the least we can do."

Mosley touched his partner's arm and shook his head at him. "We may need you to make a positive identification a little later. We'll call you. I'll explain the procedures to your parents when we get downstairs."

"Stay strong, bay," Yarbrough told her, his Seventh-Ward roots becoming more apparent. Bay was a short way of saying "baby," which was a popular term of endearment in New Orleans to establish familiarity when two people barely knew one another. "You're gonna get through this."

He reached out to pat her hand, but Twylite snatched away.

Noticing the gesture, Isis quickly said, "Thank you, Officer. She's been through a lot tonight. If you find him, would you mind if she comes to the station in the morning?"

The officers looked at each other, and then Mosley spoke up. "That's fine. We're just gonna bring him in for questioning tonight. We can't hold him for more than twenty-four hours unless we get some positive proof, so I advise you to come to the station first thing in the morning."

"We'll be there, Officer," Isis assured him.

The policemen nodded, and then left the office. Once they were left alone, Isis turned to Twylite and looked her directly in the eyes. "I know a lot happened tonight. Between what your boyfriend did to you, to getting over here by yourself, to having to bare your soul in front of God and the rest of the world, I can understand if you want to just curl up in bed and shut the world out right now."

The teen's eyes sank. Her shoulders followed suit as if Isis's words had allowed her to finally exhale.

"I want you to know this is not your fault," Isis continued. "I know you might feel that way right now, but no man has the right to put his hands on a woman, especially not in the way Peanut touched you. Even if he thought he could do it in the past, even if you let him do it in the past, no means no. You showed a lot of strength tonight, and I'm proud of you."

Twylite looked up at Isis. "What strength did I show? I let myself get caught up."

Isis slowly reached for Twylite's hand. When the teen didn't pull away, she laid her hand softly on top of the girl's. "You showed resiliency. Even if you thought it was your fault, you had the strength to report it. And you didn't change your mind when a bunch of strangers came into the room. And you held it together when your parents were clearly upset."

"I just didn't want to hurt them any more than I already had," Twylite said, shaking her head.

Isis smiled. "That's what makes you amazing. You had every right to make this night all about you, but you managed to think about your parents. Not everyone can have that strength."

Twylite pursed her lips. "If you say so."

"I do," Isis reassured her, squeezing her hand. "Trust me, I've been there, and I know weak when I see it. You, my lady, are not weak."

She pulled a business card from the front pocket of her bag and handed it to the young lady. "Here's my number. Call me anytime you need to talk."

Twylite took the card and read it. She then looked up and offered a half smile. "I will. So you gonna come with me to the police station in the morning?"

"If you want me to."

"I do. My parents will probably wanna come too, but I want you to be there as well."

"That's fine," Isis replied, rising from the sofa. "Speaking of your parents, I'd better get you downstairs before they come up here looking for you."

"Yeah, they will come up here," Twylite agreed. She looked toward the back. "I wonder if Dr. Duplessis is finished with my prescription."

"I'm sure she is."

They walked back to the doctor's office and Twylite knocked on the door. Once she heard Dr. Duplessis respond, she opened the door and peeked in. "We're finished talking. I just wanted to let you know we're about to leave."

"Okay, sweetie," Dr. Duplessis replied. Ms. Kay handed the girl a brown paper bag. The doctor explained, "Okay, Twy, in that bag is your prescription for some painkillers and some ointment for your burns. I also put a couple of samples in there to get you started for tonight, but make sure you fill those prescriptions in the next couple of days."

"I will, Dr. Duplesses," Twylite replied. "Thanks for everything tonight."

The doctor stood up and gave her a hug. Ms. Kay followed suit.

"I'll walk you guys out if you give us a minute to close up in here," Dr. Duplessis offered.

"That sounds good," Isis said. "It's pretty late."

"Yeah, it's after midnight," Dr. Duplessis said. "My husband must be dead to the world, because I know he woulda called me by now."

"Yeah, you know that man don't play when it come to you," Ms. Kay said with a laugh as she turned off the light in the doctor's office.

"Sounds like quite a guy," Isis said with a smile, ushering Twylite toward the front door.

"He's cute, too," Twylite chimed in, finally cracking a smile.

The three women stopped and stared at the teenager, then chuckled.

"Well I guess someone is feeling a little better," Dr. Duplessis remarked, rubbing Twylite's back.

"Just a little," she replied, the smile remaining, but not as bright.

# Chapter Three

"Thank the Lord today is Saturday!" Isis exclaimed, pulling her cashmere blanket over her head in an effort to block the sun's rays.

She'd been up since six-thirty that morning taking care of Twylite. Somehow the girl had talked her parents into meeting them at the police station instead of taking her there. This gave her a chance to take Twylite to breakfast so the two of them could get to know each other better.

*She was surprised to know how smart and talented Twylite was. Before the Peanut debacle, she was a straight A student with a voice as clear as an angel. Of course, Isis made her prove it as they drove to the police station, and she had to admit that she was impressed. There was no way to describe the tingle she felt on the back of her neck as Twylite sang along with Mary J. Blige's "In the Morning." It just wasn't the voice she expected from a sixteen-year-old girl.*

*Isis just couldn't understand why Twylite would sit on such a gift. At least, that was until she watched Twylite come eye to eye with Peanut. Suddenly, all of the cheer and strength she'd shown earlier dissipated once she saw her former boyfriend. Right in front of her eyes, Twylite turned into a scared young girl who'd become very unsure of herself. For a minute, Isis was afraid Twylite would change her mind about pressing charges. Peanut didn't make the situation any better. As soon as he locked eyes with Twylite, a look overtook him that could have stripped paint.*

*Although the reaction was something to be expected of a rape victim who comes face to face with her assailant, there was no getting used to seeing a young girl mentally crumble. Twylite wasn't her first case, but she was, by far, the youngest. In an instant, Isis understood the power this much-older man had over her young client. He wasn't especially tall or muscular, but the confidence in his walk and the deep-set scrunch in his thick eyebrows gave him a presence that demanded to be felt. The bass in his voice made everything he said sound like a demand. Yet, his smooth milk-chocolate skin and thin lips gave him the good looks that Isis was sure attracted the teenager to him in the first place.*

*"Twy!" he yelled, jumping from his chair. A uniformed police officer pulled him back down to the chair, but it didn't diminish his rage. "What the fuck is this? You fuckin' bust your curfew, so you told your parents I raped you?"*

*Twylite cowered closer to Isis, folding her arms tightly as if they could serve as a shield from Peanut's icy words. She opened her mouth, but nothing came out.*

*"You ain't got shit to say now?" he demanded. "I might be fired from my damn job over this bullshit, and all you can do is stand there?"*

*"You did rape me," Twylite mumbled.*

*"Why the fuck I gotta rape your ass, huh?" he shouted, struggling to get away from the policeman who continued pinning him to the seat. Other people in the station could barely file their own reports for watching the dramatics taking place before them. "I ain't gotta rape nobody!"*

*"You raped me!" Twylite fired back. The words came out a lot louder, but the fear and hurt were still evident in her voice. Isis felt helpless as she watched the scene unfold, but she knew she had to do something. She wasn't*

*about to let Peanut take away this girl's self-respect and self-esteem.*

*"That's enough!" she demanded. "Mr. Cooper, I don't know who you think you are, but you will not talk to this girl that way!"*

*"Bitch, who the fuck is you?" Peanut snapped."You best to get out my damn face with all that noise."*

*"You heard the lady," Yarbrough shouted, appearing from seemingly nowhere. "Now, shut the hell up! If you didn't do shit, then this should be easy. But let me find out this was a rape, and your ass is mine! In fact, let me stick your ass in OPP and let the girls deal with your rapist ass!"*

*"What's going on?" Earl Knight asked, walking into the station. His wife followed close behind. Neither of them looked to be in the mood for games.*

Thank God for the Knights. *They stayed calm and gave Twylite the reassurance she needed. Earl Knight never left his daughter's side, and when Peanut even looked like he was about to say another word to Twylite, Earl gave him a look that immediately made him shut his mouth and lock his jaw. Isis wasn't sure, but it seemed that that was the moment Peanut went from a violent, rage-filled monster to something darn near respectful. Either that, or Yarbrough's threat about the Orleans Parish Prison had gotten to him.*

*"Get him out of here," Yarbrough instructed the police-man who had been holding Peanut down. He mouthed a curse word and faced the family. "Mr. and Mrs. Knight, I'm sorry about that. That is not how we do business here. He was s'posed to be out the room by the time y'all got here, but I guess we moved too slow."*

*Isis shook her head as she remembered the look on Peanut's face as he was led out of the room. It almost seemed like a smirk. Like he knew the police couldn't hold him much longer because, as it stood, it was his word against hers.*

*And just as she suspected, Yarbrough brought them all into a small office. She knew it could be nothing but bad news. Had it been anything else, he could have talked to them in the main area. Once they were safely behind closed doors, he ran his hand over his head and, true to form, he got straight to the point.*

*"We don't have enough to hold him."*

*"What the hell you mean you ain't got enough to hold him?" Mr. Knight demanded, jumping from his seat and holding his arms out in expectation. "You saw my child last night. Does dat shit look like she asked for it?"*

*Yarbrough shook his head. "I know what you're sayin', Mr. Knight, but Cooper maintains they had consensual sex that just got a little rough. He said she used to sneak out all the time to be with him, and last night was no different."*

*Isis caught a glimpse of Mrs. Knight cutting her eyes at her daughter, kind of like she already knew that piece of information. That damned Peanut was good. He used just enough of the truth to make himself look good. But Mr. Knight wasn't having it.*

*"Do you see the burns on my child's face?" he asked, his hand pointed at Twylite. Even though she was dark, the redness on her right cheek was still evident, and the wounds had barely scabbed. "Dat goes way beyond getting a little rough."*

*Yarbrough sighed heavily and rolled his eyes. It was obvious his frustration was being held at bay. "I told you I'm with you, Mr. Knight, but until we get back the results of that SAFE kit or he gets a change of heart and admits he did it, we can't hold him. His ass is right back on the streets."*

*Earl Knight turned his back and began pacing.*

*"Officer Yarbrough, is there anything we can do at all?" Adele Knight asked.*

*Isis admired the way Mrs. Knight seemed to have her husband's back. She always knew exactly when to step in and when to step back. Isis vowed that if she ever got married again, she would be that type of wife.*

*"Dat bastard raped my baby, and I want him behind bars, even if I gotta put him there myself. Last night, my daughter couldn't get to sleep, and when she did, she woke up screaming. Now I don't know about you, but good sex ain't never affected me like dat."*

*Isis remained quiet because there was really nothing more she could add to the situation. The Knights asked all the right questions. They didn't need her help. Besides, her responsibility was to make sure Twylite was taken care of through this process, and she needed to stay on her job.*

Isis beat her head against her pillow as she remembered Twylite's demeanor as her parents drilled Officer Yarbrough. Had the girl's shoulders slumped any lower, Isis would have sworn she had some type of deformity. She just couldn't believe this was the same girl who'd smiled, laughed, and sung just a couple of hours earlier. All the light that had been in her eyes had flickered out. The girl from last night had reappeared, and she didn't appear to be leaving anytime soon.

Isis understood because she'd been there. She'd never been brutally raped, but the amount of men she'd slept with in her younger days had taken away her self-worth. She remembered the nights of saying yes when she really wanted to say no, all because she could no longer stand the pressure. She could still feel the judgmental stares she received when she walked into a roomful of women who just knew Isis was after their men. It was a long time before she overcame the shame that everyone wanted to sleep with her, but no one wanted to love her, not even the man she would eventually marry. The memories were more than she could bear. Leaving the police station was like a drink of ice water on a summer day. Had she sat in that station any longer, she would have suffocated. Tempers continued to rise while Twylite continued to sink deeper into her depression. Isis knew she needed to do something, but she needed time to herself to get over her own memories before she could put together a course of action for her client.

As Isis lay in bed, she was still no closer to a solution to help Twylite. This case would be nothing like her first. That lady had bounced back so quickly from her assault that when the case came back unfounded due to a lack of evidence, the lady was already ready to move on with her life. Twylite would not be so easy.

She turned over and looked at the time, which was approaching two in the afternoon. Her shoulders jumped as she grunted a laugh. She'd slept for nearly three straight hours!

"Might as well get up and try to make something out of the rest of this day," she said to herself. She rose and held herself up on her elbows, shaking out the remnants of her deep sleep. The telephone rang.

"Who in the world?" she wondered aloud. She'd only lived in New Orleans for a few months and had yet to get out and make many friends. A ringing phone in her apartment was a rare occurrence unless her parents called. Sometimes her friend Michelle would call, but she doubted she'd call in the middle of the afternoon on a Saturday.

The phone rang again, so she stretched herself across her pillows and picked up her cordless receiver. "Hello?"

"Hello, Isis?" asked a familiar but unrecognized female's voice.

"Yes? Who's this?" Isis replied. She just knew a bill collector couldn't be calling her already. Had she forgotten to pay something?

"This is Alexis Duplessis. Twylite's doctor from last night?"

"Oh, yes, Dr. Duplessis," Isis said, breathing a sigh of relief. "What can I do for you?"

"I'm sorry, did I wake you up?"

Isis laughed and rubbed her eyes with her free hand. "I guess I do still have sleep in my voice. I'm okay, I just woke up from a nap not too long ago."

"Oh, well sorry to disturb you," the doctor said. "I was just calling to see how everything went this morning. I haven't been able to get Twylite off my mind all night. I tried calling her earlier, but there wasn't an answer, although I'm not sure what I would have told her if I did get in touch with her."

"I understand, Doctor," Isis replied, finally rising from her bed. She walked into her kitchen and went straight to the refrigerator. "She seems to be quite a young lady, who got caught up with a controlling older guy."

"Yeah, I never met Peanut face to face, but from what I know of him, he was definitely a character."

"By the way, do you know that man's real name? They mentioned it at the police station, but with all the craziness, I can't remember. And if I call him Peanut one more time, I might choke!"

The two ladies laughed together.

"I know what you mean," Dr. Duplessis said. "I think his real name is Calvin. I just didn't want to start calling him that and you wouldn't know who I was talking about."

"Dr. Duplessis, you could call that boy John John, and I'd like that better than Peanut," Isis said. She had pulled out a glass and started to pour some orange juice, but decided to upgrade to a mimosa. She deserved a little something something after all she'd been through that morning.

"Well, while we're on the subject of names, please stop calling me 'Doctor.' My name is Alexis."

"Okay, Alexis." Isis took a sip from her drink. Not quite strong enough. She poured another splash of champagne into the glass and took another sip. She nodded this time. "It's nice to meet you."

They laughed again.

"So anyway, Twylite isn't doing too well," Isis continued, leaning back on the counter. "Calvin did a job on her today. That bastard had the nerve to tell the police that everything he put her through last night was consensual."

"What?"

"I know, right? He actually went off in the middle of the station. I thought Twylite's dad was going to beat his tail right there!"

"Oh, yeah, Mr. Knight don't play," Alexis noted.

"I could see that," Isis agreed. "But back to Twylite, I don't know what to do for her. I really think she should go talk to somebody, but I don't know if she and her family would agree to it."

"Why not?"

"You know," Isis began before taking another sip from her drink. "Most black people don't believe in counseling. I don't know if the Knight family is like that, but I have a feeling it would be a hard sell."

"Well, I hear what you're saying, but I also know the Knights will do what they have to do for Twylite. She's a good girl. She just got herself into a bad situation."

A silence settled over the phone line as the two women pondered the situation.

"Well, I won't keep you too long," Alexis finally said. "I just wanted to check on Twylite to make sure she was okay. I don't know if I told you, but she's kind of like a little sister to me."

"That's nice. She does seem to respect you a lot. I don't know if she would have gotten through last night if you hadn't been there."

Alexis giggled a bit. "Isis, I hope you don't mind me asking, but where are you from? Because you definitely aren't from New Orleans."

Isis smiled, wondering how long it would take before Alexis asked. Most people asked within two seconds of her uttering her first words to them. "I moved here from Killeen, Texas, but I'm from Radcliff, Kentucky."

"Wow, no offense, but that sounds like two extra-country towns."

Isis laughed again. "Well, they're not the biggest towns, but I liked them."

"And that's all that matters. So how long have you lived in New Orleans?"

"Since April."

"Wow, new in town? Is this place a culture shock for you?"

"It's different, but I'm getting used to it."

"Well, one day I'm going to have to take you out so you can see the city," Alexis offered.

"I've been to the French Quarter and Canal Street."

"Girl, that's tourist stuff. You need to see the real New Orleans."

Isis chuckled. She was beginning to like this Alexis. "Girl, you are crazy. I'll have to take you up on that one of these days."

"I'ma hold you to that, but for now, let me get off this phone before my husband snatches it out my ear. We're supposed to be going shopping for a new living room set."

"Well y'all have fun with that, but I will definitely keep in touch."

Isis smiled once she pressed END on her phone. She might have made her first friend outside of work.

# Chapter Four

"What about this one?" Jamar asked, settling into a beige C-shaped sectional. It was microfiber, with a matching ottoman that was so big it could double as a coffee table. There were also two matching throw pillows with leather accents. "Sit down. This thing is comfortable as hell."

Alexis sat down, but the look on her face showed anything but enthusiasm.

Jamar knew the look well. "You don't like it, right?"

She shrugged. "It's okay, but I really didn't have a sectional in mind."

Jamar twisted his lips. "Why did I know this wasn't going to be easy?"

"How long you been knowing me?" Alexis asked with a laugh. "You oughta know by now nothing about me is easy."

"You ain't never lyin'," he replied, shaking his head.

She swatted him playfully. "Don't be agreeing so fast!"

"You gonna get enough of hittin' on me," Jamar said, rubbing the back of his head. "You just proved my point. Another thing is you've got us out here on a perfectly good Saturday looking for living room sets when we have perfectly good furniture at home."

"There is nothing good or perfect about that mess you have us sitting on," Alexis remarked, rising from the sectional. She walked toward another living room set, knowing her husband would follow her. There was no way he could let her remark slide.

"What's wrong with my furniture?" he challenged, stopping in front of a chocolate-colored suede sofa with matching loveseat and chair with ottoman. He crossed his arms, awaiting her reply.

"It's used, baby," Alexis said, eying the set her husband stood in front of. It was nice, but way too dark for what she had in mind. Dark-colored furniture would just make the whole front room seem dark. "We're supposed to be starting a new life together. How are we going to do that with furniture you used to fart on with your little chickenhead girlfriends?"

"First of all, that's nasty. Second of all, what makes you think I had chickenheads at my house? All my women had class."

Alexis shot him a look that said "stop dreaming" all over it. "Yeah, right. What about Regina?"

"Regina was straight," he protested. "And don't even let me get started on your exes. I told you before that I was the best thing that ever happened to you."

She rolled her eyes and shook her head. "You keep saying that mess, but when are you going to prove it?" With that, she walked the other way. The truth was that Jamar was the best thing that had happened to her, but she loved giving him a hard time.

A cashmere aristocrat-style set complete with sofa, chaise longue, loveseat, and matching end tables had caught her eye. It was perfect. She ran her hand across the smooth wood frame, admiring the detailed stitching on the plush seating.

"I knew it would only be a matter of time before you made it over here, and the answer is no," Jamar said, making her jump slightly. She hadn't even heard him approach her.

"Why not?" she asked, her eyes never leaving the set. It was truly meant for a queen. She could just picture herself lounging on the chaise while drinking a glass of wine after a long day in the office.

"Woman, what do I look like sitting on this? The shit looks like it belongs in a museum!"

An older couple snickered as they walked by. Jamar looked back at them and smiled. "You feel me, huh, bruh?"

"I gotcha, chief," the man yelled back, a little louder than Jamar had expected. He frowned a bit at the man's volume, but turned back to Alexis.

"See?" he asked. Something else caught his eye. "Lexy, this shit is three thousand dollars just for the sofa! There is no way in damned hell!"

"Okay, okay." She retreated as a ringing sound came from her purse. She fished the phone from the side pocket and smiled when she saw the caller ID. "But just so you'll know, furniture is an investment. You're supposed to pay more for it."

"Not that much more!" he retorted. "Now answer the phone so we can go."

"What's up, lady?" Alexis asked after pressing TALK.

"Y'all still shopping?" asked her friend Shalonda.

"Yeah, but I don't think we're making a decision today," Alexis replied, cutting her eyes at Jamar. "My husband's being mean as hell to me right now."

"You married him," Shalonda joked. "You knew what you were getting into."

"Yeah, I know, I'm stuck with him," Alexis said, again cutting her eyes at Jamar. "So what's up with you?"

"Not much. I just wanted to see if you wanted to go somewhere tonight. I need to get out this house."

"Where you wanna go?"

"I don't care. Anywhere but this house."

Alexis laughed. "I hear you. Lemme check with Jamar and make sure he doesn't have plans for us already. If not, I'm game. I might even see if this girl Isis wants to go."

"Who's Isis?"

"She's a lady I met last night at my office," Alexis said quickly, not wanting to get into the events of last night. "I'll tell you about it later."

"Okay, that's cool. Call me later."

Alexis clicked END on her cell phone before dropping it back into her purse. She looked up to find Jamar looking at another sofa and loveseat that couldn't even compare to her dream set. She shook her head and approached him.

"Let's make a deal, sweetheart," she offered, hugging his waist from behind.

He looked at her over his right shoulder and smirked. "You just finished talking bad about me, and now you're tryin'a make a deal?"

"Baby, you know I was just playing with you."

Jamar chuckled. "Now I'm all kinds of sweethearts and babies, but before you were hittin' me and talkin' about me bad."

"I'm sorry," she purred, squeezing him harder.

He took her arm and gently pulled her in front of him, and then kissed her lips. "What's your deal?"

"If we can find a chea . . . I mean more affordable set like the one I like, I'm willing to compromise," she said, her smile showing her sincerity.

He laughed again. "Girl, it's not just about the price. It's too fancy. What do me and my boys look like sittin' on that watchin' the game?"

Alexis pulled away and folded her arms. "We're not buying our living room set for your boys. It's for our comfort."

"That's my point," Jamar interjected. "We wouldn't be comfortable on that. You might like it, but would you really want to curl up with your feet in the pillows like you do on the couch we have now? I know I wouldn't want to flop on it after I finish playing basketball. And what about those nights when we get—"

"I got your point, Jamar," Alexis interrupted with a giggle. "But can we at least find something in a similar style?"

He sighed. "We'll find something kind of like it, but it will be something we'll both agree on."

"Deal, but it's obvious we're not going to agree on anything today, so why don't we just try again next week?"

"You ain't said nothin' but a word. Let's go."

The same older couple laughed again at them as they passed by.

"You gonna bend sooner or later, chief," the man told him.

"Shoot," Jamar said, waving him off. "I'm the man in this marriage."

"Man, bring your tail on," Alexis snapped, pulling his arm. "I'm tryin'a go out tonight!"

The couple laughed again as Jamar followed helplessly behind his wife.

Before walking out, he looked back at the old man and mouthed, "I'm still the man!"

# Chapter Five

Tension hung over the remainder of the Knights' Saturday like a ton of solid concrete. To pretend that the scene at the police station didn't happen would have been impossible. Earl Knight could hardly breathe without picturing the onslaught of venom that Calvin had spewed on Twylite. Only God could tell how long he could keep from putting his hands on that boy.

If only he could have five minutes alone with Calvin. Hell, he'd only need three. Just enough time to wrap his strong hands around that boy's throat and squeeze the life out of his worthless body. Who was Calvin Cooper to think he could talk to Twylite that way? The thought that Calvin had taken everything—her self-esteem, her innocence, and even her joy—ate at his very being.

And tomorrow he would have to go to church. How could he lead devotion with these thoughts of violence running through his mind? A Christian all of his life and a deacon for the past ten, he knew the power of love and forgiveness, but God had never tested him in such a way. He sat on the bed and held his head, trying to squeeze the pain away. The telephone sitting on the nightstand caught his eye.

*Call your pastor.* He shook his head, refusing the thoughts that he knew came from God Himself. As much as he knew Pastor Lewis could help him come to grips with the situation, he just couldn't picture himself verbalizing his feelings without succumbing to emotion.

Even sadder, he wasn't sure he wanted to overcome his thoughts. The more the events of the last twenty-four hours wore on his mind, the more he really wanted to do something to Calvin. He couldn't admit that to his pastor. It was hard enough talking to Adele. For right now, it would have to be him and the Lord. No one else could possibly understand what he was going through.


Adele stood in the hallway outside her bedroom wiping away silent tears. She felt helpless. Both her husband and only daughter were hurting. And although the hurt came from the same source, it was obvious the hurt was for two different reasons, and there was nothing she could do to make it better.

Watching her husband go through his internal struggle was what hurt her most. She knew him well enough to know that she couldn't force him to talk to anyone, including her. At the same time, no one, including her, could force him out of the funk he'd fallen into. But who could blame him? Calvin Cooper had done a serious number on her family.

However, there was one thing that truly pained Adele. She couldn't help but wonder if Twylite was a coconspirator in Calvin's number. She didn't want to blame Twylite, but had she just listened to their warnings, last night would never have happened. It was a painful thought, but it was a persistent one that she hoped would stay inside and never meet the atmosphere. Voicing that concern would help no one.

Just as she prepared to walk into the bedroom and join her husband on the bed, she caught sight of Earl rising from the bed and sinking to his knees. He bowed his head and covered his eyes with his hands. Adele smiled, although her tears flowed harder. At least he knew to turn to God in his turmoil. She had yet to do the same.

Adele walked into the bathroom and turned on the faucet. *This is gonna be a long night,* she thought as she cradled the warm water in her hands and splashed it onto her face.

"Momma, is it okay if I don't go to church tomorrow?" Twylite asked from behind her.

The voice shook Adele slightly. She grabbed a towel and dried her face, hoping she wiped away any evidence of her tears. "What's wrong, baby?"

She knew it was a dumb question. Of course she knew what was wrong, but it was the first thing that popped into her mind.

"I'm just not ready to go out there right now," Twylite replied, leaning against the doorframe. "I don't want anybody asking me what happened, and I know as soon as they see my face, that's the first thing they're gonna do."

Adele nodded. It was a reasonable concern. Human nature could be so predictable. "I don't know if I want you here by yourself, Twy. Lord knows if dat boy will come around here tryin' a start something."

"He ain't gonna come around here, Ma," the teenager assured her. "He know better than that. The police are watching him. Besides, Daddy would kill him if he did."

*You just don't know how true dat is,* Adele thought, as her mind travelled to Earl back in the bedroom. "Lemme talk to your daddy about it."

"Ma, please, just let me stay home just this Sunday. It's bad enough I'ma have to go to school Monday and put up with people's questions. Just let me stay home tomorrow so I can think about some things."

"You know you can't avoid people forever, don't you?" Adele asked, folding down the toilet lid and taking a seat.

"I know, and I'll be ready Monday," Twylite said. "Just give me some time to process all of this."

"It's all right, Adele. Let her stay here."

The two female Knights looked up to find Earl standing behind Twylite.

"You sure?" Adele asked.

"The girl's been through hell da past coupl'a days," Earl said, nodding his head. "Let her stay here. Maybe dat lady Isis can check on her now and den."

"Yeah, I have her number," Twylite added, her face brightening for the first time all day.

Adele shook her head, still slightly doubtful. "Y'all act like dat woman don't got a life of her own."

"I ain't sayin' she gotta come over here and babysit, Adele, but dat's what she's dere for," Earl reasoned. "She ain't gotta be over here to make sure the girl is okay."

Adele looked at her husband, and then at her daughter. She obviously wasn't going to win this battle, so she relented. She just hoped that Isis Reynolds wouldn't be pulled deeper into this family than she needed to be.


A wave of excitement overtook Isis as she applied her makeup. It made her feel silly in a way, like she was a teenager getting ready for her first date. It was only dancing at the Perfect Fit nightclub, but it would be the first time she'd seen anything besides the inside of her bedroom on a Saturday night since she'd moved to New Orleans. And with everything she'd been through since Friday, she needed to have some fun.

Deep down, she hoped she'd meet a nice guy, although she never put much stock into meeting men at the club. She'd had enough one-night stands in her younger days back in Kentucky, and refused to go back down that road. Yet, it would be nice to meet someone who could keep her company every once in a while.

The thought of meeting someone new motivated her to carefully check her makeup. It couldn't be so light that it wouldn't be noticed, and not so heavy that she looked like a clown who was trying too hard. These were the times that she was glad she wore braids. The time she would have spent ensuring her hair was just right could be spent perfecting her makeup. She chuckled at the thought.

Satisfied with her face, she emerged from the bathroom and walked to her closet to choose a complementary outfit. Once again, she didn't want to look like a plain Jane or a hooker. Also, not familiar with the club, she didn't want to be overdressed. Then again, bump that. There was no crime in looking good. Besides, Alexis looked like a woman who never half stepped when it came to dressing. She couldn't risk looking like an ugly duckling next to her new friend.

She finally settled on a black one-shoulder jumpsuit and a pair of animal-skin stilettos. Just as she pulled the outfit from the closet, the buzz from her business cell beckoned her. Immediately her shoulders dropped, knowing it could be none other than Twylite. She'd already checked in with Ms. Delachaise, the sexual response coordinator, and her last case had been closed out weeks ago. Hopefully Twylite was okay.

"Hello?" she answered once she retrieved the phone from her purse. She dropped the outfit on her bed and sat next to it; somehow, getting dressed for the club while speaking with one of her survivors just didn't feel right.

"Isis?" Twylite asked tentatively.

"Yes, this is Isis. You okay?"

"As good as can be expected."

"I understand. What can I do for you?" Isis asked, glancing at the clock. Alexis would be there in about thirty minutes, and she wasn't even dressed yet. *Hopefully this won't be a long conversation.* Wow, she couldn't believe she thought that.

"Nothing, really," Twylite replied. "I was just wondering if you would be around tomorrow. My momma and daddy said I could stay home from church tomorrow, so I was wondering if you would be around in case I needed to talk or something."

Isis scrunched her eyebrows while breathing a quiet sigh of relief. At least she'd still be able to enjoy her evening. "Um, yeah, I'll be around tomorrow. Just give me a call if you need me."

"I will. Thanks."

"Okay, well, I have to run right now, but like I said, call me if you need me."

"Okay, well have a good night," Twylite said before hanging up.

Isis bit her lip and she dropped her cell phone back into her purse. She could already see that this case wouldn't be nearly as easy as her last one. Twylite would need to be handled with kid gloves. She was so fragile that if handled incorrectly, she'd surely break. Letting the girl call on Sunday might be a mistake. Even advocates needed a break sometimes.

"Well, what's done is done," she said aloud as she rose from the bed. She had twenty-five minutes to finish getting dressed. No need letting her mistake ruin the rest of her night.

As she slipped on her jumpsuit, she couldn't help but think of her friends Michelle and the dearly departed Kendra. They were like the three *amigas,* and went out on the town every Friday. Those were the days. She'd have to call Michelle tomorrow and check on her, and say a prayer for Kendra, who was violently murdered a few years back.

Thirty minutes had come and gone. Isis sat fully dressed in her living room, sipping on a vodka and orange juice. She checked her watch and decided to call Alexis, but before she could, her house phone rang. "Hello?"

"Girl, don't kill me," Alexis said, laughing. "Shalonda is slow as hell! I'm turning onto your street right now."

"Don't lie on me!" Isis could hear a female voice protest. She couldn't help but laugh. It was her girls all over again.

"Y'all are crazy," she said. "I'll meet you outside."

"Okay, we'll be there in about five minutes."

The Perfect Fit was packed. A little too packed for Isis's taste. It seemed as if everyone who walked past her either elbowed her or tapped her with a purse. Yet, she had to admit that the music was good. The DJ kept the dance floor packed with a healthy mixture of contemporary and old-school music.

Despite the crowd, Isis had to admit that she liked the club's atmosphere. At first, she was a bit nervous when she saw the neighborhood in which the club was located. She'd seen the hit HBO show *Treme,* but seeing the historic district in person just made her feel as if she was in a bad neighborhood. She was again nervous when she walked into the club and saw only a crowded bar and no dance floor despite feeling the bump of loud music, but when she turned another corner and saw beautiful people wearing beautiful clothing while mingling and dancing, she finally began to relax.

The colorful lights made her feel as if she were in an upscale New York dancehall. There were few tables, but she didn't mind standing. It just gave her a closer look at all of the activity going on around her. A couple of women walked past her, sporting five and ten dollar bills pinned to their dresses.

"What's up with that?" Isis asked Alexis, discreetly pointing toward the women.

"You've never seen that before?" Alexis replied. She smiled, but Isis was relieved that she didn't tease her about it. "It's their birthday. In New Orleans, when we take our friends out for their birthdays, we pin a couple dollars to their chests as gifts. On a good day, some people can go home with about a hundred dollars."

"That's my kind of birthday gift," Isis replied, laughing.

"Come on, baby, let's do the twist . . ."

"Oh, girl, that's my jam!" Shalonda exclaimed, pulling at Alexis's arm. "Come on, girl!"

"Come on, Isis," Alexis encouraged, slowly letting her friend drag her away.

"I don't know that dance," she replied, studying the line dance the crowd had formed to the Chubby Checker remix. "Y'all go ahead. I'll be fine here."

"You sure?" Shalonda asked, still inching her way to the floor.

"Go ahead," Isis pushed. "I'm fine. Y'all hurry up before the song ends."

As much as she enjoyed the atmosphere, Isis wasn't much of a dancer. Her preference was to observe the crowd. She walked to the bar and ordered a fresh vodka and orange juice, and then leaned against a nearby wall to soak in the energy around her. Alexis and Shalonda, on the other hand, had gotten lost on the dance floor. Once the Texas Twist ended, they began gyrating to a bouncy song Isis had never heard before. They seemed to be hypnotized by the beat. Every so often she'd catch a glimpse of them. Alexis would wave and try to beckon her onto the floor, but Isis would smile, shake her head, and lift up her drink as if to say she was fine.

"Girl, you know you're lookin' too good to be standin' here by yourself," a male voice laced in cigarettes and beer announced.

Isis scrunched her eyebrows and looked over her right shoulder to find a short chocolate brother sporting a mouthful of gold teeth smiling at her. She wanted to laugh out loud. What about her made this man think she would want to talk to him? But there was no use being rude. "I'm good. I'm just finishing my drink."

"Shit, your man must be crazy to leave you all alone."

This time, Isis had to laugh at the man's thinly veiled attempt to see if she had a date. "If you're asking if I have a man, no, I don't, but I'm not looking for one, either."

"Hold on, now," the man said, holding his hands up in front of him. "I'm not tryin'a be your man. You ain't gotta be mean like that."

"I'm not trying to be mean, I was just saying," Isis said, continuing to hold her smile.

"Baby, you gotta learn to take a compliment."

"And you have to learn to give one. How are you just going to walk up on me like that?"

The man laughed. "You ain't from around here, are you?"

She smirked. "How did you guess?"

"I can just tell."

Her feelings weren't hurt because she'd had similar conversations the entire four months she lived in New Orleans. To Isis, it was amusing because it seemed that New Orleanians were quick to point out an outsider's accent as if they themselves spoke the King's English. She guessed it was the same in every city with its own culture. Outsiders stood out like a sore thumb. She felt the same way when she met the soldiers who were newly assigned to Fort Knox. It was obvious from their funny talk and the way they never added the "r" sound to words like "wash" that they weren't from Kentucky.

She felt the same sentiment when she moved to Texas. Although the dialects were similar, the careful listener could tell the difference. Now that she was in New Orleans, the differences were unmistakable. People in New Orleans didn't sound like cowboys. They spoke with a relaxed tone infused with French dialect. It was almost fascinating to hear someone talk.

The brother standing near her was no exception. He sounded as if he had been born and raised in, and never left, the Crescent City. The swagger he displayed demonstrated that he had no fear and would not be deterred by her standoffish demeanor. She was almost impressed.

"Damn, girl, you know you lookin' hot tonight in that outfit," he told her, his eyes slowly tracing her every curve. His gaze nearly made her feel dirty. When he reached her feet, he smiled and shook his head. "And them shoes are just fire."

Isis cut her eyes at her unwanted escort and pursed her lips. "Is there nothing about me that tells you that I'm not interested? Please, don't make me have to be rude."

"Oh," he responded, leaning back. "You one of them uppity chicks. You probably like them white boys."

Isis rolled her eyes, letting her eyelids flutter as her pupils pointed upward. "You can't be serious. Why do you men think that just because a woman's not interested, she has to either be into white guys or gay? Did it ever occur to you that I'm just not interested in tired-ass brothas with a mouthful of gold teeth? Now please, let me enjoy my fuckin' evening in peace."

"Damn!" he reacted, taking a step back. "You ain't even hafta go there on me. Stuck-up bitch."

Isis wanted to retort that his momma was a bitch, but since she wasn't familiar with her surroundings she figured she'd let him get away with his childish remark and just walk away. It took all she had to bite her tongue and go back to people watching, but after a while, she forgot about the overage thug. There were more important things in life than having the last word.

Just as she took the last sip from her drink, she heard a male voice chuckle from behind. "I like your style."

She turned to find a tall, latte-colored gentleman wearing a black suit without a tie. His white shirt was unbuttoned at the neck, giving him a relaxed yet classy look. He wasn't bad looking, sporting a fresh curly-haired haircut and a thin goatee. The man stood with two other men who seemed oblivious to what had just transpired near them.

Yet, as good looking as he was, Isis had lost all motivation to meet anyone after the experience she'd just had. In fact, the sound of yet another man approaching her had nearly made her skin crawl. She scrunched her eyebrows and wrinkled her nose. "Excuse me?"

"You don't play, do you?" he asked, moving closer to her, seemingly oblivious to the incredulous look on Isis's face.

"I really don't," she replied, rolling her eyes.

"Don't worry, I'm not tryin'a get with you, no," the man whispered once he got close to her.

"Huh?" His statement had thrown her off until she remembered that in New Orleans many people placed yes or no behind their statements. It was a throwback to the French language. "Oh, yeah."

"What's your name, love?" he asked.

"Isis," she replied, thankful that this guy at least seemed to want to know her name before attempting what she was sure would be tired game. When were Alexis and Shalonda going to get off that damned dance floor, anyway?

"Nice to meet you, Isis," he said, extending his hand. "I'm Cain."

"Hi."

Cain continued to attempt small conversation with Isis, who couldn't help feeling like an ice princess. It almost made her feel bad. Just because some bum had irritated her, she'd elected to take out her frustration on this perfectly nice man who seemed to have no detectable agenda. She tried warming to the man so she wouldn't come off so mean. It was interesting. There used to be a time when she was never considered mean to any man. What a difference a few years could make.

"You send me swinging . . ."

"Damn, I ain't heard that song in years," Cain exclaimed. "Miss Isis, you gotta give me a dance."

"Why not?" she asked, taking his hand. She used to love the old Mint Condition song herself. In fact, she loved everything by Mint Condition.

As she followed Cain to the floor, she caught a glimpse of Alexis and Shalonda leaving the dance floor while trying to fan themselves with their hands. They looked up at her and smiled. Isis smiled and waved at them.

"It looks like your girl is starting to loosen up," Shalonda said with a laugh.

"Good, because I thought her tail was going to hold up the wall all night!" Alexis retorted.

They laughed together and went to the bar.

"Girl, it is too packed in here tonight," Shalonda remarked, scanning the crowded room. "I wish some of these people would leave so we can have a place to sit."

"I know, right?" Alexis replied, rocking to the left and right. "My feet are killing me."

"That's what your tail gets for wearing stilettos. Tryin'a be cute!"

"Oh, you got jokes," Alexis said, a tenacious smile covering her face. She wanted to be insulted, but she knew her friend was right. "You know what my grandmother used to always say."

Shalonda chuckled. "You gotta suffer to be beautiful."

Alexis nodded. "Damn right."

Her laughing stopped suddenly when she caught a glimpse of a well-dressed, caramel-colored gentleman near the corner of the dance floor. She could see him clearly, but he definitely couldn't see her. If he had, he

probably wouldn't have rubbed his escort's chin the way
he did. And he definitely wouldn't have pecked her on the
lips before leading her to the dance floor to sway to the
music. Alexis stared as the "couple" continued swaying
once the music transitioned to Anthony Hamilton's "The
Point of It All."

"That no-good bastard," she mumbled as she glared at
her husband's coworker. He was a fellow attorney at Jamar's firm who had eaten at their table, watched football
on their TV, and stood on their carpet. They'd taken rides
in the same car. This was one instance where she hoped
that birds of a feather didn't flock together.

"What's wrong?" Shalonda asked.

Alexis pointed at the couple dancing as if they hadn't a
care in the world. "Look at that shit."

Shalonda looked, but confusion clouded her face.
"What am I looking for?"

"You don't see Jamar's friend Vernon out there dancing
with that old chickenhead girl right there?"

Shalonda looked a little harder. "Oh, damn. Isn't he
married?"

"That bastard is very married," Alexis replied, folding
her arms defiantly. "And his wife is gorgeous and makes
her own money. How can he do her like that?"

"Now don't jump to conclusions, Lex," Shalonda said,
patting her friend on the arm. "You don't know the whole
story."

"Don't worry, I'm not saying a word to him," Alexis
assured her. "But you better believe I'm gonna let Jamar
know what I saw. What he does with the information is
on him. I'm not trying to get caught up in that mess."

"I hear you."

"But I will tell you this: I hope his narrow ass sees me
tonight. Let him sweat thinking I'm gonna run out and
tell Terrie what he's in here doing."

Shalonda laughed so hard, Alexis stared at her. Surely what she said couldn't have been that funny.

"What is your problem?" Alexis asked, scrunching her eyebrows.

"His narrow ass?" Shalonda asked once she recovered enough to speak. "You are really sounding more and more like your grandmother every day."

Another unintended smile crossed Alexis's face. "Shut up, Shalonda. I'm trying to be serious here."

"I know, which is why it's so funny. Now, don't let that man ruin your night."

Alexis nodded slowly. "You're right. Later for him. I wonder how Isis is doing? She acts like she's trying to break our record on the floor."

"I know, right?"

"Little Miss I Don't Dance sure is changing her tune."

"That man we saw taking her to the floor must have put something on her," Shalonda said with a smile. "You better warn her about these New Orleans men. You know they ain't nothin' nice."

"Who you tellin'? I'm married to one."

"Hell, me too."

"But I gotta give it to her," Alexis conceded when she recovered from her laughter. "The fella looks good."

"I didn't really get a good look at him, so I'll take your word for it."

"He was a nice-looking light-skinned dude with curly hair."

Shalonda grunted. "Sounds like a playboy to me. Probably checks himself out every time he passes his reflection."

"While you're playing, I've dated jokers like that."

"Here they come now," Shalonda said, pointing toward Isis and her dance partner as they left the dance floor. Shalonda waved at her to let her know she and Alexis were standing by the bar.

"It looks like you're having a good time," Alexis remarked once Isis reached the two ladies.

"Actually, I am," Isis responded, still holding Cain's hand. She looked up at Cain and introduced him to her friends.

"Nice to meet you," he said, leaning in to shake their hands. He then looked down at Isis. "I'ma let you ladies enjoy your evening. I'ma call it a night in a few."

"All right," Isis replied. "I'll call you soon."

"You do that," he said, backing into the crowd.

When she was sure he was out of earshot, Alexis smiled at Isis and patted her on the back. "I ain't mad at you, Miss Isis. He ain't bad looking. Good work for your first night out."

"Yeah, well, I was starting to think all these men in New Orleans had lost their minds, fooling with that clown who approached me earlier."

"What happened?" Shalonda asked before sipping from her newly ordered drink.

"Some ghetto-fab dude called me a bitch because I didn't wanna be bothered earlier," Isis explained.

"Oh, you've got to careful with some of these fellas," Alexis warned. "This isn't a bad club, but there are some pretty rough people who come here. You have to know how to handle yourself."

"I sure figured that out."

The rest of the night went on without incident. By the time the three women left the club, each had been approached at least three more times. Shalonda and Alexis politely turned down their advances, while Isis collected one other phone number that she didn't plan on using. Taking it just seemed like the easiest way to get rid of the man.

As they waited outside the club for the valet to retrieve the car, Isis glanced at her watch and was shocked at the time. "Goodness! It's almost three in the morning. Time sure does fly."

Alexis laughed. "It happens. I remember the first time I went to a club outside of New Orleans. I thought I was gonna have a heart attack when they announced last call for alcohol and it was only one-thirty."

"Nobody parties like New Orleans," Shalonda added.

"I see," Isis agreed. "Usually you can tell when it's time to go because the crowd starts to thin out. They just don't do that here."

"There have been times when I left the club at like five-thirty in the morning," Alexis said. "Of course, that was during my college days, when I was a bit more wild and free."

"Shoot, I was going to the club every weekend up until I got married a few years ago," Isis said.

"You're married?" Shalonda asked. "Is your husband in New Orleans too?"

"Girl, no," Isis said quickly, waving her hand at Shalonda. "I got rid of that problem about two years ago, but that's a story for another time."

"Well, it sounds like you're happy about it, so I look forward to hearing that story when you're ready to tell it," Alexis said, as the valet pulled her BMW in front of them. The ladies paused their conversation as they piled inside, Shalonda taking the front seat and Isis taking the back.

"Yeah, we'll get together sometime," Isis said once Alexis pulled away from the curb. "But I know it won't be tomorrow since Miss Twylite is planning on having me on phone duty all day."

Alexis looked troubled. "Is she okay?"

"I guess. She called me earlier and asked if she could call me tomorrow while her parents were at church."

"I guess she's staying home tomorrow," Alexis surmised. "Maybe I'll check on her, too."

"That may be good. She can probably use all the support she can get," Isis replied.

"I couldn't even imagine," Shalonda said, shaking her head.

"Yeah," Isis said reflectively, looking out of the window. She didn't want to say much more because she wasn't sure how much Shalonda already knew about Twylite's case. Although she and Alexis were best friends, she was sure that Alexis wouldn't discuss intimate details of the girl's case. It just wasn't ethical. She'd have to remember to talk with Alexis about it tomorrow.

Alexis pulled in front of Isis's Garden District apartment, which actually looked more like a warehouse than an apartment building. Isis smiled, loving the industrial charm the building offered. The outside looks gave no clue to the luxury within.

"Well, Isis, you certainly picked a nice place to live," Shalonda said. "This is a pretty uppity area."

"Yeah, you'd never believe there was a housing project not too far from here," Alexis added.

"There was?" Isis asked, looking worried.

"Yeah, but after Katrina, they went through and redid the area," Alexis explained. "They replaced them with affordable townhomes. But this area has always been nice. It's right by the mansions on St. Charles Avenue, so the property value will always stay high."

"Yeah, I usually jog down St. Charles," Isis said, relaxing a bit.

"Oh, you're a runner?" Alexis asked.

"Oh God, you shouldn'ta said that," Shalonda lamented.

"Stop hatin', Shalonda," Alexis said, turning her head toward her friend, then back at Isis. "She's just jealous because the most exercise she gets is walking from her bed to her bathroom."

"And I'm still fine," she retorted.

"Anyway," Alexis said, rolling her eyes toward Shalonda. "Now that I know you're a runner, I'm going to have to take you on some of my trails."

"That sounds good," Isis replied, climbing out of the car. "I need a running partner to get me motivated."

"Okay, I'll call you tomorrow," Alexis said. "Go ahead and get inside. Your neighborhood is nice, but crime still abounds in this city."

Isis laughed, and then turned toward her building. When she didn't hear the car pull off, she looked back to find Alexis and Shalonda still sitting there. She waved at them, figuring that they were waiting for her to get inside. She didn't feel that was necessary, but at least they seemed to be concerned about her safety. A chuckle bubbled in her stomach. What were those two women going to do if some man did snatch her up?

# Chapter Six

The sight of her bed was all it took to remind Isis that she was exhausted. It was almost five in the morning when she finally drifted off to sleep, only to be snatched from her bliss two hours later.

Since she knew Twylite would be calling later that day, attending the eight a.m. service seemed like a good idea at the time. However, her constant yawns during the sermon told her she could have used a couple more hours. It was only by the grace of God that she was able to make it home from church without dozing off.

Once she reached her apartment, she felt like she'd beaten the sleep monkey that had been perched on her back all morning. After kicking her stilettos off at the door, she went to the kitchen and made herself a mimosa. Yet, her undoing came when she strolled into the bedroom to put her Bible away. Her unmade queen-sized bed displayed her champagne-colored 500-thread count sheets and fluffy comforter. Before she knew it, she'd downed the rest of her drink, peeled off her dress, and crawled deep under the covers. She was out before she knew it.

It was nearly noon when she awoke from her slumber. She yawned and stretched without even opening her eyes. "Uuum, I needed that," she mumbled to herself.

She sat up and reached for her remote control to see if anything was on TV. As much as she paid for cable, she knew there had better be something she wanted to watch.

As she surfed the channels, she glanced at her cell phone, wondering if it had rung while she slept. The caller ID displayed no missed calls.

"I thought Twylite said she was going to call me?" Isis wondered aloud. "Maybe she decided to go to church after all."

She shrugged and continued looking for a TV show, finally settling on a rerun of *Clean House*. Yet not even the clever quips of Niecy Nash could make her mind abandon thoughts of her client. The thoughts became so powerful that she could no longer concentrate on reveal day.

Her boss, Mrs. Delachaise, had warned her about this. It was easy for victim's advocates to get so involved in their cases that they became consumed by them. Some had become so consumed that they projected the victim's feelings onto themselves, as if they were the ones going through the survivor experience. She'd even heard of some advocates having to go see counselors of their own after closing a case. It was for this reason alone that VAs had to be careful not to get too close to their survivors.

Although Isis understood the reasoning behind the warning, this case just seemed different. Her client was a teenager who had gotten caught up in a bad relationship with a grown man. Not only that, but the man brutalized her and left her in the woods when he couldn't get his way. Who did that? And from what she could surmise over the last couple of days, the abuse had started long before that fateful night.

She was surprised the girl's parents hadn't had the man arrested for statutory rape. She'd have to remember to talk to them about that. Isis could only guess that there was some emotional abuse going on on all sides. The teenager probably felt fortunate to have an older man with a job, so she let him treat her anyway he pleased. The parents tried to force her to break up with him, which only succeeded in pushing her closer to him. The girl, knowing that both sides loved her in their own way, played on that love to try to get what she wanted. It was a sad situation no matter what way Isis looked at it.

It was no wonder Twylite tried to lock herself away from the rest of the world. She thought she knew what she was doing and wound up having the whole thing blow up in her face. All she wanted was to be loved, but she got everything but that from this Peanut character. He treated her like property instead of a woman.

Thoughts of Twylite again took Isis back to the days when she had let men play with her mind and break her self-esteem so far down that she felt she didn't deserve any better. Some had given her STDs and instead of owning up to what they'd done, they berated her, accusing her of infecting them. Others seemed to smell her desire for a man like perfume, and played on it so well that she often found herself begging for just a piece of their attention.

Like Twylite, she didn't see any of this until it was too late. It was only after she married a man who had never gotten over her past that she had finally convinced herself that she deserved better. It was while she lay in a hospital bed after a brutal beating from her husband caused her to lose her baby that she finally looked back and actually learned from the mistakes she'd made. She only hoped that Twylite wouldn't wait until adulthood to learn her lessons. She could only pray that the girl wouldn't suffer nearly the same fate she did. Actually, she needed to do more than pray. Come hell or high water, she would make sure she drilled it into Twylite's head that she didn't need a man's disrespect disguised as love to make her feel special.

"I can't take this," Isis said with a sigh. She reached for the caller ID and scanned it until she reached the Knights' phone number. She then pushed the callback button and waited for the line to connect.

"Hello?"

"Hi, Twylite? How's it going?"

"It's okay," she replied, sounding as if she'd just woken up. "How are you?"

"I'm fine. I was just calling to check on you. You said you were going to call me today."

"Yeah, I was. I just haven't even gotten out the bed yet."

"You been asleep all day?"

"No reason to get up."

Withdrawal was one of the classic symptoms of rape victims. Many would act as if their blanket were the shield that protected them from the world. Like if they held it over their heads long enough, their problems would just disappear. But life didn't work that way. Eventually, they would run out of air and be forced to surface back into the real world. They'd have to face their problems if they were to ever really overcome them.

Isis had to find a way to make Twylite see that. If this rape managed to consume her now, she would have no chance at ever having a successful relationship in the future. Every person she would meet, whether male or female, would have some type of ulterior motive in her eyes. Even those with honorable intentions would never have a chance with her because of the horrible thing that happened to her when she was sixteen.

"What's on your mind, Twy?" Isis asked, pointing the remote at the television and turning it off. She turned over onto her side and propped her head onto her two pillows.

"I still keep thinking this thing is my fault," Twylite said after a pause. She sounded as if she had tears in her eyes.

The sound of her sad words broke Isis's heart.

"This whole thing is embarrassing."

"We've been through this before," Isis said. "You can't keep blaming yourself. Did you make some bad choices?

Yes, you did. But just like you had a choice, Peanut did too. And he chose to put his hands on you. You didn't make him do that. And eventually he's going to have to pay for what he did."

"How's he gonna do that? The police already said they don't have enough evidence. It's his word against mine."

"Even if he doesn't go to jail, he will pay in some kind of way. He has to answer to God for what he did."

"Do you really believe he raped me?"

And there it was: her unintentional admission that she needed an ally. Yes, her parents would always be on her side. They were her parents; they were supposed to be, whether they believed this thing was her fault or not. But this was the time when she needed a friend, somebody who really believed in her. She was willing to bet that Twylite hadn't even discussed this with friends her own age yet.

"Of course I believe you, Twylite. Why would you ask me that?"

"I just wonder if anybody else will believe me. Everybody knows me and Peanut was hangin' out. And I know people saw him pick me up the other night. They're gonna probably say I asked for it."

"Nobody asks for something like this to happen."

"Tell them that. Half those girls at Saint Francis's are jealous of me. They wish they could have a man with a ride like Peanut's."

"Was that why you were with Peanut? Because of the status it gave you?"

"No," Twylite snapped. "I loved him. He made me happy. And he never treated me like a little girl."

Isis exhaled heavily and shook her head. What was about to come out of her mouth was something she should have kept inside, but she just couldn't help herself. Why did teenage girls have to go through this? "So you're saying he respected you?"

"Yes. All the time."

"Twylite, don't get mad at me, but if he loved and respected you so much, why would he make you sneak out of the house to see him?"

Isis hoped she hadn't gone too far. She could hear the cluck of Twylite's tongue swiping the back of her teeth. Attitude was sure to follow. "My momma told you that? She never did understand the relationship between me and Peanut. Things only got bad about a month ago when Momma and Daddy made me break up with him. He couldn't handle that. We loved each other."

"Sweetie, I'm only going to say this because I care about you and I don't want you to make the same mistakes I made in life."

Twylite sighed. "Go ahead and say it, Isis. It ain't like I ain't heard it before."

"I'm sorry, sweetie," Isis said, rising from her bed. She trudged into the kitchen, stretching the kinks from her back the entire way while balancing the receiver between her shoulder and ear. This conversation made her thirsty. "But you have to think about it. A man who loves you—I mean really loves you—will not let you disrespect yourself to prove your love to him."

"Huh?"

"Think about it," Isis said, as she prepared herself another mimosa. Damn, why hadn't anyone broken this down to her when she was Twylite's age? "No relationship is perfect. Every couple has their ups and downs. But love shouldn't be stressful. Love shouldn't force anyone to lie in order to be with their significant other. You shouldn't have to fight everybody and their cousin to be together."

"Lots of people had to fight to be together," Twylite protested. "Look at Romeo and Juliet. Even Brandy had to fight with her mom to be with Wanya from Boyz II Men."

"Come on, Twylite," Isis snapped. "Are you serious? First of all, Romeo and Juliet snuck around like a couple of spoiled kids and wound up killing their damned selves. I am so tired of people thinking those two kids were the epitome of love. They knew each other for all of a day or two and were ready to go to blows with their families to be together. Had they been together maybe even a week more, maybe Romeo would have figured out that Juliet was flighty, and Juliet would have seen that Romeo didn't have much family loyalty."

"Man, Isis, you really thought about that, didn't you?" Twylite remarked.

"I read the story a few times," Isis replied, smiling in spite of herself. "I will give you that there are some people who had to fight for true love, but they are the exceptions, not the rules. But one thing remains constant: a man who truly loves you will not let you go through the drama you let yourself go through in order to be with him. If anything, you gave him power over you. He could tell you to do anything and you would do it because you thought you two loved each other."

"I never thought about it like that," Twylite mumbled after a pause.

"So many young girls sacrifice their self-respect for the sake of having somebody, but all it gets them is submission to some man's ego," Isis continued, more to herself than to the teenager she was supposed to be helping. "They get blinded by the gifts, the money, or even the bullshit words he spouts out and think they really got somebody."

"I wasn't blinded by anything," Twylite protested.

"You weren't?" Isis challenged, unable to stop the tirade. "The first thing you told me when we got on the phone was that those girls at school were jealous of you because you had a man with a BMW. It didn't matter that he had you sneaking out of the house or that he talked to you like trash. As long as you had a man with some ends, right?"

"So you do think it was my fault that he raped me," the girl said, sadness dripping from her voice.

Now it was Isis's turn to suck her teeth. "Sweetie, I'm just trying to help you see that you have to love yourself before you can get anyone else to show you real love. Yes, that man raped you, and I hope he burns in hell for what he did. But so you will never have to find yourself involved with another joker like him, learn to respect yourself and not put up with being treated like anything less than the queen that you are."

The line became so quiet that Isis thought she may have lost the girl. Had her truth been too brutal? Maybe she hung up. "You there, Twylite?"

"Yeah," the girl finally replied. "Look, I have to go. My momma and daddy will be home from church in a few."

Isis didn't want to hang up just yet, but experience told her that Twylite needed time to process their conversation. She suddenly felt sorry that she'd been so blunt so soon. It wasn't even her place to be giving advice.

She gulped down the rest of her drink and shook her head. Would she have been able to take those words when she was Twylite's age? Hell, would she have been able to take them just five years ago? "You gonna be okay? I'm sorry if I hurt your feelings."

"No, you were right," Twylite replied. "I'm good. I just wanna make sure I'm up before my parents get back."

"Okay, well, call me if you need me. I'm here for you."

"Thanks," Twylite said before hanging up.

As she pressed END on her cell, Isis again asked herself if she went too far. One of the main lessons she was taught was not to give advice. She was only to help guide the survivor's thought process so she wouldn't continue to blame herself for the rape. Isis started off doing that, but had she made a mistake in displaying too much honesty? Would she ever hear from Twylite again? Had her overzealous willingness to help finally gotten her into trouble?

"Shit, shit, shit," she hissed as she trudged back to her bedroom. She flopped backward on her bed and stared at the ceiling as if it held some undetectable answer. "Mrs. Delachaise is gonna kill me."

Her boss had pounded into her head time and time again that advocates were not to give advice, but encouragement. Why couldn't Isis remember that?

It only took a few minutes for the bed to begin feeling too hard. Her mouth watered as she thought about her temporary relief sitting in the kitchen. The thought propelled her to rise from the bed and return to the kitchen. The champagne and orange juice sat on the counter as if waiting for her to return.

She refreshed her drink and gulped down half of it. It didn't even burn as it went down.

"Damn," she mumbled. "Either that drink was weak, or I'm turning into an alcoholic."

Before she could ponder the thought, her cell phone sounded from the bedroom. She placed her glass on the counter and traced the sound to her nightstand, relieved that it wasn't her work cell this time. The number that illuminated from the display was a 504 number with the name Cain on top. She lifted her eyebrows in surprise as she pressed TALK.

"Hello?"

"Well, hello, pretty lady," Cain greeted her, his voice a welcome respite from the heaviness she felt just seconds before.

"I thought I was supposed to call you?" Isis asked with a laugh.

"I figured I would surprise you. Did you go to church today?"

"Yes, I did," Isis replied proudly, deciding to leave out how she'd struggled to stay conscious throughout the entire service. She refused to make it known to this man whom she'd just met that she was a lightweight when it came to clubbing. Her days of getting home from the club just in time to get dressed for church had faded long ago.

"I knew you was a good girl," he replied with a chuckle. "I slept right through church this morning."

Isis laughed and sat on her bed, leaning back against the headboard. She whispered a silent thank-you to God for the friendly conversation. She'd gone from zero to sixty in just a few minutes. At least, if only for a few minutes, she could focus on herself. No one else would matter except her.

"So, Miss Church Lady, whatcha got planned for the rest of the day?" Cain asked.

"I really hadn't thought about it," Isis admitted, hoping he would ask her out. She wasn't sure why, but there was something intriguing about this guy Cain. Although he had a definite rough edge to him, he came across as a gentleman. The gentleman side made her comfortable talking with him, but the rough side made him seem fun.

Maybe it was the fact that she hadn't had so much as a kiss since she moved away from Texas, but she could really see herself getting to know this man in more ways than one. She nearly laughed at herself for her slightly horny moment, but she knew there was no way she would go back down the road of her past. As fine as Cain was, he would have to agree to wait before getting a piece of her love.

"How 'bout you grab a late lunch with me? You ate yet?"

"Ummm," Isis stuttered, glancing at the clock. It was just after two o'clock, and the only thing she had in her system was orange juice and champagne. She could definitely use some food, but she was in no shape to drive, and she wasn't comfortable letting Cain know where she lived just yet.

"Awww, don't tell me you don't wanna see me," Cain said with mock hurt in his voice.

Isis laughed. "It's not like that."

"Then what, you already ate?"

"No."

"Don't tell me you already got a man."

Isis laughed even harder. "Will you stop and let me get a word out?"

"My terrible," he replied, laughing with her. "Whatcha got to say?"

"I was just going to say," she started, thinking fast," I have to run to the store a couple of blocks from my house. You mind meeting me there?"

"I can do that. What time you want me to meet you?"

"How long would it take you to get uptown on Tchoupitoulas?"

"Not long at all—about ten minutes. I don't live that far from there."

"Okay, well give me about thirty minutes."

"Sounds good, babe," he said. "I'll see you then."

"Okay, call me when you're close so I can tell you where I am."

Isis smiled as she pressed END. A date would be a welcome change from all of the heaviness she'd felt this weekend. She hadn't even realized until just that moment how lonely she'd been. Since moving to New Orleans, all she'd done was work and call back home. Now she'd met two great women who could possibly grow to be friends, and a guy who seemed truly interested in getting to know her. She hated to admit it, but out of tragedy came somewhat of a social life. Was that a fair thought?

# Chapter Seven

The moment of truth had arrived. Monday morning. Twylite knew it would be a long day when she reached over to her chair and realized her uniform wasn't there waiting for her. She'd completely forgotten that her uniform was taken with the SAFE kit. They needed it for evidence.

"Shit," she mumbled as she walked to her closet to fish out her extra uniform. She hated this skirt. It was slightly longer than her other two skirts, which she'd hemmed to just a quarter inch longer than the authorized length that the nuns allowed. That way she could still be sexy without having to worry about getting jumped on by the nuns.

The blouse was long sleeved. She'd planned to save that blouse until it was too cold to wear her favorite short-sleeved blouse. Putting on the old standby made her feel like an old woman, but what choice did she have at this point? One uniform was still in the dirty clothes hamper, while the other was being prodded through by some real-life CSI.

After donning the dreaded outfit, she looked into the mirror and groaned at all the fuzzy hair sticking out of her braids. Although she washed her hair after the attack, she neglected to wrap her braids with the satin scarf, or any scarf for that matter. She scooped a few fingers of styling gel from the open jar on her dresser and smoothed it over her braids in an effort to make them presentable. She then picked up a scrunchie and pulled them back into a ponytail, an old standby usually reserved for days when she woke up late.

"I look like shit," she mumbled as she inspected herself in the full-length mirror affixed to the back of her bedroom door.

She really didn't know who to blame for her funk that morning. Peanut certainly deserved most of the blame, and the guilt and over-empathizing from her parents had started to wear on her. But that so-called speech from Isis just topped everything. This woman had only known her for less than three minutes, and she thought she knew her like that? What was that bunk about making Peanut responsible for her happiness? She was plenty happy with or without a man. What did she know, anyway?

She'd made up her mind that she wouldn't bother talking with Isis anymore. The woman obviously knew nothing about love. She was probably some bitter, lonely woman who dedicated herself to making rape victims as bitter as she was. Self-love. She just didn't know that Twylite had more than enough self-love. She was the shit!

That thought made her smile, despite the granny uniform and horrid hair. She'd get through this day. It was nobody's business what had happened to her Friday night. Twylite was fine now and ready to meet the world. If she displayed the same attitude she normally displayed at school, she'd be just fine.

But how would she explain the marks all over her face? And what about the paper she was supposed to finish that weekend? With all the excitement, she'd completely forgotten about it. Now it was due, and she hadn't even gotten past page three.

Which reminded her, where the hell was her backpack? Dammit! Peanut had it! She wouldn't have been able to finish the stupid paper if she wanted to.

She could privately explain to Sister Victoria that she'd been attacked over the weekend and hadn't been able to finish. But then that would mean once again replaying the nightmare in her mind, and she couldn't take that.

"Twylite!" her mother called from downstairs. "You better get on down here and eat before you miss your bus!"

"Yes, ma'am!" she called back.

Maybe her mother could call the school and let them know what happened. It would mean more people in her business, but at least they would be adults. They wouldn't ask her a lot of questions or spread her business throughout the school. At least, that was her hope.


The morning actually went pretty smoothly. There were a couple of curious looks, but nothing seemed to be out of the ordinary, just the same hating girls who always stared at her. Sister Victoria even gave her a private extension on her paper. *Momma came through for me,* she thought with a smile as she headed toward the cafeteria.

"Twy!" a voice called from behind.

She turned around to find her best friend Pam walking up to her. Her toes curled in anticipation of the questions that were sure to come once Pam was close enough to see her face. Her friend didn't disappoint.

"Girl, I been tryin'a call you all weekend. What, you went outta town or somethin'? And what's up with that long skirt?" Pam's eyes batted in surprise once she really focused on her friend. "Forget the skirt, what happened to your face?"

Twylite almost laughed at the barrage of questions her friend threw at her. Pam was so busy preparing to fuss at her about not returning her phone calls that it took a minute to notice the scars.

"You all right, Twy?" Pam asked.

"It's a long story," she replied, shaking her head. "I'll tell you after school."

"It's that nigga Peanut, huh?"

"Shhhhh," Twylite chastised, looking around for a disapproving nun. "You know we can't talk like that in here."

"Well, let's go eat," Pam suggested, thumbing in the direction of the cafeteria. "But don't forget to tell me what happened, friend."

"I won't, but wait until after school," Twylite said. "I don't want any of these hatin' girls up in here to hear what happened."

She quickly cut her eyes at Yasmine, the one girl at Saint Francis's who hated her most. Twylite knew Yasmine hated her because of Peanut, but that was just something she would have to deal with. As far as she was concerned, Yasmine could have the little rapist.

Pam discreetly followed her friend's gaze and nodded. "All right. You okay though?"

Twylite nodded and shrugged. "As good as I'm gonna get. I just need for this day to be over."

Before reaching the cafeteria, Pam suddenly stopped walking and pulled her friend as close to the wall as she could. Twylite could feel the stroke of Pam's eyes as they seemed to trace the scars that decorated her face. Twylite looked away, embarrassed.

"Just tell me this much," Pam whispered, leaning in. "Did Peanut do this to you?"

Twylite nodded, preferring to stare at the cracks in the wall rather than the disapproving eyes of her best friend. She bit her lip to keep from crying again.

"Damn," Pam mumbled. "I knew I shouldn't have let you get in the car with him. It just didn't feel right, him poppin' up out the blue like that."

"Shoulda, woulda," Twylite whispered, tears stinging her eyes, threatening to fall. "Can't do anything about it now."

"Did y'all call the police?"

"Yeah, but that's a whole 'nother story."

Pam sighed and leaned back against the wall. She ran her fingers through her short, partially blond spiky hair. Twylite had always been jealous of the fact that Pam's parents let her cut and highlight her hair. Twylite's parents always pledged that she was too young for such edgy hairstyles.

"Why didn't you call me? You went through all this by yourself?"

"And say what? 'Guess what, Pam? My dumb ass let my boyfriend rape me!'"

Pam gasped and covered her mouth. "He raped you? And that nigga ain't dead yet?"

"Shut up, Pam," Twylite whispered as loudly as she could without attracting any attention. "Yes, he raped me, and there ain't shit the police can do about it. Now let's go eat before the nuns come get us."

Pam complied, but as she led Twylite into the cafeteria, she continually shook her head and punched her fist into her left hand. She could hear the loud, ragged breaths coming from her friend's nose. She sounded like a flu victim struggling to breathe.

Pamela may have only been five feet tall, but she had the spirit of a giant. She took nothing off of no one, and biting her tongue had never been in her character. She'd been in her share of fights in her four years at Saint Francis, losing very few. Twylite was actually surprised that her friend hadn't been put out of the school. She could only guess that the fact that Pam was a straight A student overshadowed her scuffles.

"Calm down, Pam," Twylite told her as they moved through the food line. "You're taking this worse than I am."

"I find that hard to believe, Twy," Pam replied as she reached for a bowl of chocolate pudding. "You had all weekend to process this, and now you're calm. You just sprung this sh . . . mess on me not even ten minutes. You're my girl, and I feel like part of this is my fault."

They silently picked up their trays and trudged to their usual table near the back of the cafeteria. Once they were settled, Twylite opened her carton of milk and slipped her straw inside. She looked up at her friend, who was still clearly bothered.

"I'm sorry, friend," Twylite said. "I just didn't wanna talk about it at the time. I needed some time to myself."

Pam nodded without looking at her. "I'm with you. I don't know what I woulda done had that happened to me."

Twylite grunted. *If Pam only knew. Every girl talks mess about what she would do if a man tried to take it from her. "I'd just kick him in the nuts. I'd slice his throat." But when you've been kicked in the stomach and punched in the face, when a man puts his full weight on you and pins you down, when he grabs you by the throat and begins to squeeze, all those claims of toughness go right out of the window. The balance of power, without a little luck, will never be tipped in your favor. Yes, every girl thinks it will never happen to her. She never looks scared. She knows how to fight. She carries a knife or gun. She might even have a killer for an older brother or family friend. But unless the girl is a quick thinker, none of that really matters.*

*Not saying she's helpless, but fear has a way of overpowering courage. This isn't an event a girl trains for every day like a soldier preparing for battle would. A soldier expects the unexpected. He trains for it, dresses for it, even practices for it. Most girls don't do that. They think they know what they'll do, but when faced with the situation, the only thing they're thinking about is getting out of the situation alive.*

At least Pam admitted that she didn't know what she would do in that situation. That made Twylite feel better. Had Pam spouted off about what she would have done and how appalled she was that Twylite hadn't fought back, she would have only succeeded in pissing her friend off. Twylite smiled on the inside at the friendship Pam showed her.

"Hi, Twylite. What the hell happened to your face?"

Pam and Twylite looked up to find Yasmine and two of her friends standing over them. She wore a smirk that showed no sign of compassion. Her friends' expressions matched hers, although Twylite was sure they had no idea why. As always, Yasmine and her friends were flawless. Yasmine wore her hair in a bone-straight, chin-length bob. Aside from a little lip gloss, she wore no makeup, but her smooth honey-colored skin needed no help. One glance at her made Twylite suddenly conscious of the road map drawn across her own face.

"Yasmine, this really isn't the time right now," Twylite said softly.

"I just asked you a question," Yasmine snapped. "You ain't gotta get no attitude."

"I'm really gonna need you to leave me alone right now before I say something I don't need to be saying," Twylite replied, struggling to hold her composure. Just the sight of Yasmine's smug demeanor made Twylite want to smack the taste out of her mouth. Who did this stuck-up bitch think she was?

"It looks like something or somebody messed you up pretty bad," Yasmine said, still smiling. "You need to be careful out there.

"I'll keep that in mind," Twylite replied, maintaining eye contact.

Pam glared as Yasmine and her girls walked away. "I do not like that girl. Be careful. Believe you me, your business will be all over this school if she finds out what happened."

# Chapter Eight

"Awww, baby, that feels so good," Alexis whispered.

"You like that?" Jamar asked, a confident sideways smile plastered on his face.

"Just a little harder."

Jamar complied, and his strong hands made his wife wince in enjoyable pain while clutching the edge of her desk. "You know, I really need to stop spoiling you like this."

"Why?"

"Because giving you foot massages in the middle of the work day is not conducive to a professional work environment," Jamar replied with a laugh. He patted her on the leg and rose from the chair that was situated in front of Alexis's desk.

Alexis watched as he walked across the office and leaned against the door, still smiling at her. "What's on your agenda today?" Alexis asked as she slid her one-inch pumps back on. As much as she loved her stilettos, they just weren't the right shoes to wear to work. Besides, many of her patients' parents thought she was a little too uppity anyway, so she tried to dress as sensibly as possibly without going straight matronly so as not to give them any more of a bad taste in their mouths.

"Not much," Jamar replied. "I have a client coming at two, and another one at four-thirty, so it might be a little late when I get home."

"That's fine. You want me to cook, or are you just gonna pick something up?"

"I'll let you know. If it looks like my four-thirty will be awhile, I'll step out and call you."

"Okay, well I'll take out those steaks just in case. Either way, you up for a movie tonight?"

"Sounds good to me," Jamar said. He picked up his keys from Alexis's desk, but froze as if he'd forgotten something. He cut his eyes at his wife and smirked. "Don't think I don't know why you're being so agreeable."

Alexis looked up at him, scrunching her eyebrows in confusion. "What are you talking about?" she asked, struggling to hold back her smile.

"Now you wanna play dumb. Okay, I'll play your little game, but don't think you're gonna get your way when we go furniture shopping again Saturday."

Alexis couldn't contain her laughter. "Wow, Jamar. Really?"

"Yes, really," he shot back with a laugh of his own. "You ain't slick, woman."

"What makes you think I'm tryin'a be slick?" she asked, rising from her desk. She placed her hand on the doorknob, but didn't turn it. Instead, she looked up at her husband and shot him an innocent smile.

Jamar laughed and shook his head. "Don't play that mess with me, no. I've known you too long for that."

"What?" Alexis asked, batting her eyelids.

"You are one silly-ass woman, Alexis," he said with a chuckle. "Let's just hope you play this crazy when we go shopping again this weekend. Just remember that, as the man of the house, I get the final decision."

She laughed and finally turned the knob. "On the real, I think we need to check the Internet first and save some time."

"That's not a bad idea," Jamar replied as Alexis led him back to the patient waiting area. "Let's check out a couple places while we're watching the movie tonight."

"Sounds good. See? I'm not that disagreeable."

The waiting room was empty, except for Alexis's cousin Lakeisha, her receptionist for the last two years.

"You gone?" Lakeisha asked without taking her eyes from the computer screen.

"Yeah, baby cuz," Jamar replied, tapping the counter twice with the palm of his hand. "I'ma catch you later."

"All right," Lakeisha replied, showing about the same amount of interest she had when the couple walked into the room. She bit into a banana, chewed, and swallowed before mumbling, "See ya."

"She all right?" Jamar whispered to Alexis once he stepped out of the waiting room and into the hall.

She rolled her eyes and shook her head. "That's just how she is sometimes. I thought you knew by now."

He shrugged. "I guess I should have. Anyway, I'll see you later."

He leaned in and gave Alexis a soft kiss on the lips. Alexis smiled. Her husband's kisses still gave her chills, and she didn't mind showing it. With everything she put Jamar through when he tried to win her heart, she enjoyed showing him that his work wasn't in vain. Besides, Jamar was the first man in a long time who showed her that being in love could actually be fun. It didn't have to be work, or stressful, or painful. When two people were on the same page, love could actually be darn near blissful. Who would have ever thought it?

Actually, if Alexis dared to admit it, her cousin Brenda and her husband Darnell were the closest example she'd seen to blissful love. They'd been crazy about each other since the day they met, and showed no signs of slowing down. However, Alexis refused to count them as a real example because, in Alexis's opinion, they hadn't been through half as much as she and Jamar had been through. And any man who would accept a woman the way Jamar had accepted Alexis—despite the fact the she couldn't give him any children—deserved some unconditional, blissful love.

"Okay, baby, get to work," Alexis said with a smile. "I'll see you tonight."

"All right, you be good today."

Alexis smiled. "I'm always good. I thought you knew."

Jamar chuckled and pinched her chin. Without another word, he backed away and headed down the hall toward the elevator that would take him to his parked car. Once he disappeared around the corner, Alexis turned and went back into the waiting room, where she found an unexpected visitor.

"Uh, hi, Twylite," she said, her eyes shooting daggers at her cousin. "How long have you been here?"

"I've been here a little while," the teenager replied, still wearing her school uniform. "I musta been in the bathroom when you came out your office."

Alexis glared at Lakeisha again. Her cousin replied with a disinterested shrug. "I didn't know you were gonna take that long."

"Sometimes I really wonder about you, Keisha," Alexis mumbled, gesturing for Twylite to follow her.

"Dr. Duplessis," Twylite said once they were behind closed doors, "don't blame Ms. Keisha. I really haven't been here that long."

"Don't worry about it," Alexis said. She sat in her chair and gestured for Twylite to have a seat next to the desk. "Everything okay? We didn't have an appointment today, did we?"

"No, I was just dropping by to say hi."

Alexis shot her a skeptical sideways look. "Just dropping by? Really?"

"Yeah," Twylite urged, trying to look convincing. "We hadn't talked since that night. I just wanted to let you know I was all right."

Alexis squinted and looked at her, trying hard to see the girl's thoughts. It wasn't unusual for Twylite to drop in on her, but something just didn't seem right today. Not even a week ago, this same girl was in here crying her eyes out after a brutal rape, and now she just wanted to talk?

"How are your cuts healing?" Alexis asked. She mentally inspected the girl's face. It still looked pretty bad, but the burns seemed to be healing normally. The swelling had gone down, but the burns were still evident. With time, they would go away with little scarring. She'd have to look closer to know for sure, but as long as Twylite was doing what she was supposed to, she wouldn't have a problem returning to normal. She silently thanked God that Twylite must have lifted her head quite a few times during the attack because she only had first-degree burns, which would heal quickly. It would have been a shame if that pretty young face would have been permanently scarred.

"They're fine," she replied, rubbing her knees, where most of the cuts occurred. "They hurt a little when I sit down and right when I stand up, but they're better than what they were."

"Good."

"I'm not keeping you from a patient, am I?"

"No, I have about another forty-five minutes, so you're good."

Twylite seemed to take this bit of news as an invitation to clam up because she began silently taking in the office as if she'd never been there before. Once she appeared to read the same comics on the wall that had been there for the last two months, Alexis found herself losing patience.

The feeling kind of made her feel bad. After all, the girl was obviously calling out for help. Why else would she be here eyeballing an office she'd seen a thousand times before? But where was Isis? Shouldn't Twylite be talking to her?

"What's on your mind, Twy?" Alexis asked quietly.

The girl continued staring at the walls, shifting nervously in her seat.

"Twy?" Alexis called a little louder.

"Huh?" Twylite asked as if being shaken from a dream.

"Okay, sweetie," Alexis said, taking the girl's hands. She looked her directly in the eyes. "What's wrong?"

Twylite looked away. She appeared to be fighting back tears. "It wasn't a good day. I shouldn'ta gone to school."

"What happened?"

"I just wasn't ready. My face still looks jacked up, I feel like everybody knows what happened, and then on the way home . . ."

"What? Did that boy mess with you again?" Alexis could feel the anger rising in her stomach. If that Cooper boy had touched Twylite again, she would kill the nigga herself.

To her relief, Twylite shook her head. "No, nothing like that."

"Then what? Did somebody give you a hard time?"

"It's just that I feel stupid. This girl Yasmine kept messin' with me, asking me what happened to my face. It was like she already knew what happened because she kept lookin' at me all funny."

Alexis squeezed the girl's hands reassuringly. "I'm sure it was just your imagination. Sometimes our minds have a way of playing tricks on us when something bad happens. You think everybody knows when, in fact, nobody really cares. You know what I'm sayin'?"

"Yeah, but when I was waiting for the bus, I saw Peanut drive by with Yasmine in his car. What kind of shit is that?"

Alexis pursed her lips. She knew what this was about. Peanut couldn't go anywhere near Twylite physically, so he would do his best to get into her mind. And it looked like he was doing a damned good job. It had only been a few days and he was already playing games. The sooner he began playing with her mind, the more he could control it.

"Twylite, you don't still want this boy, do you?"

"No! After what he did to me?"

"Exactly," Alexis exclaimed, pointing at Twylite. "And this girl, Yasmine. You two obviously don't like each other. If she knew you were jealous about her messing with Peanut, don't you think she would bother you even more?"

Twylite shrugged. "You right."

"The best advice I can give you is to ignore them both. She obviously knows what happened to you or she wouldn't be picking at you like she's doing. So if she chooses to be with a woman-beating rapist, all you can do is pray for her."

"But what if he does the same thing to her?"

Alexis cocked her head and stared at Twylite with scrunched eyebrows. Did she really care if some girl she didn't even like suffered the same fate she did? Probably not, but as a doctor, she didn't feel comfortable ignoring the question.

After a moment, she responded, "Well, first of all, you have to ask yourself if you're ready for this to get around school. Because no matter who you tell, that person's going to tell somebody, and that somebody will tell someone else. But if you really want to take that risk, you should know she's probably not going to listen to you. You can tell a mutual friend, but that doesn't mean this girl is going to leave him alone. She might even accuse you of lying to get her to leave him alone. Then you're back at square one. But the good part is that if you go that route, you've forewarned this girl, and it will be up to her to make the decision."

Twylite nodded, seemingly taking in Alexis's words. She slowly turned loose Alexis's hands and stood. "I'll think about what you said."

Another awkward silence filled the room. Alexis tried changing the subject and suggesting ways for her patient to speed the healing process of her wounds, but the subject continually turned to Peanut.

"Have you talked to Isis yet about your options concerning pressing charges?"

Twylite sucked her teeth and mumbled, "No."

The attitude didn't go unnoticed, but before Alexis could question her, there was a knock at the door.

"Yes!"

Ms. Kay poked her head in. "Dr. Duplessis, your two o'clock is here."

"Already?" Alexis asked, glancing at her watch. "Damn, she's super early."

Ms. Kay shifted her eyes, noticing for the first time that Alexis had company. "Hi, Twylite. I forgot Lakeisha told me you were here."

"Hi, Ms. Kay," the teenager replied, shooting the nurse what Alexis felt was a fake smile.

"You doing all right?"

"Yes, ma'am."

Ms. Kay nodded silently and turned her head toward Alexis. "I'll go ahead and take her vitals so you two can finish talking."

"Thanks, Ms. Kay," Alexis replied. She smiled at the nurse as she left the room, and then turned back to Twylite. "What did Isis have to say? I'm sure you two have talked at least a little about this."

Twylite sucked her teeth again and pursed her lips. "I talked to her a yesterday, but I ain't gonna talk to her no more."

Alexis drew back her head in surprise, blinking her eyes. "Why not? What happened?"

"She just doesn't know me. How I'm s'posed to take advice from her? She don't really care about me."

"I find that a little hard to believe. It seems to me that she had your back from day one."

"How is she gonna care about somebody she doesn't even know? She's only doing what she gets paid to do. I don't feel right tellin' my business to somebody like that."

In a way, Alexis could understand Twylite's reservations, but something in the back of her mind told her that there was more to this story. There just wasn't time to investigate right now. Instead, she just nodded her head and patted Twylite on the knee.

"Sweetie, I wish I could talk with you further, but as you can see, I have a patient waiting for me," she said, rising from her chair. Twylite followed suit. "Tell your mom to call me so we can set up an appointment in a week or two. I wanna make sure you're healing both inside and out."

"Okay, I'll tell her."

Twylite followed Alexis out of the office, but turned and walked toward the waiting room while Alexis went to the examining room.

"Bye, Dr. Duplessis," Twylite called before walking out of the door.

Alexis smiled and waved before entering the examining room. Ms. Kay was just finishing the notes in the patient's chart as she walked into the room.

"Everything okay?" Ms. Kay whispered, handing Alexis the chart.

"We'll see," she replied with a shrug. She quickly reviewed Ms. Kay's notes and pasted her most professional smile toward the young boy sitting on the examining table who was holding his dad's hand. "Robert?"

The boy nodded slowly, and then looked up, showcasing a salmon-pink eye.

"Awww," she said with a sympathetic smile. "I guess little boys don't like wearing pink too much, huh?"

The traffic in the Central Business District showed no sign of letting up, especially since the Saints were playing their second preseason game. Between the line of cars headed to the Superdome and the others working their way toward Canal Street, the CBD was in gridlock. A person would have to be misguided to be in that mess for no apparent reason.

Unfortunately, Isis was one of those misguided souls. She'd spent much too long at the YWCA on South Jeff Davis, listening to her boss give a lecture on survivor support. The center had a pretty successful battered women's program, so Isis felt she could benefit from sitting in on the lecture. She'd lost Twylite, but maybe the knowledge she gained from that experience could help someone else. True, it had only been day since they had spoken, but something in the teenager's voice told her that she might not hear from Twylite again. Her feeling was confirmed when she tried calling Twylite's cell phone and didn't get a response. That was hours ago, and the teen still hadn't returned the call. She'd try again tomorrow, but vowed to herself to keep her unsolicited advice to herself.

*"It's a common mistake many of our newer advocates make,"* Mrs. Delachaise told her before the lecture. *"It's hard to remember that we're not here to give advice. We're an ear to listen and a resource for finding services."*

*"I just wish I'd remembered that before I opened my big mouth,"* Isis lamented.

*"Don't be so hard on yourself. It happens. Chances are she'll be back as soon as she has time to cool off. But even if she doesn't, you did what you could. She has good parents and that doctor friend around her, so she won't be on an island by herself."*

*Mrs. Delachaise stood up and made herself a cup of coffee. Isis's eyes bucked at the amount of sugar the woman added to the small Styrofoam cup. The older woman scratched the back of her fluffy, curly black hair and took a sip from the cup, which Isis was sure tasted like pure syrup. The corners of the older woman's mouth turned down into a frown, and she added a splash more coffee into the cup, but didn't stir.*

*"Isis, you wouldn't believe how many women come through SAN who don't have the support system Twylite has," Mrs. Delachaise continued, staring out of the window. The sun still shined brightly. "Twylite will be all right. It's the other ones who come through here that I worry about. The ones who have no family. The ones whose so-called friends would rather see them down in the gutter than to lift them up. The ones who turn to drugs because they just can't cope."*

A blaring horn woke Isis from her memory. She quickly looked up to see that the light had changed to green, and she was holding up a stream of cars. She moved her foot to the accelerator and zoomed across, feeling a tinge of guilt that someone wouldn't make it across the light because of her.

"My bad," she whispered, shrugging her shoulders. She snorted a chuckle as she thought of how much someone stuck at the light had to be calling her everything but a child of God. She couldn't get mad because she knew if the tables were turned, she'd be doing the same.

Her personal cell phone rang just as she turned onto Carondelet Street, leading to the Garden District. Since the traffic had thinned out, she felt comfortable reaching into her purse on the passenger seat and fishing out the phone. A quick glance at the caller ID revealed the name that belonged to someone who was quickly becoming her favorite person.

"Hello, Cain," she sang as she coasted toward her apartment, one hand on the steering wheel and the other clutching her phone.

"Hey, cutie, whatcha up to?"

"Not much, just getting home from work."

"Good," he replied. "Perfect timing."

"What do you mean?"

"I mean you're not busy, so I can steal a little bit of your time."

"How you know? I could be busy right now," she teased.

"Nope, because if you were, you woulda said so from jump when I asked you what you were up to."

Isis laughed. "Okay, you got me. I can see that words matter with you."

"Say what you mean, mean what you say," he said.

"Okay, smart ass, so whatcha gonna do with my time?" Isis asked as she pulled into her regular parking space. She turned off the engine and began gathering her purse and messenger bag.

"Just talk with you, get to know you better," he replied. He paused, and then added, "So call me when you get settled. It sounds like you're doing a lot of moving around."

"Yeah, I just pulled up at my house. Give me about fifteen minutes and my time is yours."

"I like how that sounds. I'll be waiting."

After pressing END, Isis scooted out of her car, maneuvering the messenger bag and purse on her shoulder. She kicked the car door closed, and then scampered into the building.

As happy as she was to have the distraction called Cain, she couldn't help wondering if he had some type of hidden agenda. He almost seemed too nice. She really hated that phrase. *Women always say they want a man who won't dog them, and when they find him, they drop him almost instantly because he's "too nice."* However,

Cain seemed to fit that category, but in a different way. He in no way seemed like someone she could walk all over, but he was nice in the way that made him seem like he was up to something, like he hoped to get into her pants sometime soon.

"Stop that, Isis," she mumbled to herself as she unlocked the door to her apartment. She had to remind herself that she no longer lived the life she used to live. While there was nothing wrong with keeping her guard up, she had to remember not to build the wall around herself so high that no man would be able to get through it. The best thing she could do was take the lessons she learned from the past and apply them to her present. There was no use in carrying her past mistakes because there was nothing she could do about them.

What she could do, though, was let Cain prove himself. If he was up to no good, he would reveal himself without any help from her. Until then, why not enjoy some friendly company? It's not like she had a parade of men beating down her door. It was time to start enjoying the Big Easy.

She thought back to their lunch date on Sunday. The conversation wasn't deep by any stretch of the imagination, but she still had a blast. They laughed and cracked jokes, and she didn't care that all the champagne she'd drunk on an empty stomach had given her a splitting headache. He couldn't believe that she had moved to New Orleans from Texas, but was actually from Kentucky.

"What black people actually live in Kentucky?" he'd asked with a laugh. "I knew you sounded funny."

"Like you folks in New Orleans speak the King's English, baaaaabay!" Isis had retorted.

They went back and forth like that for the nearly two hours of their date. Isis laughed at just the memory of that day. She glanced at her watch and realized a half hour had passed since she had gotten out of her car.

"Oops," she mumbled as she fished her cell phone out of her purse, which lay next to her on her bed. She dialed Cain's number and braced herself for whatever smart remark he'd come up with for her calling back so late.

"Man, what the hell you want now?"

The fire in Cain's voice nearly singed Isis's ear. She furrowed her eyebrows and pulled the phone away to make sure she'd dialed the right number. Yep, she'd definitely called the right number.

"Um, did I, uh, catch you at a bad time?"

"Aw shit!" he moaned. "Isis, baby? Girl, I'm so sorry. I didn't even look at the screen when the phone rang."

She sighed with relief, glad his wrath hadn't been directed at her. "It's okay. Did something happen in the last thirty minutes I need to know about?"

"Uh, naw, I'm good. One of my, um, cousins called asking for some money. You know how family members get when they know you got a li'l bit. They start treatin' you like damn Chase Bank."

Isis offered a dry chuckle. "I know how that can be. It doesn't happen to me too much since I moved, but my girlfriend Michelle is in the Army, and her family thinks she's rich."

"That's what I'm sayin'," Cain said with a laugh. "I work hard for what I got. I don't make this paper just to give it away with no interest."

"Well, now that I know you're not mad at me, tell me what you wanted to do with my time," Isis said, trying to change the subject. She hated conversations about money. She hated people who bragged about what they had just as equally as she hated people who claimed to be broke all the time. "Live your life" was the rule she tried to live by.

"Well, I do have a bone to pick with you, though."

"What?"

"That fifteen minutes seemed a lot like forty-five!"

Isis laughed again, this time throwing her head back and covering her mouth. "What were you doing? Sitting by the phone and watching the clock?"

"I mighta been. You always keep brothas waitin' like that?"

"Now you know I was just getting home from work. Cut me some slack!"

"Uh-uh. You disrespected my time, now I'm gonna have to stop speakin' to you for the next ten seconds."

True to his word, Cain sat on the phone without a word, despite Isis continually calling his name. She laughed. "You are so childish."

After a couple more seconds, Cain chuckled. "Now, let that be a lesson to you."

"Wow, really?"

"So when can I see you again?" Cain asked, quickly changing gears.

Isis looked at the clock. It was nearly seven. She clicked on the TV and searched for the Saints game, figuring that if she couldn't go to the game, she could at least watch it. And after the day she'd had, she preferred to watch the game with her favorite person: herself.

"How about tomorrow?" she asked, kicking off her shoes and reclining against her headboard.

"How 'bout tonight?" he countered.

She had to admit that his assertiveness was a turn-on, but she'd try to stick to her guns. A giggle escaped as she told him, "Sweetie, I just got comfortable, and I'm about to get into this Saints game."

"You mean to tell me you're about to watch my boys play and you're not gonna let me come over and watch them with you?"

Isis smirked. "Are you serious? I've only known you a couple of days and you want me to let you in my house? We don't know each other like that."

"Yeah, but we can get to know each other. And don't worry. I'm not gonna let you take advantage of me."

"Take advantage of you? What planet do you live on?"

"Mars. You didn't read the book?"

Isis laughed again. "Boy, you are so stupid."

"Naw, just anxious to get to know a certain young lady a little better. Now lemme come keep you company. I promise to behave."

Isis thought about it for a second. *Why not?* she wondered. *Because I don't know this man. And why put myself in a situation I can't get out of? But didn't you say you wanted to finally have some company?* Her phone beeped as she went back and forth in her mind.

"Hold on, Cain," she said. "My other line is ringing."

"Saved by the beep, huh?"

"Shut up," she said with a laugh. "I'll be right back."

"I'll be right here."

Isis looked at the caller ID, and when she saw that it was Alexis, she quickly clicked over. "Hey, Alexis, what's going on?"

"Hey, lady," Alexis greeted her. "I was just calling to check on you."

"That's nice of you. I'm good, can't complain. How are you?"

"Cool, on my way home, fighting this traffic."

"Yeah, I just got out of it not too long ago."

"Hey, I was calling to let you know that Twylite stopped by my office today."

"She did? How is she?"

"So I guess you really haven't talked to her."

"Not today. She kinda stopped talking to me after I gave her some advice."

"What did you tell her? Then again, that's not my business. It was probably something she needed to hear anyway."

"It was, but I'll have to tell you about it later," Isis said, remembering that Cain was waiting on the other line. "I'm on the other line with that guy Cain I met at the Perfect Fit last week."

"Oh," Alexis said, sounding impressed. "Girl, get back over there and handle your business. He seemed like a nice guy."

"We'll see," Isis said, smirking. "He's trying to get me to let him come over and watch the game."

"Girl, let that man come over. You're not a teenager anymore," Alexis encouraged. "I think you know what to do if he gets outta pocket."

Isis laughed. "You're right. Well, let me get back on this other line before he hangs up on me."

Alexis laughed with her. "Okay, call me tomorrow and we'll talk."

Isis hurriedly clicked back to the other line. "You still there?"

"Yeah, but as long as you had me waitin', I hope you're about to tell me to come on over."

"Yeah, you can come over, but you better behave."

"You ain't gotta even worry about that. Now, what's the address?"

# Chapter Nine

"Twylite, baby, it's time to get up," Adele Knight said, swinging open the door to Twylite's room.

"Ma, it's Saturday," Twylite mumbled without opening her eyes. She turned over and pulled the covers up toward her neck.

"Yeah, but it's eleven o'clock. You gonna sleep your life away."

"So? It's my life."

Adele felt tempted to storm into the room and slap the sleep right out of her daughter for that comment, but she had to remind herself that Twylite was going through some things. To Adele, rape was an unimaginable reality. She knew it happened, but she'd never met anyone who it had happened to. She had no idea how the healing process worked, or how long it took. All she knew was that she would have to show some patience, and for a woman who grew up in the means streets of New Orleans's Lower Ninth Ward, patience was not a virtue.

She left her daughter's doorway and trudged downstairs and back into the living room. Her husband Earl sat in his favorite brown leather recliner watching the latest report on the Iraq War on CNN. The president had changed the operation name from Iraqi Freedom to Operation New Dawn, but so far, no one had seen much of a difference in the way the troops were being killed by roadside bombs. They could only pray that Earl's nephew Victor, a lieutenant in the Army, would come home safely. With only two months left in his deployment, he'd already been hit twice and walked away from both incidents unscathed. Who knew if the third time would be the charm?

"She up yet?" Earl asked.

Adele shook her head. "I don't know what to do about dat girl."

"Just give her time," he replied. "She'll come around when she's ready."

"When will dat be, Earl?" Adele challenged, taking a seat on the sofa. "How long is it supposed to take? And what are we supposed to do in the meantime? Don't get me wrong. I'm not rushin' the process, but I don't know how I'm supposed to act in this situation. Just a week ago, I sent my smart, beautiful daughter with a bright future ahead of her to school. She returned beaten, raped, and bitter. How am I supposed to handle dat? How does she get over dat? I feel like if we don't do something, she'll never get over this."

Earl turned from the TV and sighed as he regarded his wife. She looked back at him as she struggled to keep the tears from falling. She looked away and took a deep breath to regain her composure.

All her life she had to be the strong one. The oldest of six girls, she grew up quickly, learning to be the caretaker, the decision maker, and sometimes the backbreaker. She rarely took anything from anyone, and her sisters learned to respect her strength. They often consulted her with their problems, be it indecision on what to wear, issues with their respective boyfriends, or financial advice. Even her parents grew to depend on her strength as she got older. She was the first to graduate from junior college, the first to get married, the first to have a child. She wasn't rich, but she knew how to stretch a dollar until it hollered. She could make groceries last two months with her knack for sniffing out deals and sensible recipes. Why wouldn't she know it all?

Yet, none of her problem-solving ever hit home like this situation. It was always easy for Adele to tell everyone else what they should do because what they did never really affected her. Now that she was knee-deep in the problem, a sensible solution just didn't seem to exist. What she wanted was what she knew in her heart that Earl wanted as well—to go out and blow Calvin Cooper's penis into next week! Yet, as a Christian woman and a law-abiding citizen, she knew that wasn't a possibility.

"So whatcha want me to do?" Earl asked, seeming to read Adele's mind.

She dismissed the question with a wave of her hand and stretched out on the sofa. "Ain't nothin' we can do right now. All we can do is wait for her to get out this funk."

A silence fell between them as they contemplated the situation. Soon, the silence grew so heavy that Adele could hardly breathe. It felt like a weight had settled on her chest, causing her to nearly hyperventilate. She popped up and stormed to the guest restroom.

The room was no larger than a closet, but the bright yellow wallpaper and beige tile made it feel bigger than it really was. It was at least a welcome respite from the suffocation she'd felt a minute earlier. She turned the faucets for the hot and cold water, and once she felt the right mix of warmth, she cupped her hands together under the flow. Once they filled, she bowed her head close to the sink and doused her face. She repeated the process a few more times, trying to rid her eyes of the dryness.

She couldn't cry even if she wanted to, yet the thought of crying pissed her off. Why did women have to cry when they felt helpless? Why did they have to be so damned emotional in the first place? Why did her hands feel tied?

Adele stared into the mirror over the pedestal sink, watching the water drain down her forehead and cheeks, dripping from her chin. She looked a mess, but she didn't give a damn. At least her face felt cooler and she could breathe easier. Maybe now that her head was clear, she could think better.

A towel appeared over her right shoulder. She turned and gave her husband a grateful look as she took the towel and dried herself off. The sink, wall, and floor were soaked. She'd clean it later. With any luck, by the time she got around to cleaning it, the water would have dried.

"You ever think about calling Dr. Duplessis and seeing what she think?" Earl asked, gently rubbing his fingernails across Adele's back.

Adele responded with a shrug. "I've talked to her before, and she's adamant about staying out of this. She told me she's just Twylite's doctor, and ain't nothin' she could do about the situation."

"Dat could be true," Earl said, nodding. "What about that Isis lady? She'll probably know more about the situation."

"Yeah, I could call her," she said, drying her hands. The water drops finally bothered her enough to use the towel to wipe off the sink. She then dropped the towel in the sink, neglecting the water that still glistened from the tile. "You know where her number is?"

"I thought you had it."

"I did, but I don't know where I put it."

"Well, you better find it, because you know Twy ain't gonna give it to you."

"Why she won't?"

Earl looked at his wife as if seeing her for the first time. "You serious, Dele? You really think your headstrong daughter is gonna help you tell Isis how difficult she's being?"

Adele nearly smiled, almost embarrassed at the thought. If anyone knew Twylite, it was definitely Earl. She was Daddy's girl through and through. "Well, you gonna go upstairs and help me find it?"

The search took all of about ten minutes. Adele only had three decent purses, so it was just a matter of remembering which one she'd taken with her to the hospital that night. Once she located the brown leather shoulder bag on the floor of the closet, she found Isis's business card sitting neatly inside the zippered pocket.

She and Earl sat on the edge of their bed and she dialed the number. Adele nearly hoped Isis wouldn't answer, as she still wasn't sure what she would tell the woman. Her hopes were dashed when Isis answered on the third ring.

"Hello, Ms. Reynolds?" Adele asked quietly, too quietly for her own taste. She felt like a teenage girl begging her teacher for an extension on her homework.

"Yes, this is Isis."

"Yes, hello, um, this is uh, Adele Knight. Twylite's mother?"

"Yes, Ms. Knight. How are you?"

To Adele, Isis sounded nearly as nervous as she did. Her words came quick, but tentative.

Adele flapped her hand toward the door, indicating for her husband to close it. If she was going to have this conversation, it was best to eliminate any chance of Twylite walking up on her.

"I wanted to talk to you about Twylite," Adele explained, the confidence returning to her voice. Her eyes cut at her husband. She could see in just that slight glance that she had his full support and attention.

"Um, can you hold for a quick minute?"

Adele could hear muffled shuffling. She couldn't tell for sure, but she wondered if she'd interrupted something.

"I'm sorry, Mrs. Knight," Isis said, sounding more clear. "Is everything okay?"

"I was actually gonna ask you dat," Adele replied. "Twylite don't seem to be gettin' much better, and we're gettin' concerned about her."

"I'm sorry to hear that."

"Yeah, me too. I know you can't tell me all dat y'all talk about, but has she said anything to you about why she might be in this funk? How long does it usually take for these girls to come outta it?"

Adele's question was answered with an uncomfortable silence. The silence lasted too long in Adele's eyes. "Isis? You still there?"

"Yes, I'm sorry," Isis replied. "It's just that I haven't spoken to Twylite in a week. I've called a couple of times, but all I get is her voice mail, and she never calls back. I thought she told you."

"Say what?" Adele asked, drawing concern from her husband. He scooted closer, as if he could hear Isis through the telephone. Maybe if Adele were on a cell phone, his tactic would work. But a landline would give him no clue. He would have to guess the conversation by listening to Adele's words. "She ain't told us nothin' like that. Why she not talkin' to you?"

"I think she got a little upset with me because of some advice I gave her."

"Dat girl could use some advice. What, you hurt her feelings or somethin'?"

"I just told her that she had to love herself before anyone else could love her," Isis explained. "I kind of told her that Peanut didn't respect her as much as she thought he did."

"Shit, da truth hurts, don't it?" Adele remarked. She'd been trying to tell her daughter that same thing for months.

"What she say?" Earl asked.

"I'll tell you in a minute," Adele told him before turning back to her conversation with Isis. "Well, Isis, I'ma tell you Twylite ain't doin' herself no good staying to herself. She's not talking to me, her daddy, or you. She might be talking to Dr. Duplessis, but I don't know how much good dat'll do. Believe you me, she'll be calling you before this weekend is out. She might be callin' today!"

"Mrs. Knight, you can't make her talk to me. That's not what the advocacy program is all about."

"The hell I can't!" Adele retorted almost too loudly. At this point, she really didn't care if Twylite overheard her. Who was that girl to make such a decision without talking with them? If she were capable of making such a decision, she wouldn't be getting worse instead of better. Why did teenagers think they ruled the world?

"I'll tell you what," Isis suggested. "Maybe you can talk with her, see what's bothering her. But let her call me when she's ready. If you make her, she'll only come back into the situation with a closed mind. That won't do anyone any good."

Adele nodded, but she was cynical. Isis didn't have any kids, so how would she know what it's like to raise a teenage daughter? *These new-age women, they really do think kids should be allowed to make their own decisions.* Well, Adele wasn't by any means a new-age mother, and there was no way in hell Twylite would win this one.

"I hear you, Isis, and I'll think about what you said," Adele said, already formulating her plan of attack.

"Thanks, Mrs. Knight," Isis said. "Dat's all I ask."

"Okay, well, I'll call you in a couple of days and let you know how things go."

As Adele hung up the phone, she yelled, "Twylite!"


"Everything all right?" Cain asked, leaning across the kitchen counter.

"Huh?" Isis asked, still staring at her cell phone. She slowly placed the phone on the counter, not knowing whether to frown or laugh. Twylite's name in the tune of Adele Knight's angry shout still rang in her ears. She knew there was no way that woman would listen to her. In just her short encounter with her, Isis could tell Adele was stubborn and tough, like her own mother.

"I asked if everything was okay," Cain repeated.

Isis smiled at her shirtless friend. She was happy that she'd stayed true to herself and refused to have sex, but Cain looking as good as he did didn't make things any easier.

"I'm good," she replied, her eyes tracing the outline of the four abdominal muscles below his pectorals. He wasn't exactly Mr. Universe in the muscle department, but with his oak-colored skin and smooth complexion, he could certainly make money as an exotic dancer if he wanted to. His jeans fit him just right—not too baggy, not too tight. She hated men who sagged, and despised men who wore skinny jeans. "Just talking to the mother of one of my clients."

"She sounded a little irate," he stated.

"She was, a little, but I can understand. What mother wouldn't be when her daughter's been raped?"

"I hear you. I know I would kill a muthafucka, he did that to my sister," Cain said, punching his right fist into his left hand. "That's the worst shit you can do to a woman."

Isis winced a bit at the language, but she couldn't judge him. She was known to throw around a curse or two, herself. Yet, there was something violent in the way Cain swore. It was almost scary. She shrugged the thought away, thinking maybe she was being oversensitive.

"How many sisters do you have?" she asked, turning toward the refrigerator. They had slept the morning away after a night of movie watching, so she figured she'd make some lunch.

"Just one, but I also have a brother," he replied, his voice relaxing a bit. "My sister is eighteen, just graduated from McDonogh 35 High School, and my brother is thirty, but he lives in Baton Rouge."

Isis waited for him to elaborate more on his family, but his silence told her that he was done speaking on the subject. "That's cool," she mumbled as she placed cheese and frozen French fries on the counter. She wondered whether she should tell him more about herself, since he seemed to be guarded with his own information. She still wasn't even sure what he exactly did for a living. "You want a grilled cheese sandwich?"

He smirked. "Grilled cheese? I ain't had one of them since way back in the day! I use'ta love them thangs."

Isis smiled, glad to find a little common ground with her mysterious friend. She preheated the stove and began spreading the French fries on a cookie sheet. She loved baked fries. They were less greasy. "I still love them. And they're perfect for a lazy Saturday. I don't think I'm going to do a thing today."

Cain smiled at her. "I wish I could sit here and be lazy with you, but I gotta run after we finish these sandwiches. I got some business to take care of."

Isis frowned. "Really?"

"Yeah, babe. Saturday is my busiest day. That's when all the buyers have time."

"Huh?"

"Never mind," he said, chuckling. "I'll have to tell you about my job one of these days. Right now, let's get these sandwiches started."

*And the mystery continues,* Isis thought as she began spreading margarine on the bread slices.

# Chapter Ten

"Okay, so we have a deal?" Alexis asked once Jamar climbed into the driver's seat of his black Cadillac Escalade.

"Yeah, but we'll see if you stick to it," he remarked as he started the truck. "You're still gonna pick the most expensive set you see."

"You really shouldn't doubt me so much. It's not a good look."

Alexis smiled at the glimmer in her husband's eyes as he backed out of the driveway of their two-story, four-bedroom home amid the nineteenth-century mansions on beautiful Esplanade Avenue, in the heart of Treme. Although Alexis and Jamar made enough to have bought a home in Lakeshore or the West End of New Orleans, they'd loved the charm of historic Treme long before the HBO TV show made it famous. The tree-lined streets and peaceful atmosphere down the street from City Park made the country's oldest African American neighborhood look like something right off a historic postcard.

Esplanade Avenue was once known as "Black Millionaires Row" to the Creole elite of Louisiana back in the nineteenth century. Although the homes looked normal from the outside, many hid three floors of hardwood maple flooring and spacious bedrooms, and were surrounded by historic sites, bed and breakfasts, and quaint cafes. The neighborhood was also a stone's throw from the Central Business District, where Jamar's office was located. Some of the city's best hotels were located on nearby Canal Street, which made it convenient for their occasional out-of-town visitors.

Alexis also had fond memories of marching in the Treme Parade during the Mardi Gras season as a child with Phillis Wheatley Elementary School's majorette team. Back then, she didn't know the value of the parade, nor did she even realize that Treme was more than just the name of a parade. To her, it was just a two-mile walk in the cold while wearing tapped boots with pompoms on them, and trying not to drop her batons.

Once she got older, the significance sank in, and the memories stayed forever. Although nowadays when people think of Treme they think of the Indians or the popular TV show, natives like Alexis could remember when all the schools in Treme paraded through the streets and put on their best performance for the residents. The neighborhood still did a smaller version of the parade, but it was nothing compared to her days back at Phillis Wheatley, which was permanently closed and torn down after Hurricane Katrina.

Alexis lay her head back and closed her eyes as she and Jamar rode, continuing their quest for the perfect living room set. The week had been trying, but nothing stood out more than her talk with Twylite. What could Isis have said to her to make her cut ties with her all of a sudden? The vibrator on her cell phone buzzed from her purse. She dug the phone from the inside pocket of her purse and glanced at the caller ID.

"I guessed I thought that up into existence," Alexis mumbled, pressing TALK.

"Who's that?" Jamar asked.

"Twylite," she mouthed before turning to the phone. "Hey, Miss Lady, what's going on?"

"Not much," Twylite said. "Just wanted to let you know I'm supposed to go see Isis Monday."

Alexis lifted her eyebrows. "Really? That was a quick change of heart."

"It wasn't my decision. My momma called Isis, and when she found out I stopped talkin' to her, she went off and pretty much ordered me to go see her."

Alexis laughed, imagining how that conversation went. Adele Knight loved her daughter, but she didn't play at all. "You gonna be all right?"

"I'll be fine. I'm really not looking forward to it, though," Twylite said, scorn dripping from her words. Alexis couldn't tell if it was directed at Isis or Adele. "But I'll tell you one thing: she might be making me go, but she can't make me talk."

"You have got to give the woman a chance," Alexis said, trying hard not to sound like the other adults telling her what to do. "It's not like she cussed you out and told you to kiss her tail."

Twylite chuckled. "Yeah, you're right. I'll give her a chance, just for you."

Alexis laughed as well. "Well, thanks. Glad to feel so special."

"It's nice how you're always there for that girl," Jamar said once Alexis dropped the phone back into her purse.

"Yeah," she replied. "Twylite is a special girl. She's been my patient since she was a kid, so we've gotten to know each other pretty well."

"I guess with everything she's been going through, she needs someone like you who's more like a friend than an authoritarian."

"I feel the same way. You haven't met her momma, but she's a trip. I'm sure Twylite gets more than enough authority in her life."

"Kinda like your momma, huh?" Jamar said with a smile and a wink.

Alexis cocked her head back and shot him the stink eye. "I know you're not talkin' about my momma!"

"And I know you're not trying to pretend your momma ain't mean as hell!"

They laughed, both knowing Jamar's words were true. As much as Alexis loved her mother, she'd be lying if she said Adele didn't draw a strong resemblance to Mary White. Mary said what she wanted, when she wanted, and there wasn't a soul who could do anything about it. Her husband, Alexis's stepfather, was the only person who could possibly stand up to her, but even he knew when to draw the line. However, no one could say that either Adele or Mary didn't have love in their hearts, because both would go to hell and back for the people they loved.

"You know my momma has a heart of gold," Alexis said, smiling at her husband.

"Yeah, but it took months before I figured that out," Jamar retorted. "Don't get me wrong. You know I love Ms. Mary like she's my own mother, but her sharp tongue has cut me more than a little bit. If Twylite's mom is anything like her, any boy who comes close to her has got his work cut out for him."

"Yeah, I just wish that was the case with that Cooper boy," Alexis said. She looked sadly out of the window as they turned onto Broad Street, headed toward Metairie, where their quest for the perfect living room set would continue. As confident as Alexis was that the search would end that day, the conversation about Twylite had brought a dark cloud that seemed to refuse to go away.

She so wished there was something she could do for Twylite besides being the disinterested buddy. Maybe if she had been more than the disinterested buddy, she could have convinced Twylite to leave that Cooper boy alone before things even got to this point. She had that opportunity when Adele came to talk with her, but she was so busy trying to be professional that she refused to get involved. Twylite trusted her and respected her like a big sister. Wouldn't she have listened if Alexis had stepped in?

*It wasn't my place.* Alexis continually tried to convince herself of that fact, but it did no good. She was going to have to take some of the responsibility in this situation.

She chuckled a bit. "I feel like my cousin Brenda right now."

"How so?"

"You know how she takes everybody's issues as her own, almost to the point where she stresses out?"

"Yeah, I've seen that."

"I feel like I'm doing the same thing with Twylite."

Jamar let out a playful grunt, causing his shoulders to jump slightly.

"What?" Alexis asked.

"You really have changed over the years," he said. "When I first met you, you were about as mean as your momma. You did what you wanted, and said what you wanted. If somebody's feelings were hurt, it wasn't your problem. I think this is the first time I have really seen you take this much of an interest in somebody other than your family."

Alexis wanted to shoot him such a smart comment, but as she thought about his words, she had to admit that he was right. She had been a handful growing up, and even just before she accepted Jamar's proposal. She actually could have lost Jamar forever if he hadn't been so stubborn. He knew he wanted her, and wouldn't relent until she admitted that she wanted him just as much.

"I do have a heart," she said with a smile. "If I didn't, we wouldn't be together."

"You've got that right," he said.

They drove in silence a few more minutes. Once they reached a red light, Jamar turned slightly and regarded his wife. "I'm glad to see you take such an interest in this girl, but I don't want you to let it overtake you. I know you care about her, but you have other patients. You have a family. You have friends like Shalonda whom you haven't talked to in a few days. Don't forget to take care of yourself."

"I know you're right," Alexis admitted, "and I'm not going to get too caught up. I know how Brenda used to get, and I'm really not trying to go there."

"Good," Jamar said, continuing down the road once the light turned green. "Right now, let's concentrate on getting this living room set because I'm about ready to end this chapter in my life."

"Yeah, and I'm tired of sitting on your old sofa!"

"So let's agree now on what we want before we get in the middle of the store fighting again like we did last week."

"I can agree with that," Alexis said, thankful for the diversion. Everyone should have a husband like Jamar, and she thanked God that her attitude hadn't run him off for good.

They had already agreed on shopping local. There were a couple of furniture dealers who had been in New Orleans longer than they'd both been alive, so they decided to visit those stores instead of fighting the malls. Besides, post Katrina, it was more important than ever to support their local businesses.

"Too bad Rosenburg's isn't around anymore," Alexis said with a laugh.

"You mean '1825 Tulane'?" Jamar replied, singing the familiar tune that every true New Orleanian knew without even thinking about it. The local furniture store had closed years ago, but everyone who grew up in New Orleans could still quote their commercials.

They laughed together as they reached the busy traffic of Metairie. As they fought their way through the traffic, they bargained and agreed on selecting fabric instead of leather, separates instead of a sectional, and earth tones over bright colors. Since they had no kids, stain resistance wasn't a concern for them, although Alexis pointed out that it would be a plus for accidents. And Jamar was sure to point out that he didn't mind contemporary, but the set had to have a masculine touch. He refused to walk into a living room that looked like only women lived there.

By the time they pulled in front of Hurwitz Mintz, they were no closer to knowing what they did want, but they knew exactly what they didn't want. However, once they walked into the store, a smile spread across Alexis's chocolate face.

"I see it, baby," she exclaimed. "Follow me!"

Before Jamar could protest, he was already being led directly to a cream-colored micro-suede sofa with matching loveseat. It had just enough contemporary styling to make Alexis happy, but not so much that Jamar would feel ashamed to call it his. They sat and nearly became lost in the oversized cream and black pillows that lined the back of the loveseat.

"Now if we can find a recliner to match this set, we're in the house," Jamar said.

"So you like it?" Alexis squealed.

"I think we found our set," he replied.

She clapped excitedly, and ran off to look for a salesman.


An air of satisfaction filled the Escalade as Jamar and Alexis maneuvered through the traffic. They had decided to grab lunch since they found their set so quickly, but

Saturdays in Metairie could be relentless. It would be awhile before they reached Drago's Seafood Restaurant, but the thought of charbroiled oysters kept them both motivated. As they drew closer to the restaurant, Alexis's cell phone rang.

"What's up, Shalonda?" Alexis asked once she fished it from her purse and hit talk. "Girl, you gonna live a long time because we were just talking about you earlier."

"You and who?" she asked with playful attitude painting her voice.

"Girl, relax your shoulders and let the air out your chest," Alexis replied with a laugh. "Jamar had just pointed out that we hadn't talked in a while."

"That's true, and that's why I called. So I could fuss you out for not keeping in touch!"

"You know I've been busy," Alexis said, as they pulled into the small Drago's parking lot. "Plus, Jamar and I were out again searching for that living room set."

"So did you two finally agree on something?"

"Yes, and it's beautiful," Alexis said. "Once we get it set up at the house, you guys will have to come over and see it."

"You know we will. But you two handle your business. Give me a call when you get home."

"Okay, friend," Alexis replied. "I'll call you tonight."

"Who was that? Shalonda?" Jamar asked, opening the passenger door for his wife.

"Yeah, I guess you talked her up," she replied as she climbed out.

"Yeah, I'm good like that."

"And humble," Alexis mumbled.

Jamar laughed, and then led Alexis into the restaurant. A hostess greeted them and led them to a table near the back of the restaurant. They each ordered charbroiled oysters. Jamar chose to wash them down with a beer from the tap, while Alexis ordered a margarita.

Once the waitress left the table, Alexis again reached for her phone, much to the dismay of her husband.

"I know, I know," Alexis apologized. She would have had to be blind to miss the scorn on Jamar's face. His eyes could strip the wallpaper off the walls. "I just want to check on Isis and then I'm all yours for the rest of the night."

Jamar sucked his teeth. "You owe me big. I'ma throw that thing out the window. You never see me on the phone as much as you."

"You're right, and I'm sorry," Alexis said, still dialing Isis's number. "I won't be but a minute."

Before Jamar could respond, Alexis was already holding the phone to her ear and greeting whoever was on the other line.

"Hey, Isis, how you doing?"

"I'm good, just hanging out with Cain."

"Sounds like you two are really hitting it off. I'm happy for you."

"Yeah, he's okay," Isis replied, laughing. Alexis imagined that he had to be sitting close enough to hear her remark.

"Maybe you two can double date with me and Jamar one day," Alexis suggested. She glanced up just in time to see Jamar's mouth curl into a smirk. The waitress set their drinks in front of them and quickly walked away.

"Sounds like a plan," Isis said. "I'll talk to Cain about it."

"Cool, but what I really called you about is Twylite," Alexis said, her voice dropping a bit. "She called and said she was going to see you Monday. Y'all all right?"

"I'll know Monday. Her momma made her come see me. I know she can't be too happy about that."

"Yeah, she was kind of pissed, but I told her she needed to give you a chance."

"I appreciate that," Isis said. "I figure I'll let her do most of the talking so she won't think I'm trying to tell her what to do again."

"Good idea," Alexis said, stealing another glance at her husband. He wasn't happy. "Well, lemme go. My husband looks like he's planning on divorcing me on the grounds of talking on the phone too much."

Isis laughed. "I understand. Thanks for calling, though. I'll let you know how things go."

"Okay, you take care." Alexis pressed END and dropped the phone back into her purse. She looked at Jamar and smiled, propping her chin with her two fists. "All yours."

"Whatever, man."

"What do you mean whatever?"

"You're gonna think of someone else to call, or else somebody's gonna call you," Jamar stated before taking a sip from his beer. "You're not gonna be satisfied until you get caught up in some shit that ain't even your business."

"You're overreacting," Alexis replied, waving her hand at him. Yet, as much as she protested, she had to wonder if Jamar's words were more fact than opinion. His words also reminded her that she had never told him about her seeing his friend Vernon at the Perfect Fit with another woman.

"You know, while we're on the subject of me being all up in people's business," she said before taking a sip of her margarita, "I meant to tell you I saw your boy the other night when we went out."

"Who?" Jamar asked, scrunching his eyebrows.

"Vernon." She paused as the waitress returned with their oysters. She reached for a slice of French bread and dipped it in the buttery sauce. "And he wasn't with Denise."

Jamar looked even more confused. "I'm guessing since you're talking like that, he wasn't with his boys, either."

"Nope, and he looked real damn cozy with that chick he was with."

"Ain'tcha business."

"You know he's cheatin' on Denise, don't you?"

"Ain'tcha business."

"You men are a trip!" Alexis exclaimed, trying hard to keep her voice down. "Y'all would stick together and cover for each other, knowing that woman is at home being made a fool of?"

Jamar stabbed a piece of his oyster with a tiny fork. "Woman, calm down. First of all, it's not your business. Second, I didn't tell you I was covering for anything. I don't need to tell you everything that's going on in my boys' families, just like I don't tell them all our business. Now, did I know he was playing around? No, but I didn't ask him. Do I condone it? Hell, no. But his drama is not about to ruin the good day I'm having with my wife. Now, leave it alone and eat your oysters."

Alexis had never grown used to the way her husband could shut her without raising his voice or even cursing. Had she lost her edge? Had she put up with this attitude before they'd gotten married without noticing? A part of her wanted to snap at him and ask who the hell he was talking to, but another part had to admit that she loved the way her husband took charge. But make no mistake, he was still the only man who could.

"You're lucky I love you," she mumbled.

He smiled and winked at her. "I know."

# Chapter Eleven

"Whatcha got goin' on after school today?" Pamela asked as she and Twylite walked toward the cafeteria. Today was one of the few days they both got to school in time for breakfast, so they decided to take advantage of the situation. A little cereal and fruit never hurt anyone.

"My momma's makin' me go see that bitch Isis," Twylite grumbled. Just the thought of the way her mother tore into her Saturday made her flesh crawl. Truthfully, that was the real reason she'd gotten to school so early. She needed the escape. Between her mother yelling at her and her father pretending he didn't hear anything, she didn't think she could take any more.

She planned to stay as far away from home for as long as she possibly could. She'd play the game and go see Isis, and then maybe walk around Loyola University since Isis wasn't located far from there. The quiet Jesuit university was pretty, and would be a safe place to hang out for a while. Who knew; maybe she'd even apply for a job somewhere.

She hoped that by the time she did go home, her parents would either be asleep or too tired to light into her again. What was wrong with them, anyway? It was like they'd been old for so long that they forgot what it was like being a teenager. But then, being a teenager in the sixties was nothing compared to growing up in the new millennium. The sooner they realized that, the easier life would be for all of them.

"Why you calling her a bitch?" Pamela asked, interrupting Twylite's thoughts.

"Because she think she knows every damned thing."

"How?"

Twylite stopped walking just short of the cafeteria and
faced her friend. "You wanna go with me to meet her
today?"

Pamela's eyes widened in surprise. "You sure you want
me in your business like that?"

"Why not?" Twylite asked. "You know everything else
about me. Ain't like you don't know what happened."

"I guess, but that's kinda personal, huh?"

Twylite sighed and blew out some exasperated air.
"Just come with me. Then you can see for yourself how
she is. Then we can hang out when we finish."

Pamela still looked unsure, but softened when Twylite
said, "Come on, Pam. I could use the company."

"Okay, I'll come, as long as you're sure."

"I'm positive," Twylite said, leading her friend into the
cafeteria. "Thanks, boo."

"You got it," Pamela said. "But I still don't think this
lady is as bad as you keep saying she is."


Once school let out, Pamela and Twylite met up at their
usual spot and walked to the bus stop. A bus was already
loading once they reached the stop, but since so many
girls had boarded, they decided to let it go and wait for
the next one.

A new bus came about fifteen minutes later. It was
still crowded, but the girls managed to find seats toward
the back. As usual, the ride was fairly quiet, with only a
couple of soft random conversations. For the most part,
everyone seemed to be wrapped in their own business.
Some listened to iPods. Some played games on their
phones. Others took the opportunity to take a quick nap.

Even Twylite had grown a little drowsy, but when she saw that Pamela had already fallen asleep, she decided not to risk missing their stop.

"Pam, wake up," Twylite mumbled, tapped her friend's forearm.

Pamela slowly opened her eyes and looked around. Finally recognizing that they'd reached Canal Street, she nodded and slipped her backpack over her shoulder. They stood next to the back door and waited for the driver to bring the bus to a halt. The bump of a brass street band in full force greeted them as they debarked and walked toward the St. Charles Streetcar.

The high-spirited, heart-pumping music known as second line music was a staple in the Big Easy. No matter when or where it was played, it always managed to attract and keep a crowd. The music was most often heard following a funeral processional. Once the deceased had been buried, the music would begin and the people would dance, celebrating the deceased's passing from one life to the next. Today, almost befittingly, the music would be heard at clubs and parties, signaling that the festivities had come to an end.

Normally, Twylite and Pamela would stop right where they were and begin twisting their hips to the tunes, and dropping low to the beat. But it didn't seem appropriate right now. Twylite wasn't in the mood, and she was sure her friend wanted to dance, but wouldn't for fear of hurting her feelings. Twylite looked over and watched young and old men dip and jerk to the beat right in the middle of the street, moving to the sidewalk only when the occasional car passed. She rolled her eyes and kept it moving. Maybe next time she would join them.

Her cell phone rang as they reached the streetcar stop. Twylite's face tightened when she saw Isis's name appear on the screen. Just as she said hello, a streetcar approached.

"Hi, Twylite," Isis greeted her. Her voice could barely be heard over the screech of the trolley stopping in front of the girls. "I was just calling to check on you."

"Yeah, we're on the way," Twylite said, handing the conductor her transfer slip. She spied two empty seats near the middle of the car and led Pamela in that direction. "I said we were comin', didn't I?"

"We? Your parents are coming too?" Isis asked, obviously ignoring the edge in Twylite's tone.

"No, I asked my friend Pam to come," Twylite responded, sliding in the seat toward the window. Pamela sat next to her and watched her, looking worried. Twylite knew her friend thought she'd made a mistake by coming.

"Oh," Isis said, her word sounding almost like a whisper. "Are you sure you want to do that?"

"It's fine. Pam knows everything about what's been going on. We've been friends for like five years."

Isis remained quiet, as if considering this revelation. Finally, she said, "Okay, if you're sure, I'm sure. Just know that I don't want either of us to hold back. The only way I can help is for us to be straight with each other."

"I know," Twylite said, nodding her head. In a strange way, Pamela had actually encouraged her. Maybe having her friend there for support wouldn't be so bad after all. Pamela had always had a way of bringing the bravery out of Twylite. Maybe today would be no different.

Isis sat at the table, drumming her fingernails as she waited. She couldn't help but accept the butterflies that swirled around her stomach. Her last conversation with Twylite hadn't gone very well, and the teenager had avoided her since. She was convinced that she'd lost the girl, but when Mrs. Knight called her, she felt a turning point. This time, she'd offer her help at all costs, even if it meant begging every professional she knew to give Twylite the advice she couldn't.

She refused to lose this girl to the statistics. She'd seen the statistics that proved that girls Twylite's age were more likely to lose their virginity to older men. The long-term repercussions of such unions were depression and low self-esteem in the girls. Isis could already see this in Twylite, because she'd experienced it herself. Isis had never seen herself as very pretty in high school, so when a twenty-one-year-old dream of a man began showing her some attention, she decided that she would do whatever it took to keep his attention.

Unfortunately, that relationship and way of thinking opened the floodgates to promiscuity and bad decisions, including marrying a man who saw her as nothing more than a recovering whore. Although she'd never cheated on her husband and had done everything in her power to make her marriage work, he'd convinced himself that she had slept around, leading to the beating that changed her life forever. If Isis could help it, Twylite would never experience the same fate Isis did. She couldn't change her past, but she would try damn hard to shape Twylite's future.

The trick was she had to figure out a way of helping her without blatantly pushing advice down the girl's throat. She still wasn't sure how she would do that, but she had to try. She saw too much potential in this girl to let her throw it all away over some mail carrier who thought he was God's gift to teenage girls.

Her cell phone's shrill ring snapped her away from her thoughts. She smiled when saw it was Cain. She'd have to get him a ringtone soon. The factory-provided ringer just didn't fit his personality.

"Hey," she whispered after pressing TALK.

"Hey, you," he replied. "I'm just checkin' on you. How's it going?"

"It's not yet. I'm still waiting on her to get here."

"What's taking her so long?"

Isis laughed. "She had to take the bus. Not everyone has a fancy truck like you."

He chuckled. "Yeah, I do have it going on, don't I?"

"Oh, God," she groaned, laughing even harder. "You can come back down to earth anytime now."

"You know you like it."

"Whatever!"

Just as she had settled into a good laugh with Cain, she noticed two girls wearing school uniforms enter the deli.

"Hey, sweetie, they're here. I'll call you later," she said.

"Okay, but I'll call you," he replied. "I have to work late tonight, and I won't be able to answer if you call me."

Again, Isis wondered what in the world type of job this man had, but she didn't have time to get into it with him. Instead, she said good-bye, and had just barely dropped the phone into her purse when Twylite and her friend approached the table.

Twylite's face looked a bit hard to read. There wasn't anger, but she certainly didn't see joy. But then again, why should she show joy? Isis could imagine the venom in Adele Knight's voice when she practically threatened Twylite with death for breaking contact with her. Twylite wasn't here of her own volition. She was here because her mother told her to come. And who wanted that?

"Good evening, ladies," Isis greeted them, smiling at the two teenagers. She motioned toward the empty seats across the table from her. "Have a seat."

The girls did as they were told, as if awaiting an invitation.

"Would you like anything to eat?" Isis asked, trying her best to hold on to her smile. The key to getting Twylite to talk was to make her as comfortable as possible. She needed to show the girl that there were no hard feelings, and she was willing to play by Twylite's rules. To an extent. "My treat."

The girls glanced at each other and simultaneously picked up the paper menus in front of them. The restaurant was fairly quiet, save for some muted conversations coming from a few tables away. Isis appreciated its peaceful nature, and came here often whenever she needed to get away. Not even Cain knew about this spot because she wanted to keep it her personal hideaway. She was sure Twylite was no threat to her little secret.

"You see anything good?" she asked.

"Ummm, what did you have?" Twylite asked, looking at the empty plate in front of Isis.

"I just had a turkey and cheese," Isis replied. "It was pretty good."

"I think I'll try that," Twylite's friend chimed in.

"Me too," Twylite agreed.

Isis signaled for the waitress and placed their orders, while ordering herself another orange pekoe tea.

"So, I'm sorry, but what is your name again?" Isis asked once the waitress left.

"Pamela, but you can call me Pam."

"It's very nice to meet you. I think Twylite said you two have been friends for about five years."

"That's right," Pamela responded. "We met in the sixth grade."

"That's awesome. I wish I had kept in better touch with some of my childhood friends. I moved a little too much for that to happen."

"Why did you move so much?" Twylite asked, leaning in a bit.

Isis smiled. "I was born in Louisville, Kentucky, but when I got old enough, I came up with the bright idea to move to a small town about an hour away so I could live on my own. I made a few mistakes along the way, but I managed to get married and move to Texas with my new husband. He was in the Army. Unfortunately, that fizzled out after a few years, so I moved back to Louisville. Later, I found a job in New Orleans, so here I am."

"How long have you lived here?" Pamela asked.

"Since April."

"You like it?" Twylite asked.

Isis laughed on the inside at the way the girls tag-teamed their questions at her. She felt like she was being interviewed, but at least they were talking. "New Orleans is nice, although I admit that I haven't gotten out much to explore the city. I plan on it, though. Maybe you two could give me some suggestions on where to go."

"Just stay out the French Quarter," Pamela said with a grunt. "Everybody thinks that's all there is to New Orleans. Every time my parents' friends come to town, we gotta drag them down there. It's like they don't even know we have other parts of the city."

"They know," Twylite said. "They just don't care. All my parents' friends want to do is tour the Ninth Ward so they can see the poor black folks who got washed out by Katrina. Like those people wanna be on display like a damned zoo!"

Her eyes widened once she realized she'd let a cuss word slip. She covered her mouth like a little girl. "Oops, sorry."

"That's okay. It happens. Where do you like to go, Twylite?" Isis asked.

"I actually like it right here on St. Charles Avenue," she replied, a shadow of a smile crossing her face. "We have Audubon Park down the street. My cousin got married there a couple years ago. It was nice. The zoo is right behind there, even though I ain't been there in a while. And right across the street from the park are Loyola and Tulane Universities."

Isis smiled. "You seem to know a lot about the city. Maybe you should become a tour guide."

Twylite laughed: her first genuinely easy gesture since arriving at the restaurant. The waitress returned with their sandwiches, placing a plate and bottle of juice in front of each girl, and the tea in front of Isis.

"I just love my city." Twylite shrugged.

Isis nodded. "I can tell. Most of the people I run into here feel the same way."

The table fell silent as the girls indulged in their sandwiches. Isis sipped her tea as she awaited the right moment to begin talking again. She knew from recent experience that the sandwiches, fully dressed on a whole wheat bun, were delicious. No need in ruining that experience with some heavy talk.

A few more minutes passed before Twylite took the last bite of her sandwich and washed it down with a swallow of her fruit juice. Isis waited until she sat back. Pamela seemed to still be working on her sandwich, but she wasn't the focus at the moment.

"So, Twylite, I just wanted to apologize to you for coming down on you the way I did the other day," Isis said after taking another sip of her tea. She reached for her tiny silver teapot and refilled her cup. "That wasn't my place."

Twylite nodded and looked at Pamela, who was busy ripping her last bite of sandwich in half. Probably trying to savor the moment.

Isis continued, treading lightly. "Believe it or not, I really care about you. I just don't want to see you make the same mistakes I did when I was your age. I know you need to make your own mistakes and you have to learn your own lessons, but some things don't always get better with time."

The teenager nodded again, this time leaning forward and propping up her right cheek with the palm of her hand. "I know what you're saying. You were just trying to help."

"Yeah, but it doesn't look like I was much help, huh?"

"You were cool. I just wasn't in the mood to hear it at the time."

Twylite's honesty shocked Isis. The anger she'd had when they'd spoken days ago seemed to have dissipated. She wondered if Adele had actually gotten through to daughter amid the screaming. After all, they were mother and daughter. She was sure they knew how to talk with each other, and they probably had a great relationship, just like Isis had with her own mother.

"So we're cool again?" Isis asked, smiling cautiously.

Twylite shrugged. "Can't stay mad forever, and like my momma said, I ain't doing too good gettin' over this by myself."

"Your mother told you that?"

"You met my momma. She can be mean sometimes!"

"You ain't never lied!" Pamela chimed in.

They all laughed.

"But seriously though," Twylite said, "it was pretty cool of you to apologize. Most grownups don't do that. Pam told me I needed to give you a chance, and I'm glad I did."

"Well, thanks for your help," Isis said, turning to Pamela. "Your friend is a special girl, and I just don't want to see somebody like Peanut take her light away."

"Me either," Pamela said. "I wanted to kill him when Twy told me what he did."

"Well, all we can do is pray that the SAFE kit turns up the results we think they will," Isis assured her.

"What's a SAFE kit?" Pamela asked.

"It's the kit Dr. Duplessis used to poke and prod me that night," Twylite explained.

Isis smiled. "You make yourself sound like a science experiment."

"Shoot, that's what it felt like."

They chatted for a while longer, the conversation flowing easier. Walls had come down, and trust began building on both sides. Finally, Isis began feeling as if she could actually help this girl. She wouldn't push too hard. She'd follow the lessons she learned from her boss and let Twylite determine the pace.

Isis glanced at her watch when she noticed the daylight waning outside the window. "It's getting a little late, ladies," she said. "You want me to drive you home?"

"That might be a good idea," Twylite said, thinking her walk around Loyola would have to wait. "Lord knows I don't need my momma fussin' at me again for being out by myself."

Pamela grunted. "I don't know what you're talkin' about, but I would take a ride over the bus anytime."

They laughed again.

Isis tapped the table with her palm and rose from her seat. "Let me just go use the restroom and we'll be on our way."

"She was pretty cool," Pamela said once Isis was out of earshot, "and her braids were bangin'."

"She was cool today, and it was nice of her to apologize," Twylite replied absently. An Asian lady carrying an armload of papers had captured her attention. She was pretty, standing at approximately five feet eight inches with bone-straight hair that hung halfway down her back. Her eyes weren't slanted like most of her friends thought Asians had, but were brown and striking in their own way.

The lady walked directly to the counter as if she had important business to discuss. Something told Twylite that the lady had done this a time or two before.

"Hey, Frankie," the lady told the man standing behind the counter. "I'm gonna put up a couple fliers in here. Is that cool?"

Her dialect surprised Twylite. She didn't have a hint of an Asian accent. In fact, if she hadn't been looking, she could have sworn the lady was black. She didn't sound all stereotypical, but she had a swagger in her voice that Twylite had only heard in her girlfriends' speech.

"Do your thing," Frankie said with a shrug. "Are you guys doing another poetry event?"

"Yeah, we got a coffeehouse Friday night in the Wolf Den," the lady answered as she pinned a flier to the bulletin board next to the counter. "We're trying to get a big turnout for this one because we have some poets coming from a few other campuses."

"Sounds like a nice event," he said.

"Yeah, it's gon' be on," she said, scooping up her fliers from the counter. "Mind if I pass a few to your customers?"

"You know you don't have to ask."

She shot him a thumbs-up and began circulating the room, dropping fliers at empty tables and talking with customers. When she reached Twylite and Pamela, she shot them a winning smile and handed them each a flier.

"Hey, li'l ladies," she greeted them. "Do you like poetry?"

"My girl Twylite here sings, but I don't think she's ever written anything," Pamela said.

"Yeah, I don't write, but I love to hear it," Twylite added, her eyes scanning the purple flier with the wild writing. It was definitely a college event. The paper said the coffeehouse would take place on Loyola's campus in the student center. "We're in high school, though. Can we get in this?"

"Girl, we ain't servin' no alcohol!" the lady said almost a little too loudly. She laughed. "I'll tell you what—if you'd like to come, you two can be my special guests."

"That's cool," Pamela said.

"That is nice of you," Twylite said. "What's your name?"

She laughed. "I guess I never told you that, huh? I'm Sue."

Isis returned to the table, shooting the group a puzzled look. "What's up?"

"This is Sue," Twylite introduced. "She just invited us to a poetry set at Loyola Friday night."

"Your mom?" Sue asked.

"Girl, no," Isis said. "I'm not nearly old enough to have girls this big. These are two of my good friends."

Sue shot her a funny look, and then smiled. "My bad. Didn't mean to offend."

They girls laughed again.

"Well, I gotta get going," Sue said, checking her watch. "My number is at the bottom of the flier, so if you decide to come, give me a call."

"We'll do that," Pamela said. "Thanks again."

"Anytime," Sue said as she backed away. She threw her free hand up and waved. "Y'all have a good night."

Twylite and Pamela followed Isis out of the restaurant a few minutes later. Twylite again glanced down at the flier. She'd never been to a college event. Maybe this would be a good start to getting prepared for life after high school, not to mention getting over Peanut. She'd always wanted to visit Loyola, and this seemed like the perfect opportunity. Now, the hard part: convincing her mother to let her go.

# Chapter Twelve

"You must be out your damned mind if you think I'ma let you go to some college campus by yourself!"

Although the conversation went as expected, it still wasn't the answer Twylite wanted to hear. Deep down, she knew why her mother was apprehensive, but she was willing to fight for this. Going to the poetry set was just too important to give up on just because of her mother's fears. It would be the first normal thing she'd done in weeks.

"But, Mom—"

"To hell wit' 'but, Mom!'" Adele snapped, wheeling her neck toward Earl for support. He remained silent, pretending to be engrossed in a *Times-Picayune* article. She cursed under her breath and turned back to Twylite. "Twylite, you have been through enough. Why would you think I would let you go to a college campus with some Chinese teenager I don't even know, in a situation you're not even familiar with, to hang out with some drunk-ass college kids?"

"Ma, it's not even like that," Twylite pleaded, flopping back against the sofa. "It's a coffeehouse, not a bar. And the lady isn't a teenager; she's a student at Loyola."

"Yet and still, I don't know the woman, and you don't, either," Adele retorted. "You can't even tell me her last name. You're lucky I even let you go see Isis by yourself. Now, you're just pushing it."

"Ma, please, I really wanna go to this. You told me you wanted me to get out more."

"Then start with church. You ain't been there in a while. Shit! Why this so important to you, anyway?"

Twylite knew the exact answer to that question, but she knew her mother would never understand. She probably thought it was about meeting some new guys or something, but it was nothing like that. All she wanted was to get away for a minute. Be around people who weren't just interested in cars and clothes. Spend time with people who wouldn't ask her if she was okay. She wanted to feel grown for a minute, and not feel like the dumb ass who got herself raped by her boyfriend. She could finally feel anonymous.

She looked at her father, hoping she could get the support he hadn't given to her mother. Nothing. He remained seated in his recliner, engrossed in the paper. Twylite was convinced that he wasn't even reading anything. He would let them fight this out by themselves.

"Ma, why you being like this? Dag!" Twylite whined. What was so unreasonable about her request?

"You mean why am I being a goddamned parent?" Adele charged. "It's my goddamned job, Twylite! You better come correct when comin' to me with some bullshit like this, because I ain't the one."

"But Pam and I promise to watch each other's back," Twylite reasoned.

Adele sucked her teeth and threw her hand up. "Girl, you better stop while you're ahead, because one more silly word outta your mouth might get my foot in your behind."

Although she had more fight left in her, Twylite was smart enough to realize that this was the end of discussion. Adele Knight didn't make idle threats.

Frustrated, she rose from the sofa and stomped off to her bedroom, slamming the door behind her. She threw herself across the bed and clamped her eyes shut, refusing to give way to the tears that burned the backs of her eyes. Her mother may have won this battle, but come hell or high water, she was determined to get to that poetry set.

She reached for her cell phone and dialed Pamela's number. It was late, but knowing Pam, her phone was on vibrate and hidden under her pillow. Sure enough, her friend answered before the first ring stopped.

"Hey, what's up?" Pamela whispered. "Whatcha momma say?"

"Shit," Twylite replied, her voice just as low. "Whatcha think she said? She said hell no."

"Mine said the same thing. She even had the nerve to ask me if I wanted the same thing that happened to you to happen to me."

"Pissssh," Twylite hissed. "That's some cold mess. Everybody ain't like Peanut. Besides, you think I'ma let the same shit happen twice?"

"I know what you're saying, but she kinda had a point. We don't know Sue from Eve. How we know she got our back? I heard some of those fraternity dudes can get kinda wild."

"It's not like we're going to a fraternity party, Pam. We'll be all right. Plus, Isis doesn't live that far from the campus. Maybe we could get her to take us."

"I don't know, Twy," Pamela said. "She seems cool and all, but I don't wanna feel like we have a babysitter."

"Yeah, that is true."

The line grew silent as the two girls pondered their dilemma. There was no way either of them could convince their parents to take them, and neither of them knew anyone in college besides Sue. At least no one local. Twylite's cousin went to the Southeastern Louisiana University, and Pamela's brother was way out in DC attending Howard.

"Maybe we should just chalk this one up to the game," Pamela suggested.

"Damn, we might have to, but God knows I don't want to," Twylite relented. She could kick herself. She'd finally found an interest in something, but she was blocked by circumstances. Life just wasn't fair sometimes. "I'll see you at school tomorrow. Hopefully we'll have thought of something by then."

School ended just as uneventfully as it began. Neither Twylite nor Pamela was any closer to a solution. It looked like attending their first college poetry event would be nothing more than a pipe dream.

Twylite had toyed with the idea of calling Sue and asking her to talk with Adele, but she knew that would be a bad idea. What college girl would want to take responsibility for a couple of teenagers she didn't know? And black teenagers at that? And top that off with one of the teenagers having been raped less than two weeks ago. Sue seemed cool, but Twylite was sure she wasn't that cool.

She thought again about breaking down and asking Isis to take them. Isis was there when Sue gave them the flier, and Twylite was sure Isis sensed their excitement. But Pamela had made a good point. They would be the only people in there with a babysitter, which would make them stand out like a couple of kids. And who wanted that? Besides, Twylite was sure Isis had her own plans. She never mentioned having a boyfriend, but she was pretty enough. Twylite guessed there was some kind of man in the mix.

Asking Dr. Duplessis was certainly out of the question. By the time the coffeehouse started, Dr. Duplessis would be on her way home. Asking her would require her to leave work early, drive across town to pick them up, and then drive them back uptown. Not to mention having to sit through a two- or three-hour event Twylite had never heard her express any interest in. She felt like a jackass for even considering the notion. The entire situation made her angry all over again.

"Maybe we could put on our own poetry set at church or something with the youth department," Pamela suggested as they boarded the bus to head home.

Maybe if Twylite had been in a better mood, she would have considered the idea, but now wasn't the time. She shook her head and glanced out the window. She caught sight of Yasmine rolling past in Peanut's BMW. Why did he like high school girls, anyway? At this point, she didn't care why. "It's not the same."

They remained silent throughout the rest of the ride home. Once Pamela got off at her stop, Twylite pulled out her cell phone and began playing *Angry Birds* to pass the time. Just before she could pull pack the sling with the tip of her finger, her phone rang. She didn't know whether to smile or cry when she saw the name on the caller ID.

"Hey, Isis," she groaned.

"You don't sound too happy," Isis said. "What's wrong?"

"My momma shot down that poetry set so quick, I couldn't even respond."

Isis chuckled a little. "Sorry to laugh, but you had to know she wasn't going to agree to that."

"Yeah, but this sounded like such a cool event. It's not like I asked her to let me go to some wild party or something."

"You're right, but you have to understand that just like this is a tough time for you, your parents are having it just as rough," Isis explained. "They might have let you go under different circumstances, but in light of everything that's happened, you can't blame them for wanting to keep you close."

"If you say so," Twylite sulked, refusing to admit to herself that Isis made sense. "They let me go to school by myself. They let me come see you by myself. What's wrong with going to this by myself?

"Twylite, are you serious?" Isis asked. "You go to school in the daytime. You came to see me in the daytime. This poetry thing is at eight o'clock at night, across town from where you live."

"But you live near there," Twylite protested. Her eyes quickly scanned the bus to see if any of the passengers sitting nearby could hear how pitiful she was sure she sounded. She felt like a ten-year-old kid begging to stay up past nine.

"Yeah, but how do you know I don't have plans Friday? You can't just plan other people's time around your plans."

Twylite grew silent, unsure of what to say next. If she managed to piss off every adult around her, there was no way in the world she'd be able to go anywhere, let alone the poetry set.

Isis sighed, probably sensing the sadness clouding Twylite's face. "Let me think about it. I'll call you later this evening and let you know."

Twylite smiled for the first time all day. "Really?"

"I haven't made any promises yet," Isis warned. "I just said I would think about it."

"Well, that's a start. Thank you, Isis!"

"Yeah, whatever," she muttered.


"How do I get myself into these predicaments?" Isis asked herself, slamming her cell phone on the bed.

She had a feeling that she'd somehow get roped into this poetry thing as soon as she saw the girls talking to that student. It was inevitable that Adele would say no, just like it was inevitable that Twylite would ask her to take her. The fact was, as much as she understood that this thing would do a lot to lift Twylite's spirits, she really didn't want to go. There were countless other things she could think of to do with her time than sit in a smoky room with a bunch of twenty-year-olds listening to revolutionary and sex rhymes.

But it wasn't about her. It was about Twylite. This was the most excited Twylite had been about anything since she met her two weeks ago. Maybe if she went, Twylite would rediscover her interest in singing and acting. She'd start focusing more on college and less on Peanut.

Damn, she hated calling that child Peanut. How did he get such a silly, juvenile nickname anyway? And why could she never remember his real name? She'd only laid eyes on the man once, but she knew she hated him. Any person who could so callously take away a young girl's innocence the way he did deserved every horrible punishment imaginable. As a Christian woman, she knew she shouldn't think such things, but as a black woman who had seen too many young women suffer the same fate, including herself, she couldn't help it.

Thinking back on her own youth, she remembered men like Peanut who took advantage of her naïveté. Men who played on the fact that she didn't think she was pretty or smart enough to attract a man who would like her for more than just her body. Men who knew she felt the only way she could keep them was to give herself to them. Men who knew that even if she did say no, they only had to touch her a certain way, or say just the right words to convince her to change her mind almost immediately.

The sad part was that she didn't learn her lessons as a teenager. It took low self-esteem, a physically and mentally abusive marriage, and a lost baby to convince her to get her act together. And although she knew she could feel herself becoming too involved in Twylite's case, she couldn't bear to watch her client go down the same road she'd worn a path on.

With that thought in mind, she sighed and picked up her cell phone. She tapped it lightly against her chin, hoping she was making the right decision. Finally, she sighed again and quickly dialed the numbers before she could change her mind.

"Hello, Mrs. Knight?"

# Chapter Thirteen

There are some days when the hours seem to just fly by. Everything just seems to click, and the to-do list gets smaller. Before you know it, the day has drawn to an end, but you've been lulled into the zone. It's the zone that makes you lose all track of time.

Unfortunately, it was already nearing six-thirty by the time Isis realized she'd been lulled into this zone.

"Damn, when did it get that late?" she mumbled after taking a glance at her watch.

It seemed as if only five minutes had passed since she checked her e-mail and saw the message from Mrs. Delachaise asking for the update report on Twylite's case. In actuality, a full three hours had passed as she searched out her original files, racked her brain for details she'd forgotten to write down, and typed the information into a readable format.

All of this was on top of preparing the closeout report for her prior case. That case was nothing compared to this one. Why couldn't all of her survivors be older women who knew exactly what they wanted? They didn't cut her off at the drop of a dime. They didn't flip-flop over their perpetrators. They didn't need their mothers to make decisions for them. And most importantly, they didn't try to talk Isis into taking them to college functions she really didn't want to attend.

Every time Isis thought about what she'd committed herself to, she wanted to scream. Now that she'd finally allowed her day to come to an end, the reality of the rest of the evening set in. Instead of letting Cain rub the stress from her tired shoulders, she'd be sitting at Loyola University, babysitting two teenagers.

"Now, that's what I call a good time," Isis mumbled as she rose from her chair and grabbed her messenger bag from her desk. She took another deep breath and stared at the ceiling before leaving her cubicle. "Maybe it won't be so bad."

She couldn't help but glance into Mrs. Delachaise's window as she strolled toward the door. As usual, the older woman was still burning the midnight oil, her mug of overly sweet coffee sitting next to her computer. Isis considered sneaking past, but why? There was no work left that night to be given, so she stuck her head in her boss's doorway and waved.

"See you Monday, Mrs. Delachaise," she said.

The older woman looked up and straightened her glasses on the bridge of her nose. "Oh, good night, Isis. I didn't realize you were still here. Most people run out of here on Fridays."

"Normally, I would have too, but I wanted to finish those reports. Did you get them in your e-mail?"

"I did. I was gonna go over them tonight, but I think it can wait 'til Monday."

Isis smiled, satisfied with herself. When she'd first begun working for Mrs. Delachaise, she felt she could do no right. Being from the Fisher Projects, one of New Orleans's roughest and most infamous housing areas, the old woman took her job very seriously. She'd seen too many cases go unsolved, too many mistakes made that cost a survivor her sanity.

No report went without review, and every new advocate underwent a strenuous training process. Nothing was held back: graphic training videos, body parts referred to by their street names, exhausting role plays, or rehearsals, as Mrs. Delachaise liked to call them. She made it her mission to ensure that every advocate in the Survivors Advocacy Network could handle any situation and could set their clients up for a successful recovery.

This was a tough pill for Isis to swallow at first. While she felt Mrs. Delachaise's goals were admirable, she hated her boss's methods. She'd never felt so micromanaged in her entire professional life, including her time working with Army public affairs soldiers. Having her work checked and rechecked was something she detested.

Fortunately, she decided to play the game, figuring that if Mrs. Delachaise continued to check her work and saw that it was done to standard, Isis could earn the autonomy she craved. For the next couple of months, she checked and rechecked her work before handing it over to her boss. She looked for every window of opportunity Mrs. Delachaise would have to criticize. Eventually, her hard work paid off, and she earned her boss's trust, as evidenced by tonight.

"Well, I'd better get out of here," Isis said after a few moments. She straightened and adjusted her messenger bag on her shoulder. "I promised to take Twylite to a poetry thing, and I'm already running late."

Mrs. Delachaise looked up from her computer and scrunched her eyebrows, but fortunately for Isis, she didn't comment. Well, not directly. "Be careful."

"I am. I will."


It was after seven by the time Isis made it to her car. There was no way she could make it to Twylite's house, pick her up, and get to St. Charles Avenue before eight. Between the traffic and the distance, it was mission impossible. She knew in the back of her mind that Twylite was probably cursing her very existence, but she would just have to deal with it.

Isis reached into the front of her messenger bag and dug for her cell phone as she maneuvered through the traffic. Once she finally felt it, she pulled it out and held it near the steering wheel so no one would notice her scanning the phonebook for Twylite's number. She quickly pressed CALL and enabled the Bluetooth earpiece she'd recently purchased. After dropping the phone in her lap, she placed her hand back on the wheel and continued down the road.

"Hello?" Twylite answered after the first ring.

"Hey, Twy, I'm sorry I'm just calling, but I just got off work."

"It's okay. I understand. It happens."

Isis scrunched her eyebrows and glanced down at her phone to see if she'd dialed the right number. Was this the same Twylite? The one who called her on the verge of tears just earlier this week because her mother wouldn't let her attend the event alone? "You're not disappointed?"

"I was at first, but it's okay. Pam and I just decided to do something else. I figured something must have happened when I didn't hear from you by six."

Isis's shoulders dropped in guilt. She was sure all of Twylite's understanding words were just a façade. She was probably being cursed out three ways from Sunday in the back of her client's mind. "You sure you're okay?"

"I'm good, Isis. I promise. You go on ahead and get you some rest."

"Okay," she replied, the guilt still lingering. "I'll call you tomorrow."

"Okay. Good night."

"Good night."

Isis continued her drive home, partially glad she could salvage her Friday night. Maybe she could call Cain and see what he was doing. Maybe they could go to a movie or get a late dinner. Maybe . . .

Something didn't seem right. Twylite had never been that agreeable or understanding. Isis played the conversation back in her mind. *"Pam and I just decided to do something else." Something else? Something else like what?*

A chuckle bubbled in her stomach as she merged onto Interstate 10 from I-610. *That girl thinks she's slick. No wonder she was so understanding.* When she hadn't heard from Isis by six, she decided to take matters into her own hands. Isis wondered what kind of lie Twylite came up with to get out of the house. She and Pam were probably on the bus while they were talking. No wonder she got off the phone in such a hurry.

"That girl must have forgotten I was a teenager too," Isis mumbled. "Well, I got a surprise for her li'l ass."


"I didn't think I was gonna hear from you two," Sue said as she pulled into the parking lot outside of Loyola's Danna Center, the student center that housed the Wolf Den. "Y'all 'bout had me late, drivin' all the way down St. Charles like that."

"We're sorry," Pamela said. "It was just getting too dark to walk down here."

"Why y'all ain't take the streetcar?"

"'Cause it was takin' too long," Twylite explained.

"I hear you," Sue said, nodding. "They slow down the later it gets."

Hip hop music greeted them once they walked into the building. They followed the sounds into a dark room set up with four-top tables with tiny candle centerpieces. A single microphone stood at the head of the room, next to the DJ, who had his eyes closed, his head bobbing to the beat, seemingly lost in his own rhythms.

Twylite marveled at how different college people looked from high school kids. For years, both public and private school students in New Orleans wore uniforms. Plaid skirts, solid-colored pants, and white shirts were the only reality Twylite ever knew when it came to attending class. But these students were like nothing she'd ever seen before. While some looked pretty normal in jeans and T-shirts, others looked to be from a different world with colorful dreadlocks, earthy ankle-length skirts, and shorts short enough that nothing was left to the imagination. The guys wore sweater vests with ties, while others wore button-down shirts and slacks. Everyone seemed to have their own identity. Twylite felt nearly self-conscious and vanilla in her sundress and jacket.

Sue, herself wearing skinny jeans, stilettos, and a tank top, walked through the crowd with the same air that Twylite noticed at the deli earlier that week. She seemed to know exactly where to go and what to do. She was like no other Asian woman Twylite had ever seen. Not that she knew a heck of a lot. Actually, Sue was the only Asian she'd ever met outside of the couple of girls who went to her school. But even they didn't seem to act like Sue did.

Twylite's eyebrows rose when she saw Sue wrap her arms around a muscular African American guy wearing a blue fraternity T-shirt. *This girl really does think she's black,* Twylite thought.

"You see that?" Pamela whispered, as if reading her friend's mind.

"Ummm hmmm," Twylite replied, nodding. "You think she's a wannabe?"

"Naaaa," Pamela replied. "She's probably just doing her."

They took a seat at a table near the back and watched as Sue worked the crowd. She certainly did have a way with people. Everyone she spoke to seemed to be taken with her. Twylite admired how easily she laughed with the African American students around her, as well as the few white students scattered throughout the room. She fit in perfectly, yet at the same time she seemed to be herself. Pamela was right. She didn't try hard to be black. She was herself. She didn't try to talk like those around her, and she didn't try to impress anyone with her Asian heritage. And yet, Twylite was definitely impressed.

"Sue is cool as hell," she whispered to Pamela.

Pamela smiled and nodded, but before she could respond, the brother Sue had hugged earlier took the stage.

"Ay, y'all," he greeted them with a boyish grin. The music, which had transitioned from hip hop to soft jazz, softened, but continued to play. "Welcome to Soulful Rhythm. I'm your host for tonight, Malik Tyler, also known as M-Tempo. You know how we do it each first Friday night in the Wolf Den. This is the spot where you will hear the most soul-stirring, mind-tingling, pulsating verses in the Big Easy!"

The crowd responded with cheers and clapping, along with a few whistles. Even Twylite and Pamela got caught up in the energy. Excitement bubbled inside Twylite as she realized she was finally experiencing what she'd anticipated all week. Finally, she could be a young woman kicking back with her best friend and getting a taste of college life. Her parents, Peanut, Yasmine, none of them meant anything tonight. This would be her attempt to snatch back some of what Peanut stole from her long before he ever raped her.

"Tonight, before we bring up our first act, I got a treat for y'all," M-Tempo said, his eyes glued on Sue. "Y'all all know my girl, Sue, right?"

"Yeah!" a few of the guys shouted through a round of applause and lustful whistles.

"Well, my baby is about to grace your ears and touch your hearts with a new original piece."

Twylite and Pamela glanced at each other with surprised eyes as Sue stepped on the stage. Twylite was sure Sue was a poet due to the way she met her, but a feature act?

"What's up, y'all?" Sue asked, her voice a bit lower and sultrier than it had been when she drove the girls earlier. "It's good to be here at another coffeehouse tonight. I can't think of another way I would rather spend my Friday night." She glanced at M-Tempo and let the corners of her mouth turn up. "Well, almost."

The crowd chuckled knowingly. The two teens giggled.

"So I've got this new piece I've been working on, right? I got the inspiration from watching some of the girls around here let themselves get treated any kinda way by some of these so-called men around here."

"I know that's right!" a young woman shouted from the audience, followed by a chorus of hoots and hollers.

"No, no, no," Sue exclaimed, laughing as she held up her hands defensively. "I'm not saying everybody. Ain't no hate intended. Y'all know I love everybody! And I'm Korean, so you know what my heritage is. Our ladies are taught to be silent and submissive. But American sisters, y'all got swagger. I just don't understand why some of us ladies let our men talk to us crazy, breaking down our self-esteem. So I wrote this lyric to help us to remember to be the queens we are. If it doesn't apply to you, cool. Take it and share it with somebody else. If it does, take from it what you will."

With that, she looked down, and slowly pumped her shoulders. She then slowly raised her head and gazed into the audience, staring at everyone, but looking at no one. Twylite squirmed a bit, feeling as if Sue's eyes bore into her soul.

"And it goes a little somethin' like this," she said.

The essence of a lady isn't in the way she wears her hair, or the clothes she wears

It isn't how loudly she shouts, or how effectively she pouts

It isn't about the amount of men she pulls, or how hard she rules.

It isn't about how often she's called fine, sexy, thick or bad

Or how much thigh her skirt displays, or how much breast she shows, a lot or just a tad

Yet if we don't talk to our young girls

If we don't counteract the isms of the world

They will become lost in a lack of self-esteem

And fall victim to the challenges the opposition may bring

You see, I know because I could have been that girl who felt she was nothing more

Than what people thought of her:

Ugly

Dumb

Gullible

A whore

But thank God He took my hand and helped me rise above

Those terrible words and showed me I deserved to be loved

Not just by men, but also by me

Because I'm a queen, a lady, God's child. You see?

I found that I didn't need to wait for affirmation from anyone

Because I knew who I was: a child of the Son!

That is the true essence of a lady

She demands respect and awe when she walks into anyplace

Because her confidence and smile just light up her face.

She will not stand to be called anything but the name her mother gave her.

If you can't respect that, then, brother, I'll see you later.

She bridles her tongue when she gives you the business,

Yet will encourage and comfort you with word or kiss.

If she's wrong, she'll tell you.

But if she's right, she won't tell you "I told you so."

She is the muse of Lionel, Babyface and Raheem

She's beautiful. She is a lady. She is a queen.

"Wow," Twylite mumbled as she clapped. She quickly stopped when she realized she and her friend were the only ones clapping. They then raised their hands over their heads and began snapping with everyone else.

"That joint was fire," Pamela exclaimed in an excited whisper.

"I know, right?"

Twylite wanted to respond, but something made her stop short, her hands still over her head. There was no way her eyes were playing tricks on her. Isis was actually watching her from the doorway. And she didn't look happy.

*Busted.*

# Chapter Fourteen

Isis's eyes narrowed into slits once they connected with Twylite's. She was tempted to smile at the panic written all over the girl's face, but she fought the feeling, not wanting Twylite to think she was okay with the situation. At the same time, she didn't want to fly off the handle too soon since she still wasn't sure if the girl had lied. She was more than sure that Twylite had lied, but there was a chance that Adele had had a change of heart.

"Yeah, right," Isis muttered as she moved toward the girls' table.

She watched as Twylite whispered something to her friend, Pamela. Pamela then looked toward her and matched the panicked expression Twylite had worn earlier. Her lips mouthed a curse word, and then she whispered something back to Twylite.

"Yeah, that's right," Isis muttered again. "Get your little story together. You picked the right one tonight."

Isis needed to get her own game plan together. As she wormed her way through the crowd, she ran over in her mind the best way to handle the situation. This wasn't the time to play buddy. She had to stick to her guns and let Twylite know that she was not to be used this way. Or any way, for that matter. There was no way in hell she would be dragged into any game concocted by two teenagers who didn't understand that sometimes life happens. And it didn't always happen in their favor.

She reached them and took a seat in the only other empty chair at the table. Silently, she folded her hands in front of her and looked first at Pamela, and then at Twylite. They both broke eye contact, looking everywhere but at her. Isis took a deep breath and rubbed her forehead before speaking.

"Ladies, start talking," she said, her voice even and authoritative. She was even impressed with herself. Lord knew she had no idea how this situation would turn out. "And before you say one word, I'ma tell you now that I will detect a lie a mile away. I'm not the one to be played with right now."

Pamela and Twylite looked at each other and back at the floor, neither of them ready to offer an explanation.

"I'm waiting," Isis coaxed.

Still no response.

"Okay, then allow me," Isis said, growing angrier by the second. "I was running late, so you decided to take it upon yourself to get here the best way you could. You probably told your momma that I told y'all to meet me somewhere and I would take you the rest of the way. Am I about right?"

Twylite glanced at Pamela, but when she didn't get a return glance, she rolled her eyes upward and sighed. The college-age poetry continued, surrounded by occasional agreement and cheering. The world hadn't stopped because the two teenagers in the room had gotten busted. It was possible that no one had even taken notice.

"I'm sorry, Isis," Twylite mumbled.

"Sorry? You could have ruined my credibility had I not been the first one to figure out your silly little plan," Isis retorted, trying hard not to raise her voice. "You're lucky I hadn't noticed the missed call on my phone from your mother when I called you. You see, I felt so bad about causing you to miss your little event that you were the first person I called when I got off work. Had I called your momma back, your whole little scheme woulda blown up in your face. You're damned lucky I'm here by myself, because I'm more than sure Adele woulda beat me here had I called her when I figured out how you tried to play me for a damned fool."

"It wasn't like that," Twylite pleaded.

"Does your momma think I brought you two here?"

Twylite bit her lip and looked away. "Yes."

"Case closed," Isis said, tapping her palm on the table. "Now, I'm trying not to embarrass you two in here, so you have five minutes to tell your friend Sue, or whatever her name is, good-bye so I can get you two home. I'm not about to be responsible for this hot mess here."

Pamela stared at her from under raised eyebrows. "How you know about Sue?"

"I was there when she invited you two to this thing, genius," Isis snapped. "I'm sure you didn't come here and not speak to her."

Pamela whipped her head back in surprise and looked like she wanted to say something in response, but thought better of it. "Come on, Twy."

Her friend followed her to the side of the makeshift stage, where Sue stood with her arms around a handsome African American guy, who Isis presumed to be a student at the school. Isis watched as they walked up to the couple and said a few words to them. Sue looked up and started to walk in her direction, but Twylite stopped her. Isis understood the move. Why let someone else know she'd lied and gotten busted? The situation was embarrassing enough.

Isis stood once she saw the girls head for the door. They didn't even slow down to wait for her. She knew they were pissed, but that wasn't her problem. They were wrong, and would have to deal with the consequences.

It was only five minutes after nine when they arrived at the Knight home. Isis was sure Earl and Adele would notice that there was no way the girls could have gone to an event across town, enjoyed it, and gotten home in an hour. But the way she felt right now, she couldn't even think of a lie to cover for them. And frankly, she didn't want to.

Yet, at the same time, as much as she wanted Twylite to get the beat down of a lifetime, she felt funny being the cause of it. Being the recipient of many a whipping herself growing up, she couldn't picture herself bringing that type of wrath on someone else. Yet, Twylite deserved to face the consequences of her actions, right?

She silently thanked God that the ride home was quiet. Both girls sat in the back sulking, probably wondering what fate lay ahead. Part of her wanted to do what her own mother would do in this situation—lecture them for the duration of the entire trip. Isis's mother was a quiet woman, but when her wrath was riled, no one would want to be in her path. Her words could hurt worse than any spanking ever could, not because she would curse and insult, but because she expected so much more from Isis and her sister Cleopatra. She would constantly lecture them on how they'd disappointed her, how they were so much smarter than what they'd shown her, how they needed to grow up if they expected to make it in this world.

Isis considered imparting the same words on Twylite and Pamela, but she didn't know them well enough to say something like that. The effects of her last badly timed lecture to Twylite still rang in her head. She also didn't want to come off sounding like anyone's mother. At thirty-four years old with no serious husband material in her life, she wasn't sure if she would ever have her own child. And her miscarriage years ago was still too close to her memories to even think of going down that road again.

The silence in the car was excruciatingly loud. The girls could at least talk to each other if they weren't going to beg for her forgiveness and mercy. At least if they did that, she'd have a reason to stay mad. Their flimsy excuses would fuel her strength, kind of like Samson's dependence on his hair. If they talked, they'd be bound to say something dumb that would keep her angry and make her want to bust them out to Adele and Earl. Turn and walk away without a care or regret in the world.

That would be what they deserved, right? After all, Twylite had lied and put herself and her friend in danger. Shouldn't she learn a lesson for what she'd done? It was only right that she caught hell.

But then again, she couldn't help but remember her own life as a teenager. Outside of her parents, she'd never had an adult whom she could trust to talk to. Maybe if she had had an advocate back then, someone in whom she could confide and trust to give it to her straight, maybe she wouldn't have gone through the sexual turmoil she'd put herself through. Maybe, just maybe, she wouldn't have made the silly mistakes she made as an adult because she wouldn't have felt the need to hide so much.

Looking back, hiding her sexual activity didn't make her more refined and experienced. It only made her more of a target because no one had taught her to say no. No one had taught her that giving it up on demand didn't make her girlfriend material, but jump off material.

Isis wanted so badly not to let Twylite make those same mistakes. She'd seen enough cases to know that rape didn't always scare people straight. Sometimes it only made a volatile situation worse.

Would getting Twylite in trouble for what she'd done tonight help or hurt her? Would she really learn a lesson? She thought of Earl and the pain that reflected in his eyes each time he looked at or spoke of his daughter. She was sure he would never get over knowing that his daughter was raped and there was nothing he could do about it. Something was taken from his daughter that even a justifiable homicide couldn't get back.

Adele felt the same pain, but where Earl handled it internally, she was more than vocal. Isis knew Adele would bring the pain when she found out about this situation, but that would only force Twylite further inside her shell. If that happened, no one would be able to get through to her.

There was Alexis, but Isis had to admit that a selfish corner of her mind didn't want to turn to her newfound friend. Although she knew Alexis would always be Twylite's unofficial advocate, she hoped that the girl would learn to depend on her, instead. That was the reason she'd become a victim's advocate in the first place. If she had to depend on other people to get through to her clients, then what good would she be? She knew her feelings were selfish, but there was no way possible to overcome it.

Isis glanced into the rearview mirror. The light from a passing car illuminated the sadness on her client's face. The silence in the car spoke more words that Twylite could ever think to utter.

The silent standoff needed to end.

"I know you really wanted to go tonight, but was this poetry thing really that important?" she asked, stealing another glance into the rearview mirror. "You compromised the trust that both I and your parents had in you, not to mention my credibility. What do you think would have happened had your mother gotten in touch with me?"

Silence was the only response.

"Now, you don't have shit to say. Forget everybody else, just as long as Miss Twylite gets her way, right? Right?" Isis repeated, irritated.

"It wasn't like that, Isis," the girl finally mumbled.

Thankful to have finally received a response, Isis stole another glance and caught Twylite giving Pamela the side eye. Isis felt her pain. There was nothing she could say in front of her friend without looking pitiful. Sneaking out was probably Twylite's idea, and now that the plan had failed, she was most likely wondering how she could save face.

Isis realized that Pamela hadn't said a word throughout the entire trip home. She probably wanted to say "I told you so," but was too good a friend to dump more coal on Twylite. Isis wished she'd had a friend like that when she was their age.

She decided to leave the situation alone for the moment instead of embarrassing her client even more. They were nearing Twylite's house anyway. The silence would give her a chance to decide the best way of handling this situation. And once she pulled into the driveway, the answer entered her mind.

*What went wrong? How did she figure it out?*

The question played over and over in Twylite's mind as they took the green mile home. She was sure she'd covered all her bases. They were home free. At least that's what she thought until Isis showed up at Loyola University with venom in her eyes. She just knew Isis would curse them out all the way back home, her parents would curse her out some more when she got home, and Pamela would finish cursing her the first chance she got.

She barely heard anything Isis said as they zoomed down I-10. She needed to get her story straight, and hoped against hope that Pam read her mind. They needed to be in sync, and since she couldn't talk out loud, she had to figure something out that would be quick and easy.

But then again, lying was what had gotten her into this situation. And since she was sure Isis would rat her out, she figured she might as well face the music and hope that she hadn't gotten her friend into too much trouble. As much as she hated to admit it, Isis was right. She'd not only gotten herself and her friend in trouble, but she could have cost Isis her job.

The stomach pangs began as soon as the car pulled into her driveway. The time had come to prepare herself for the ass beating she was sure was coming. Isis shifted the gear into park, and laid her forehead on the steering wheel.

*Dag, she's taking this a little too damned hard,* Twylite told herself. She gestured for Pamela to get out of the car, and then followed suit.

"I'm sorry," she mumbled to her friend as the trudged toward the front door. The porch light immediately popped on. Someone knew they were home. Twylite hoped it was her dad.

"Don't worry about it," Pamela muttered back.

Adele opened the door and looked at them with a puzzled expression. "It's over already?"

Before Twylite could reply, Isis called out to her. "You forgot something," she called.

"I'll be right back," she told her mother and friend as she backed toward the car. She walked to the driver's side, wondering what she could have forgotten. All she had was her purse, which hung safely on her shoulder.

Isis took a deep breath once the girl reached her window. "I'm not going to tell your parents about what happened tonight."

Twylite took a deep sigh of relief, but before she could say thanks, Isis continued. "Don't make me regret this. Your parents have a lot of trust in me, and I don't want to violate that. Not only that, I could get fired if I allow you to involve me in anything immoral. Don't ever use me like that again. Sometimes life happens, and it sucks, but you just gotta live with it."

Twylite nodded, not knowing what else to say. She wasn't going to get ratted out, but something told her that she hadn't fully gotten away with what she'd done.

"I know you're going through a lot right now; and I'm trying my best to help you through it," Isis continued. "But that doesn't mean that people will cater to you and give you everything you want. That attitude will not help you through this. You need to grow up, and you'd better do it quick, because pulling shit like you did tonight will only make things worse for you. I know you hate when I give you advice, but this is something that needs to be said."

Twylite nodded again and then backed away from the car. "I'm sorry, Isis."

"Don't apologize. Just do better."

With that, she backed out of the driveway and disappeared into the night.

"Everything all right?" Adele asked once Twylite returned to the house. "Why y'all back so early?"

"The show was shorter than we thought," Pamela said before Twylite could respond. "Kind of a waste of time. I coulda stayed home and watched *Def Poetry Jam* or something."

Twylite laughed, relieved that Pamela had taken away the opportunity for her to lie. There was no way she could get them both into trouble. "Yeah, but Sue was really good. That Asian girl got some soul."

"Is that right?" Adele asked, smiling genuinely. The smile warmed Twylite on the inside. It was the first smile she'd seen from her mother in a long time. "I hope you thanked her for inviting you two out."

"We did," Twylite replied, looking around the room. "Where's Daddy?"

"He went to grab us something to eat," Adele said. She smiled again and winked. "We thought we were gonna have the house to ourselves for a while longer."

Twylite laughed, tapping her friend and pointing upstairs. "We're gonna watch TV in my room. Thanks for letting us go."

"All right," Adele replied. "Y'all don't be up too late."

"We won't," the girls said in unison.

"Thanks," Twylite told Pamela once they reached the safety of her room.

"It's all good," her friend replied. "There was no use in both of us getting our asses whipped, and since Isis didn't tell on us, I figured I'd leave well enough alone. She gave it to you pretty good in the car. What did she tell you when she called you back?"

"That she wasn't gonna tell on me, but you know she had to give me another speech, too."

"I figured that. At least you know she cares about you, though."

"Why you say that?"

"Because, anybody else probably wouldn'ta come to get you."

Twylite shrugged. "She was just protecting her job."

"Maybe, but it seemed like it was more than that to me. She still coulda told your momma, but she didn't."

"That's true," Twylite mumbled. Maybe there was more to Isis than she gave her credit for. She thought back to the smile her mother gave her. It was good to see her relaxed, not all uptight. Maybe if she listened to Isis, she'd see her mother smile a whole lot more.

# Chapter Fifteen

Twylite took a deep breath as she walked into choir rehearsal for the first time in weeks. She knew Sister Max, her choir director, had been asking about her. She'd managed to avoid her phone calls, and wasn't sure if her mother had told her about the rape. The urge to sing still hadn't returned, but she knew she couldn't avoid the choir forever. Pretty soon, they would come knocking on the door, and knowing Sister Max, the excuse that she just didn't feel like singing wasn't going to fly for long. Besides, she was afraid that her dad would begin making good on his threats to take away what little freedom she had if she didn't start singing again.

The sounds of "How Excellent Is Thy Name" filled the sanctuary and filled her ears as she trudged down the center of the aisle and took a seat on the third row, where her family usually sat when they attended service. Clarence, a tenor with a voice that reminded Twylite of Chris Brown's, caught a glimpse of her and smiled as he lifted his eyebrows in greeting.

The gesture didn't go unnoticed by Sister Max, who turned to see what had broken his concentration. When she saw Twylite sitting there, a wide grin broke across her face, and she waved her hand toward the organist to stop the music. "Well, praise the Lord, the prodigal child has returned to the flock!"

A few choir members cackled in laughter, prompting Twylite to smile in spite of herself. "Hi, Sister Max."

"Hi, yourself," she replied. "You just paying us little folks a visit, or are you here to use the talent that God gave you?"

"I'm here to sing," the girl replied, embarrassed at once again being the center of attention. She knew there were other people who never missed a Friday rehearsal or a Sunday service, so she felt kind of badly that she had taken some of their attention. Was she really that special?

"She probably forgot how," Clarence taunted, his eyes boring a hole into hers. Had he not been smiling, Twylite would have sworn that he was irritated.

"That's all right, because she wasn't that good anyway," chimed in Doretha, the oldest member of the choir. She had been singing in the young adult choir since she was fourteen, and was now finishing her first year at Dillard University.

"I'm better than you," Twylite snapped. She knew Doretha was only playing, but it was no secret that the two of them had a bit of an unspoken rivalry. Where Doretha had experience, Twylite had a natural talent. Yet it wasn't an unfriendly rivalry like she had with Yasmine. They respected each other, and teased one another to bring out the best in each other. To Twylite, her friendship with Doretha was the most productive friendship she had, even more so than with Pamela.

"If you were, you never woulda left."

"All right, that's enough," Sister Max interrupted. "Sister Twy, if you're really back, then get yourself into this stand and rehearse this song before you find yourself in that same spot come Sunday."

"Yes, ma'am."

She popped up and speed walked to the alto section, taking her normal spot right next to Doretha and in front of Clarence. Without another word, Sister Max raised her hands, recapturing the choir's attention. On cue, the organist began the chords, and Sister Max moved her hands and prompted the group to sway left to right.

"'Oh, Lord, how excellent, how excellent, how excellent,'" Doretha sang. "'How excellent is thy name.'"

Twylite wasn't surprised that Doretha had been chosen to lead the song. Her voice had a soft bravado that gave the song a reverent feel. Twylite could feel the tears tease the rims of her eyes before the chorus even began.

"I'm glad you finally came back," Doretha said after rehearsal. They sat in the back of the church awaiting Twylite's parents to take her home. "It's hard trying to carry this choir by myself."

Twylite smirked, knowing her friend spoke the truth. Church choirs weren't like professional choirs. Anyone who had the desire to sing could join, even if they couldn't carry a note in a sack. Sister Max had a way of making their voices blend and sound harmonious, but it was obvious during practices who had real talent and who only had desire.

"I'm sorry. I just had a lot goin' on the last couple of weeks."

Doretha shifted in her seat. "I heard."

Twylite shook her head in frustration and embarrassment. "Does everybody know?"

"Girl, you know there are no secrets in this church. Everybody knows. When you disappeared out of the choir, people started asking questions. Then somebody, I won't say who, decided to put your business out in prayer meeting, pretending they were asking folks to pray for you. It just went downhill from there."

"Why am I not surprised? More people's business gets put out during prayer meeting than a little bit."

Doretha chuckled a little. "I know, right? Your parents were hot when they found out, but Pastor told everybody that your family needed to handle this privately and to let you talk about it when you were ready."

"That's good."

"You doing okay?"

"As good as can be expected. He's still walking the streets like nothing ever happened, but I guess that's the way things go sometimes."

"Well just pray that he gets his in the end. No one deserves what he did to you. I admire you for continuing to live your life after all this. It takes a lot of strength to be able to do that."

"Really? I don't feel like I did anything special. I'm only here because my daddy said he wanted me to start singing again."

"But you didn't have to listen. Trust me, I run into all kinds of people with all kinds of issues at school, but you seem to have bounced back better than some people who have experienced much less. I'm proud of you."

"Wow," Twylite said, surprised at the amount of pride Doretha's words had given her. No one had ever called her strong before. She'd always depended on her parents for everything, and for a long time, Peanut had made her believe she could do nothing or be nothing without him. "Thanks for saying that. I really needed to hear that more than you might think."

"Then I'm glad I said it, because it's the truth. Don't you let that man steal God's gift from you."

Twylite was still smiling when Earl walked into the church to take her home. Her head still echoed Doretha's words. It had been a week since Isis had told her that she needed to grow up, and now Doretha had placed the exclamation point on her words. Was God really trying to tell her something?

"Daddy, do you think I can get past all this?"

Earl sighed and shifted nervously in his seat. He'd wanted to have a heart-to-heart with his daughter ever since the night of the rape, but continued to put it off because he could never find the right words to say. For him, it was easier to leave all the vocals to Adele. He looked around, the scenery telling him that they would be home in five minutes.

"Get past what?" he asked, stalling as he struggled to find the words she needed to hear.

"I mean, I've heard the stories about these girls who get raped and they never have a normal life again," Twylite stammered, as she stared out of the window. "I don't wanna be like that."

"You don't have to be."

"I just don't know if it's as easy as that."

"Why would you think that?"

Twylite shrugged. "I just don't know what makes me so different from those other girls. I mean, Doretha said I was strong, but I don't feel it. I haven't done anything special."

"Wait, wait, wait," Earl said, pulling into a grocery store parking lot. They were right around the corner from the house, but this was a conversation that needed to be had now. "I can't speak for nobody else, but as for you, you got a momma and daddy who would walk to hell for you. We gonna do whatever we have to do to help you through this. Even if that li'l nigga never pays for what he did, I'll be damned if I let you pay the price."

Earl saw the nervousness on his daughter's face and stopped, realizing that he'd had more venom in his voice than he'd intended. It made him wonder if his hatred for Peanut had overtaken his love for his daughter.

When he first saw the movie *A Time to Kill*, he knew he identified with Samuel L. Jackson's character, Carl Lee Hailey. What man wouldn't want to kill anyone responsible for bringing harm to his only daughter? But he hadn't been in this situation back then. It was easy to say what he would do when it was just a movie, but now that it was real life, he realized that even the thought of taking another man's life just wasn't that easy. He wanted to believe that the police would handle it eventually, but what if they didn't? Could he just walk away and shield his daughter with love? Or would he kill Peanut and risk going to jail, where he would be no use to his wife or daughter?

"I'm sorry, baby girl," he said, pulling back the force his previous words had displayed. "I know this whole thing has been hard on you, because it's been hard on me. Your momma has been hard on you because this thing has been hard on her as well. But, baby, you are the most important thing in all of this. I'm not gonna let that boy win by watching you turn into a shell of yourself. If you do that, you're gonna give him just what he wants."

"He wants to see me fail?" Twylite asked, scrunching her eyebrows.

"Twylite, I'm a man and I know how men think," Earl said, patting her knee. "When a woman leaves us, or even when we leave a woman, we don't want to see her do better. We wanna see her broken down, like she ain't nothin' without us. I know dat boy told you stuff like dat."

She looked down and nodded.

Earl continued, "I'll be damned if I let you prove him right. You're a beautiful girl, Twylite, and before you got mixed up with dat boy, you were doing good in school, singing in the choir, and had started showing interest in acting. Now, you just mope around the house feeling sorry for yourself. You're better than dat, Twylite."

She pursed her lips, probably feeling the sting from her father's words. "But I went back to choir rehearsal today."

"And I'm proud as hell dat you did. You don't know how it hurt my heart looking in dat choir stand and not seeing you there the past few Sundays. I don't wanna see you waste your gifts."

Twylite wiped a tear away, a move that didn't go unnoticed by her father. He felt badly that his words had made her cry, but he knew what he said was what she needed to hear. He loved his daughter more than he loved himself, and all the tiptoeing the women in her life were doing wasn't doing any good. She needed to hear it straight from a man who cared about and loved her. Someone who wanted nothing from her except her love.

He reached out and turned her chin toward him. "You hear me, Twylite? You're gonna get through this because you are more than what he told you you are. You're my child. And more important, you're God's child."

A hint of a smile pulled at the girl's lips. "Thanks, Daddy."

He nodded and started the car. Before placing it in reverse, he again looked at his daughter and asked, "You okay? You got anything else on your mind?"

She shook her head. "I'm good. I'm glad we got a chance to talk. You been so quiet, I didn't know how you felt about all this."

"Just because I'm quiet don't mean I don't care. I ain't gon' ever stop carin' about you."

"I know you won't."

He placed the car in reverse and began backing out of the parking lot. His talk with his only daughter seemed to do them both some good. Yet, he still couldn't shake Peanut from his thoughts. The way he yelled at her at the police station still rang through his mind. He only hoped that Peanut would stay as far away from the Knight family as possible. Earl could stay a Christian man for only so long before Carl Lee took over.

# Chapter Sixteen

"On your backs!" Peanut proclaimed as he slammed the double five domino on the table, earning thirty points and winning the game. The other three men groaned and cursed, drawing a cackling laugh from Peanut. "Y'all niggas can't mess wit' me! I done tol' y'all!"

He stood up at the table and looked around the bar. It was still early in the evening, so only a few tables held customers. The atmosphere was relaxed, with Mel Waiters's "Got My Whiskey" flowing through the jukebox sitting against the wall. The few patrons in the place swayed back and forth in their seats as they drank from their beer bottles and mixed drinks. A couple bobbed their heads while playing pool on the bar's lone table near the back of the room.

"Anybody got next?" he shouted to anyone who might be listening. "These bustas ain't ready!"

"Hey, I gotcha," replied a young man sitting at the bar adorned with colorful Christmas lights. It was still three months before Christmas, but it appeared that the owner felt that the lights would be a cheap way to add ambiance to the bar.

Peanut scanned the man using only his eyes. He wore a green, white, and blue Rocawear shirt and a pair of sagging jeans. His face didn't look readily familiar to Peanut, but he thought nothing of it, figuring the man could be new to the area.

He turned to the table and looked at Rick, who sat nervously tapping two dominoes together. It was obvious he knew who would be moving to make room for the new guy.

"A'ight, Rick, you know the deal," Peanut told him. "Low man gets his ass up."

"Why Boe can't get up?" Rick protested. "It was his ATM ass dat gave you all dat money."

"Aw, nigga, you cain't change the rules just 'cause you lost," Boe shot back, leaning back in his chair and laughing. "Get ya ass up and make room for the new blood."

"Dat's some bullshit," Rick mumbled, scooting back from the table. He stood and allowed the new guy to take his seat. Rick shot his eyes around the table and looked down at the newbie, who had already begun to scramble the dominoes. "Watch they cheatin' asses."

The entire table erupted in laughter.

"Man, get your sore-losin' ass up outta here with noise," Peanut retorted, dismissing him with a hand wave. He turned back to the new guy. "What's your name, playboy?"

"Cain," the man replied, pushing the dominoes back to the center of the table.

"Cain? I heard dat name before," Peanut replied, looking at him skeptically. He reached in and chose his seven dominoes, never taking his eyes off the new guy.

"I get around."

"Why I ain't never seen you in here before?"

"Damn, man," Cain protested, his smile remaining on his lips. "Is this li'l hole in the wall a private club now? I was making some rounds in the area and decided to stop for a drink. That all right with you?"

"Aw, hell," Joe remarked, smiling at Peanut. "Looks like we done met somebody else who ain't takin' your shit."

The table again erupted in laughter, but Peanut looked at Cain and winced. "You ain't had to get all smart. I just asked your ass a damn question."

"And I just answered it, so can we play some bones, or what?"

Peanut tapped his domino on the table and turned toward Boe. He would let the situation go for now, but had a feeling that Cain was someone he'd need to watch. "This motherfucka here got some mouth and some heart."

"It don't take much," Cain responded, winking at him.

"Man, whose turn is it?" Joe asked. "Too much damn talkin' and not enough playin' goin' on."

"You ain't neva lied," Cain agreed. He then looked back at Peanut and smiled. "Hey, man, you like yogurt?"

Peanut looked at him and winced. "What?"

"It's yo' play."

Everyone in earshot laughed again.

"I like dis mothafucka here," Boe shouted.

Peanut laughed as well, but the remark solidified his thought that he would definitely have to watch Cain. He wasn't sure why his name sounded familiar, but if there was some funny business going on, he would damn sure find out.

The game continued, and after the first two rounds, Peanut began to relax a bit. Cain seemed to be okay. He talked noise at all the right times, and seemed to be more concerned with the game than he was with the people playing it. Some might have thought Peanut was overly suspicious of people, but in his line of work, everyone was a suspect.

Peanut might have been a mailman, but packages and envelopes weren't all he delivered. He was also a small-time hustler, selling weed part time and running a small call girl service in the evenings. The money he made was decent for now because he was paid well from the post office. However, he was always on the lookout for a bigger payout.

He had planned to add Twylite to his service, but everything had gone wrong that night. Where did she all of a sudden get all that mouth? Before, if he told her to jump she wouldn't even bother to ask how high. She'd just do it. If he told her he wanted to see her at two o'clock, she was there at one fifty-five.

This was why he was shocked when she just up and broke up with him. He knew her parents were giving her a hard time about being with him, but he could handle that. His other girls had gone through the same thing, but with a few sweet words whispered in their ears about how he loved them and could take care of them, nothing their parents said even mattered.

He didn't fight it when she broke up with him, though. Instead, he laid back and maintained military silence for a couple of weeks. This way, she'd begin to realize how much she missed him. Then all he'd have to do is show up one day and she'd be begging him to take her back.

At least, that was the way it was supposed to go. That's what had happened with his first girl. But Twylite just had to get bold. She even had the nerve to try to put her hands on him. As far as he was concerned, that basic bitch needed to be put back in her place. He didn't mean for it to go as far as it did, but since he hadn't heard anything else from the police, it was time to move on and chalk the thing with Twylite to the game. She'd just have to be the potential that got away.

"'Scuse me, fellas," Cain said, interrupting Peanut's thoughts. He reached for the vibrating cell phone clipped to his pants pocket. "What's up, lady?"

Peanut sighed and tapped his domino impatiently on the table. A glance back and forth told him that Boe and Joe shared his sentiment. No one had patience for a domino game being stopped for petty reasons. The way they saw it, you either got your ass off the phone and played, or left the table.

"Yeah, I'll be there as soon as I finish breaking these backs," Cain told his caller.

And he had the nerve to talk shit, too? This clown didn't know who he was dealing with!

"Nigga, play or talk!" Joe shouted. "We got women we need to get home to too!"

"Baby, lemme go," Cain said. "Shit just got serious in here."

After ending the call and replacing his phone, Cain took his turn and claimed ten points. "I don't know why y'all in such a rush to get y'all asses kicked."

"Man, fuck you," Boe retorted. "You talkin' a whole lotta shit to be down by half a house."

"Just temporary," Cain said with a smile. "All money ain't good money."

"That shit only applies to dominoes," Peanut said. "'Cause a nigga like me is gon' get his money!"

"Believe me, I got mine too, but even in life all money ain't good money."

"You tellin' me you would pass up some dollas just because?" Peanut asked. The wheels in his mind began to turn again.

"Bruh, money has to benefit me more than just the here and now in order for me to go after it," Cain said. "I don't chase money. That shit comes to me."

"Dat's some deep shit, right there," Boe said, nodding. The light finally went off. "Man, I thought your name sounded familiar!"

Cain just raised his eyebrows, not out of fear or shock, but out of acknowledgment.

"The hell you doin' around here?"

Boe looked confused. "Who the hell is he?"

"Don't worry about it," Peanut told him. "If you don't know, you don't need to know."

"On your backs, and twenty when I go!" Joe announced, rising from his seat. "All that talkin' and you ain't payin' attention the board. It's my time now!"

Peanut and Cain leaned back in their seats, never taking their eyes off of one another.

"Good game, bruh," Cain told Joe. "You got me this time. I might hafta come back over this way and play again."

"Yeah, you do dat," Joe replied. "You got some game in you."

"You right about dat," Peanut said.

Cain backed away from the table and stood. "All right, y'all. I'm out. There's a fine-ass woman waitin' on me."

"Do your thing, playboy," Boe said, shaking hands with Cain.

"Nice meetin' y'all," Cain said, throwing up his hand in farewell before walking out of the bar.

Boe turned to Peanut, who had already begun placing the dominoes back in their tin. "All right, Nut, now dat he's gone, who the hell is he?"

"You ain't never heard Cain's name before?" Peanut asked. He looked around to ensure no one could hear him, and leaned toward Boe, lowering his voice. "His name is short for Cocaine. He's like the second-biggest coke dealer in New Orleans. Dat nigga got dollas on top of dollas, and he ain't never been caught!"

"Sounds like somebody we need to know."

"You ain't lyin'. I just gotta figure out how to do it."

# Chapter Seventeen

"Girl, you've got some legs on you!" Alexis exclaimed through a series of huffs and puffs. She bent at the waist in an effort to stretch her hamstrings before they began tightening.

Isis paced back and forth, her hands clutching the small of her back as she breathed in the oxygen from the trees surrounding them. "What are you talking about? I thought you were going to leave me in the dust a couple of times."

"I was just trying not to let you show me up," Alexis replied with a laugh. "You said you hadn't run in a while, so I didn't want to look like I had been half stepping."

Both ladies laughed as Shalonda approached them, her arms pumping and propelling her speed walk. Well, slow walk.

Alexis shook her head at her friend. "You are so sad."

"I ain't even thinking about you, Lex!" Shalonda snapped. "You're lucky I even came out here at all. You know I don't do this."

Isis smiled. "Well, I'm glad you're here. It's nice to have some company."

"Whatever," Shalonda said, waving her off.

Isis had decided to get back to taking care of herself the night before when she'd tried on an old pair of jeans that had obviously shrunken with time. She managed to pull them up, but was unable to get the zipper all the way up. After mentally kicking herself and lamenting over the good old days when she maintained her fit figure by exercising five days a week, she called Alexis and asked her for a good running trail. Alexis suggested she go to the running trail at City Park, and then asked if she could join her.

Isis had jumped at the chance to spend some quality time with who she hoped would become a good friend. She still hadn't met many people since she'd moved to New Orleans. The Twylite case had taken so much of her time and energy that she'd nearly forgotten about being social. Something had to change.

Shalonda showing up was just an added bonus. Isis loved the interaction between Alexis and her. It reminded Isis of the days when she hung tight with Michelle and Kendra. They never held their tongues when it came to expressing themselves.

Alexis and Isis had done two laps around the two-and-a-half-mile track while Shalonda only walked one. Each time they passed her, Alexis would tap her on the shoulder and shout, "Move your ass, woman!" Shalonda would stick her tongue out at her and shout, "Shut up!"

"You two are hilarious," Isis said.

"Nothing wrong with making exercise fun," Alexis replied. "But in the meantime, I need to scoot out of here so I can get ready for work. It's already seven-thirty."

"Yeah, me too," Shalonda agreed. "I have to admit that it was nice getting up early and exercising. I don't believe I'm saying this, but I wouldn't mind doing this again."

"Really?" Isis asked, her words only echoing the shocked look on Alexis's face.

"Why y'all so surprised? I don't like to exercise, but I value staying in shape too."

"I just never thought I'd see the day," Alexis replied, still astounded. "We'll see how long this lasts."

"I'll just have to show you better than I can tell you," Shalonda challenged. She turned to Isis. "How often you wanna do this?"

Isis shrugged. "Monday, Wednesday, Friday?"

"That's cool, but I'll probably do a longer run on the levee on Saturdays," Alexis said.

"How long?" Isis asked.

"Well, that levee is about ninety miles long, but I try to do about ten miles on it. Five out and five back."

Isis and Shalonda looked at each other and back at Alexis before simultaneously saying, "You can keep that."

"Baby steps, Shera!" Shalonda added.

Alexis laughed. "I didn't say y'all had to come. My man usually joins me for those runs. I told y'all before, all this doesn't just happen. I work hard for this body. The older I get, the harder it gets."

"I agree, and maybe one day I'll be there with you, but I'm just starting this journey again," Isis said. "I have to get back to that level, but I'm not even sure I was ever there."

They stood around chitchatting a while longer before Shalonda glanced at her watch.

"Well, ladies, let's get out of here before we're all out of a job," she announced. "It's almost seven forty-five now."

"Ooo, let me get out of here!" Isis said, backing toward the parking lot. "I have a meeting at nine-thirty, and I know the traffic is going to be ridiculous. I'll see y'all Friday!"

Isis jogged back to her car. She really had to credit herself for even getting up that morning. Cain had spent the night, and although they still had not gotten physical, he kept her up all night making her wish she could easily break her celibacy. His kisses made her melt, his arms made her feel comfortable. Five o'clock had come way too soon.

It took everything she had to leave Cain's arms, get dressed, and drive across town to run five miles in the cool air, but she did it. Now, she was on her way to losing the proverbial ten pounds that would make her clothes fit better and welcome the numbers on the scale like an old friend.

She reached her apartment building in record time, considering the traffic. She'd already called Mrs. Delachaise and told her she would be running a few minutes late, promising that she would be on time for the meeting. As soon as she entered her apartment, she headed straight for the shower, peeling off her clothes with each step.

"We're going to have to find some running trails closer to my house," Isis mumbled as the water hit her face. She washed off quickly, and dried off just as fast.

Her cell phone rang as she slipped into a pair of slacks that she knew would fit.

"Shit, I don't have time for this," she mumbled again. A quick glance at the clock as she found her cell phone told her that she had just less than an hour left before the meeting began. "Hello!"

"Isis?"

She looked at her cell phone, puzzled. Why would Twylite be calling her this early in the morning? Shouldn't she have been in school? "Yes, this is Isis. Is everything okay?"

"Kind of. Can I meet you after school today? I really need to talk with you."

"Of course, is something wrong?"

"I'll tell you later."

An exasperated sigh escaped Isis's lips as she tossed the phone into a purse. "It's always something."

Twylite knew she had probably freaked Isis out with the early-morning cryptic phone call, but she wasn't sure what

else to do. Peanut had dropped Yasmine off at school yesterday as he had been for the past couple of weeks, but this
time she didn't look so good. Her hair usually had shiny
curls that cascaded over her left shoulder, and she wore
makeup that rivaled some of the makeup artists she'd seen
on YouTube. So when she got out of Peanut's car looking
like she'd just woken up, Twylite could tell right away that
something was wrong.

She knew Peanut had seen her when he drove past her.
Lately he'd gone from staring at her to just ignoring her
altogether. Today was no different. He'd driven past her
as if she just blended in the atmosphere. It used to bother
her, but lately she shrugged it off as his lame attempt to
avoid her. Yet, she couldn't get Yasmine off her mind. She
hated her, but would never wish her harm.

"You all right?" Twylite asked the girl as she walked
past her in the hallway.

Yasmine just sucked her teeth and rolled her eyes. "I
don't think how I'm doing is any of your fuckin' business."

Twylite cocked her head back in surprise, although she
knew it was to be expected. Yasmine had hated her since
middle school, although she could never understand why.
She guessed Yasmine had thought her unworthy of her
friendship. "You the one lookin' all crazy at school. I was
just tryin'a be concerned."

"I don't need your damned concern. Now leave me the
fuck alone!" Yasmine said a little too loudly. All the girls
within earshot looked up to see if a fight would break out.

"You know, you a dumb-ass bitch," Twylite said before
she could catch herself. "You best leave that nigga alone
before he kill your ass."

"And you better get up out my business before I kill
your ass!"

Before Twylite could respond, Sister Beatrice stepped
between them and broke up the argument. Both girls

knew better than to defy the sister, who had been teaching at the school for the last ten years, so they shot each other one last glare and went their separate ways.

"Girl, why you wastin' your time arguin' wit' that girl?" Pamela asked later. "You not jealous 'cause she's messin' wit' Peanut, are you?"

"Ain't nothin' to be jealous of," Twylite snapped. "She came here lookin' crazy, so I just wanted to see if she was okay. I didn't know she was gonna snap on me like that. She ain't gotta worry about me saying nothin' else to her."

And she meant that until Peanut pulled up at the bus stop with Yasmine sitting in the passenger seat the next morning. She looked all too content to watch as Peanut cursed Twylite out in front of everyone.

"I told your basic ass to stay away from me!" Peanut shouted. "Keep my mothafuckin' name out your mouth and don't ask my girl shit about me."

Twylite was so shocked at the display that she could do nothing but stare with her mouth wide open. It was a good thing Pamela was there.

"You old-ass, rapist-ass bitch, get away from my girl before I call the police on ya ass!" she shouted, stepping between Peanut and Twylite.

"Rapist?" Peanut spat. "You better be careful of what the fuck you say out here. I will whip both your li'l young asses."

"You just try to touch either one of us, and your ass will be in handcuffs so fast so your damn head will spin."

Twylite finally got her bearings back and tried to pull Pamela away. "Go 'head, Pam. He ain't worth all this."

The bus stop had gotten crowded with students. Even some neighborhood people had come out of their homes to see what all the commotion was about.

"That's right, you better pull her ass back," Peanut said, backing toward his car. "You know damned good and well what happens to chicks wit' too much mouth."

"That's enough!" yelled an older woman who was also awaiting the bus. "You need to get back in your car and leave these two girls alone. You are too old for this."

"Man, shut up and mind your own business," Peanut shouted back.

"Oh, hell no," the woman said, walking up on him. "I'm a grown-ass woman, not a teenage girl. You don't know who the hell you're messin' wit', so I suggest you take your ass on and stop disrespectin' these kids."

A chorus of "yeahs" and "damns" rumbled from the crowd. Even Twylite was impressed. She'd never seen a woman talk to a man that way, and judging by how fast Peanut got back into his car, he obviously hadn't either. She was even more astounded by the fact that the woman didn't even look their way once Peanut left. She just stood there with her girlfriend and continued to fuss about "these disrespectful-ass men" thinking they could scare people, and that she wasn't "the one."

It was that scene that prompted Twylite to call Isis. She needed to find out how she could find some of the power and strength that woman had shown. She wasn't dressed the best, and she was waiting for the bus just like Twylite was. She didn't speak with the King's English, but her words demanded respect. She refused to back down, and Twylite admired that.


Isis was speechless when she heard Twylite's recount of the last couple of days. In her mind, she'd risen from the table and pounded the streets in search of Peanut. Once she found him, she'd punch him right in his abusive mouth, drag him to Orleans Parish Prison, and throw him under the jail. But she knew that wouldn't happen. Even if it could, it wasn't her place. She needed to focus on what was most important—Twylite's well-being. Although she had to admit that it was getting harder and harder to stay focused.

"How do I get like that?" Twylite asked.

"Get like what?" Isis asked before taking a sip of her tea.

"Bold, like that lady this morning. She didn't take anything from anybody."

"That lady could have put herself and those other people around you in danger. What if he had pulled out a gun?"

"But he didn't."

"But what if he did?"

Twylite pursed her lips and looked away. Immediately, Isis felt bad. She didn't mean to shut the girl down, but she needed her to realize the importance of the situation. Fighting in the streets was no game. Isis had never fought, herself, but she knew well what it was like for a man to put his hands on her. Her final night in the house with her husband, Vincent, whom she heard had died in Afghanistan two years ago, was still bright in her mind. That night caused her to lose her baby, but it strengthened her resolve to never depend on someone else's love for happiness.

"Don't get me wrong, Twylite," Isis said. She touched the girl's arm, causing her to look back at her. "I know what you're asking me. I just want you to be careful. You never know what someone else is thinking, and you could put yourself in a bad situation if you're not careful."

"So do I keep going through life being afraid?" the girl asked, tears teasing the corners of her eyes.

"No, that's not what I'm saying at all. I'm saying don't put yourself in the situation."

"How do I do that?"

Isis started to open her mouth, but quickly shut it. She'd been here before. The last time she tried to give Twylite advice, it had blown up in her face. She was just starting to make progress with the girl, and didn't want it all to be for naught.

"Twylite, you're not going to make me go there," she said. "You promise not to stop speaking to me if I tell you what I'm thinking?"

"I'm sorry about that, Isis. I was just doing bad at that time. I really wanna know what you think about this."

"Why don't you talk to your parents?"

Twylite scoffed. "You know how my momma is. And I did talk to my daddy, but every time I talk to him about this stuff, he looks all sad, and then he looks mad like he's about to do something."

Isis nodded, picturing Earl Knight going through the different stages of grief. She made a mental note to ask Mrs. Delachaise if there was any help she could offer him to get through this.

"So what can I do?" Twylite asked again.

She really wanted help! Twylite was actually asking for her advice! Although Isis knew she had to tread lightly, she couldn't refuse to take advantage of this opportunity. It was what she'd wanted all along.

"Well, the first thing you need to do is stop walking around like you're in the dumps all the time," Isis said.

Twylite nodded, but she still seemed unsure. "I can't just act like nothing ever happened."

"Why not? Did you know that when you carry the world on your shoulders, you give the world power over you?"

"Huh?"

"Let's put it like this. Peanut did something horrible to you. Something you or I wouldn't wish on our worst enemies," Isis explained, pushing her empty teacup aside. "Does it change things to walk around mad at the world or sad that it happened?"

"I guess not."

"It doesn't minimize what happened to walk around with your head held high. It shows people that you may have been cast down, but you're not destroyed, as the scripture says."

Twylite smiled. "I remember singing that song with my choir."

"I sang it too when I was in the choir back in Kentucky."

"You used to sing?" the girl asked, her eyes wide with surprise.

Isis sighed, remembering her days back in Kentucky. She missed those days. She may have been a little wild sexually, but she felt so much closer to God back then. She prayed daily to change her life, and rarely missed a Sunday in church. It made Isis realize that she needed to stop playing around and affiliate with a church family sooner rather than later. "Yeah, but that was a long time ago."

"You don't sing anymore?"

"I haven't found a church to join yet. I've been visiting, but I haven't found one I really like yet."

"Maybe you can visit my church," Twylite suggested. "It's not like you won't know anybody. I'm back with the choir, and my daddy and momma are a deacon and deaconess."

"That's true," Isis said, nodding. "I'll think about it. But in the meantime, back to you, young lady."

Did she just hear Twylite chuckle?

"I'm really happy that you began singing again. You have a gorgeous voice."

"Thanks. I hope to get a contract one day."

"You can do it, but that takes dedication. You don't get that by quitting the one activity that allows you to sing on a regular basis."

"Yeah, after you busted us at the poetry thing, and Pamela covered for us, I figured I'd better start doing what my parents want me to do."

"Yeah, well I'm staying out of that one," Isis said, lifting her hands in surrender. Truthfully, she was glad that Pamela had lied. It actually let them both off the hook.

"But anyway, that's all you need to regain some of that power you think you lost. Continue to do you. Do what makes you happy, and walk around like your stuff don't stink."

Twylite laughed again.

"I'm serious," Isis said, beginning to enjoy the conversation. "I don't mean become stuck-up and unapproachable, but when you live life as if other people's actions and opinions don't affect your opinion of yourself, you'll be surprised at the level of confidence you'll start to feel."

"I can get with that," Twylite said, nodding.

"But there's another thing."

"What?"

"You can't allow people to speak to you in a disrespectful way," Isis warned. "Once you do that, it won't matter how you carry yourself. I'm telling you this from experience. Love and friendship shouldn't hurt. If a person really cares about you, they won't say things that will hurt you. They may say or do something they don't realize hurts you, or they may say or do something because they know it hurts you. Either way, it's up to you to let people know what you will and won't stand for."

"I don't wanna come off all touchy or sensitive."

"I don't know about you," Isis said, playfully pointing at her young client, "but I would rather be thought of as sensitive than a pushover. No one respects a pushover. People think they can say what they want with no repercussions. I believe that if I had been more vocal back in the day, I'd still be married."

"I hear you."

"Yeah, I let myself get disrespected more often than I'd like to admit. I used to think I was satisfying the men who wanted me, but all I was doing was giving them a chance to get their rocks off."

Isis shook her head at her unexpected trip down memory lane. She stared at the table as if it were a movie screen broadcasting her past. She hadn't realized how deep she had gotten until she caught a glimpse of the uncomfortable teenager in front of her. Once she saw the girl shift as if searching for the right words, the personal turn the conversation had taken became apparent. This was not the side she was supposed to show her young client. It was time to bow out gracefully while she was ahead. "It's getting a little late, Miss Lady. You want a ride home?"

"If you don't mind," Twylite replied, gathering her books and jacket. "Thanks for taking the time to talk with me."

"You're welcome. I just hoped something I said helped."

"It did."

Isis struggled to hide her smile as she followed her client out of the restaurant. Who would have thought that Hump Day would be her best day of the week? She woke up in a man's arms, ran five miles with her new girlfriends, made it to work on time, and gave some solicited and well-received advice to her client. Twylite actually walked with a bit more bounce all of a sudden. She wished it were Friday, because there was no way her week could get any better than this!

# Chapter Eighteen

Thoughts of power and money consumed Peanut's thoughts. It was all he could think of ever since meeting Cain. If he could hook up with him, he was sure he could come up faster and leave the mail carrier thing alone.

Sure, the mail-carrying gig gave him a chance to meet women. It was how he met the two chicks he had working the street, not to mention that silly-ass Twylite. Even though it didn't work out between them, he was happy that she had unknowingly made it possible to meet Yasmine.

He turned his head and watched his new girl as she slept. A slight smile tugged at his lips. She lay on her back with the sheet only pulled up to her waist, exposing her perfect tan-colored breasts. Yes, she would do fine.

Peanut had been working on ways to increase his business for the last two years. He'd added pimping to his repertoire back in January. He preferred to use high school girls because they rarely asked questions. As long as he broke them off with a few dollars and drove them around in his car, they felt special.

He also liked the young girls because their bodies were ripe. Most of them hadn't been ruined by having babies and drinking alcohol, so they didn't have to worry about wrinkles, obesity, or stretch marks. They also exercised at least three times a week, at his "strong encouragement," just to make sure they stayed that way. With New Orleans being one of the top obese cities in the country, he didn't want to take any risks of losing his business before it was time. He could always market his women as being extraordinary, not the average kind you saw in the streets every day.

His cell phone rang. Peanut looked up and saw the iPhone sitting on the dresser across the room.

"Ay, Yaz," he said, shaking the girl from her sleep. "Go get that for me."

"Damn, Peanut, I'm 'sleep," she mumbled, snatching her arm away from him.

"Girl, get your ass up and get me the phone before it stops ringin'."

The force in his voice propelled Yasmine to pop up and grab the phone. She even hit TALK to ensure the caller wouldn't hang up.

"Here," she said, jabbing the phone at him. She tried to crawl back in bed, but Peanut stopped her.

"Go in the kitchen and fix me a Hen and Coke on ice," he instructed before turning his back to her. "What's up, playboy?"

"Ay, Nut, I found out where ya boy Cain be hangin'," Boe said.

Peanut glanced around to make sure Yasmine had left the room. Of course she had. "Whatcha find out?"

"He be at the Perfect Fit sometimes, but he don't go to clubs like talkin' 'bout it," Boe explained. "He actually be uptown a lot, eatin' at them restaurants on St. Charles Avenue."

"Get the fuck outta here!" Peanut exclaimed. "I ain't goin' in that bougie-ass area. I bet his ass be eatin' that cheesecake at Cheesecake Factory and shit."

"The hell you know about Cheesecake Factory?"

"Nigga, I seen the place, it don't mean I been there," Peanut said. He turned his face away from the phone. "Girl, where the hell my drink at? Hen and Coke don't take that long to make."

Yasmine trudged back in to the bedroom, her lip poked out as far as it was when she left five minutes ago. She slammed the glass on the nightstand, grabbed her clothes, and charged back into the living room.

Peanut shook his head at the spilled liquid on his oak furniture. She hadn't wasted much, but it was enough to soak the corner of his notepad that sat near the lamp. "These fuckin' young girls gon' be the death of me."

"Which one you got over there?"

"Yasmine's dumb ass," Peanut whispered, cutting his eyes at the doorway. He could see her take a seat on the couch and turn on the television. She was mad, but that wasn't his concern at the moment. "I'll talk to you about that lata. Finish tellin' me about ol' boy."

"You wanna go up there and talk to him?"

"Hell, naw. That shit would look obvious and desperate, especially since I don't roll on St. Charles. I ain't chasin' behind nobody. We'll just hafta thinka some other way to do this."

"All right, playboy," Boe said. "Let me know when you come up wit' somethin'. I did my part."

"A'ight, bruh, I'll check ya out lata," Peanut said. He clicked END without another word and took a sip from what was left of his drink. "This silly broad here."

As if on cue, Yasmine reentered the room, this time fully dressed. She walked right up to him with her arms folded, her lip looking like a shelf protruding from her face. "I gotta get back home. My momma got me watchin' my li'l brother tonight."

Peanut stood and reached for a pair of jeans that had been thrown over a folding chair next to the bed. "That's fine. I got some shit to do this evening anyway."

Yasmine remained in place and glared at him as he got dressed.

"What?" he asked, feeling the prick of the daggers she shot at him.

"You tell me how much you love me, and you even say I do you better than Twylite ever could, but yet, you keep talkin' to me like I ain't shit."

*Here we go.* He sighed and turned to face the girl. A deeper look told him that she really wasn't that pretty without makeup, and she had the potential of being a worse problem than Twylite ever was. He would have to think harder on whether it was time to put her out on the street. Maybe he would try her on the Westbank with one of his other girls and see how that went. But, for now, he'd have to play it cool until he could come to a decision.

"Baby, come here," he said, holding his arms out for a hug.

She responded by sucking her teeth and looking away.

"Yasmine."

The sound of her name coming from his lips must have touched her because he could actually see her melt before his eyes. Her face softened, her bottom lip moved back, and her arms slowly unfolded.

"Come here, baby," he beckoned, knowing he had her. There was nothing like having a woman's mind as well as her heart. It was almost better than having the world. Almost.

She walked into his arms trying to look strong, but the tears had already begun to fall. He patted her back like a father comforting a baby, encouraging her to let it all out.

"Why you gotta keep treatin' me like this?" she whimpered. "You said I was your woman. If you don't want me here, say that then. You ain't gotta talk to me like that."

"Shhhhh," he hissed, trying to calm her down. "You know I'm goin' through some things right now. With Twylite tryin'a bring me up on charges, my money actin' crazy, and now this stress with you, I got a lot on my mind."

"You work enough hours at that post office," Yasmine said. "Why they can't give you a raise or something?"

*Damn.* Why did he have to say something about money? Yasmine knew nothing of his marijuana sales, and he wasn't ready to let her in on the prostitution ring just yet. "That's what I'm hopin' for."

Then again, maybe her thinking his money was bad could turn out to be a good thing. If she loved him enough, she would do what she could to help him stay on top, wouldn't she? He might have to seed the nest a little, but it just might work. Just a little more observation needed to take place just to make sure.

He thought about exploring her sexual prowess once more, but knew it wasn't possible. The faster he got her home, the faster he could make some deliveries and stack some money. It was time to make a move.

He reached into his wallet and pulled out two hundred dollar bills. He kissed her and slipped them into her bra. "Take this and get yourself something nice and get your hair done tomorrow. I'm gonna handle some business and I'll call you in a couple days."

"A couple days?" Yasmine protested.

Before the pouting could make its return, Peanut explained, "I tol' you I got some things I need to take care of. Now if you wanna see me happy, you'll let me do what I gotta do."

Yasmine nodded, but she still wasn't happy. She looked up at him with a halfhearted smile. "You could at least give me another hundred. My weave by itself is gonna eat up half of this."

He pursed his lips, but did as she asked. *This is an investment,* he told himself.

After checking on his other two girls and collecting their earnings, Peanut headed back to the bar to meet

Boe. He couldn't help but notice the overstuffed mail-boxes outside of some of the homes he drove past. This was what made him hate being a mailman. *People are quick to complain about their mail being late, but when it does come, they let it pile inside their mailboxes. Just take your business inside before somebody steals your crazy check.*

He chuckled to himself at that thought. He knew not every person who received a check from the government was mentally disabled, but he'd seen enough of those en-velopes to know what they looked like. Why more people didn't just get direct deposit, he would never understand, but it least it kept him with a job.

A police car stopped next to him at the red light. Peanut glanced at the officers, and quickly moved his eyes back toward the road. He hated how nervous the police made him feel. He could handle it when he was selling weed, but things just hadn't been the same since the rape charge. It always felt like they were watching him. Like they were waiting for him to mess up. Like they didn't truly believe that it was consensual sex that had gotten out of hand.

Truthfully, it wasn't, but they didn't know that. As far as they knew, it was he said/she said, and no one witnessed it so no one could say anything different. And if he could just calm his nerves and watch his back, it would stay that way.

He found a parking spot right in front of the bar, but remained in his car. The cars of the customers he was to meet were nowhere to be found, so he figured he had some time to kill until they arrived. He turned up the radio when Jay-Z and Kanye West's "Gotta Have It" began, tapping his hands against the steering wheel and bobbing his head to the beat.

An older man wearing a grey church suit walked past his car, seemingly oblivious to Peanut's private party.

The man stopped at a house about half a block from the bar. Peanut craned his neck to look closer, more out of nosiness than curiosity.

"Muthafuck," Peanut mumbled, and smiled. "Ain't dat Twylite's old man? Don't tell me he's creepin'."

The man carried a plate wrapped in aluminum foil. Peanut watched as he rang the doorbell, and waited to see what kind of young thing would open the door. He struck Peanut as the type who would like young girls. Probably messed with a couple of women at the church, pretending he was praying over them. That was why he didn't go to church now. Like Michael Baisden said, there were too many pimps in the pulpit.

Disappointment took over when he saw an elderly lady in a wheelchair come to the door. Earl Knight bent down, kissed her on the cheek and handed her the plate. Peanut sucked his teeth when he saw Earl Knight take a seat on the steps and begin laughing and talking with the lady.

"Damn sick and shut-in visit," he mumbled. "Shoulda known he was just a square-ass, borin' nigga."

A red Toyota pulled behind him, and he saw one of his customers get out of the car. Worry again set in because he didn't want Earl Knight to see him, but getting out of the car or blowing his horn would attract attention. Not that he was afraid of Earl, but he really didn't want the drama. There were more important things on his mind.

His customer was just about to walk past him, when he hurriedly put down his window and called out to him. The customer looked around, surprised when he saw Peanut sitting in his car.

"You comin' in?" the customer asked, pointing at the bar.

"Naw, man, get in the car," Peanut snapped. "And don't get no mud on my interior."

The customer did as he was told. "Dis a nice ride you got here."

"Nigga, I know. Dat's why I bought it."

"What's wrong wit' you?"

Peanut reached into a backpack sitting behind the passenger seat and pulled out a plastic bag filled with marijuana. "Nothin' man. I'm just in a hurry."

The customer nodded, and after paying Peanut for his product, got out of the car and walked into the bar. Peanut wanted to tell him to just leave so his next customer could pull in his spot, but he disappeared before he could say anything.

"Nut!" a voice called out. "Da hell you doin' in the car? Bring your ass in here and get a drink."

*Shit!* Peanut wasn't the only person searching for the voice. Earl Knight and the old woman were looking as well. Earl stood up from the porch and watched Peanut as he got out of his car and cursed at the owner of the voice—his friend Joe.

"Damn, man, you know better than to be callin' my name all loud!" Peanut said, not caring about his audience. "I oughta punch you in your damned mouth!"

"What's wrong wit' you?" Joe asked.

"Man, you know what's wrong," Peanut said, turning down the volume on his voice. "You better start learning what goes on around you before you do shit like dat. Now let's go inside."


"You know dat boy?" the old woman asked.

Earl Knight's eyes never left Peanut. He would know his face for as long as the Lord kept him on this earth.

"Brother Knight?" the woman asked again.

"Huh?" Earl asked, shaking himself from his trance. He kept his eyes on Peanut as he spoke. "Yeah, I'm sorry, Mother Jeanie. Dat was da boy dat attacked my daughter."

"My God," she said, looking back toward the bar. "Why he ain't in jail?"

He shook his head, barely able to understand the situation, himself. Peanut went into the bar, allowing Earl to think straight. He turned to the old woman and frowned. "Dey didn't have enough evidence."

"What more they need? Dey seen da girl's face."

"Yeah, but it ain't dat simple. He said she consented to it, and we waitin' for da rape kit ta come back to see it'll show dat she was raped."

"My Lord. So he get to run around scot-free?"

"Looks like it so far, but if I ever get da chance, dat boy is goin' down for what he did."

Mother Jeanie looked toward the bar and shook her head. "I cain't stand dat dere bar. Ain't nothin' good ever came outta dere."

"I see."

"Well, how is Twylite doin'?" she asked, slightly changing the subject.

"She doin' all right," he replied, reflecting on his only child. "She gettin' better. She joined the choir again."

"Oh, now dat's just beautiful. Dat girl got a voice like an angel. She's truly blessed. Despite da circumstances, you and Adele did a beautiful job wit' dat girl. She gone be all right. Just you see."

Earl smiled. He loved hearing people shower his family with compliments. And it did his heart well to know that the situation hadn't caused people to look down on him and his family. If anything, they had given them more support than before. Yes, there were a few unfavorable whispers, but the people who mattered were the people who cared.

"Thank you, Mother." He rose from the porch and dusted off his pants. "I better be goin'. It's gon' be dark soon, and I gotta be home for dinner."

"I understand. Thanks for comin' see 'bout me, and tell Pastah I'll be back befow he know it."

"I know you will," Earl replied, bending for another kiss on the cheek. "I'ma see you next week. You might wanna warm dat plate up a little."

"I'll be fine. You go on, now, and stay safe."

Earl waved as he headed back toward his car. He couldn't help but stop at Peanut's green BMW. It was a late model, probably a 2010 or 2011. The dashboard rivaled something he would see in an airplane. The seats were leather, and except for the backpack sitting on the floor in the back, they were in pristine condition. *How a mailman get to drive somethin' like dis?* he wondered. He shrugged and continued on to his car. *Guess it's possible.*

# Chapter Nineteen

"Girl, I'ma need you ta get off dat computer and help me wit' dinner," Adele ordered.

"I'll be done in a minute," Twylite said. "I'm finishing my Facebook profile."

"You still doin' dat?" Adele asked, wiping her hands on a dish rag. She walked behind her daughter and peered at the computer screen. "You been on dat thing all day."

"Well, number one," the teen started, happy to be laughing with her mother for a change, "you wouldn'ta noticed that if you woulda let me have my own computer a long time ago. And two, since I'm the last of my friends to even get a Facebook profile, I got a lotta catchin' up to do."

Adele snapped the dish rag at her. "Don't get smart. And this is reason one why we never let you get a Facebook. You been on dis computer since you got up dis mornin'."

Twylite continued typing in silence for a few minutes, and finally logged off. She turned to her mother and smiled. "Well, Mommy, you'll be happy to know that I haven't been on Facebook the whole time. I also set up a YouTube account, a Twitter account, and I started looking for jobs."

"What in the world is Twitter?"

Twylite laughed. "You ain't never hearda Twitter? Dag, Ma."

"Girl, you know I don't mess around on no Internet too much," Adele said, waving her daughter off. "If it ain't the church Web site or my e-mail, I ain't got no use for it."

"That is so sad. You need to get wit' the times."

"Look at you. Been on da Net for alla ten minutes and think you know it all, huh?"

"I know I applied for three jobs, and I already have two hundred friends on Facebook."

"All right, now, Miss Career Woman," Adele said, returning to the kitchen. "I don't mind you gettin' a job and having funny of da Internet, but don't let it interfere wit' school. And please don't let it interfere wit' choir. Ya daddy'll have a fit."

"What I'ma have a fit about?" Earl asked, closing the front door behind him.

"Hey, Daddy," Twylite greeted him. She gave him a kiss and joined her mother in the kitchen. Since Earl was home, dinnertime wasn't far behind.

"Ya daughter been on da Internet all day lookin' for jobs," Adele reported, as she pulled a pan of chicken from the oven. "Twylite, stir those greens for me. I don't want 'em stickin' to the bottom of the pot."

"I got it, Momma," Twylite assured her. She never admitted it, but Twylite actually loved cooking with her mother. Adele Knight always made her meals from scratch, so Twylite learned to make cornbread, collard greens, dressing, and many other dishes the old-fashioned way. The only thing she hadn't mastered yet was Adele's famous gumbo. For Twylite, that would be the ultimate feat, so she planned to stay tight at her mother's side on Thanksgiving.

"What made you start lookin' for jobs, baby girl?" Earl asked from the living room. His favorite recliner sat near the kitchen doorway, so he could hear both of them clearly.

"Why not?" Twylite replied, shrugging her shoulders. "If I made my own money, I wouldn't have to ask you guys for money so much. Plus, I'll be a senior next year, and if I had a job, I could pay for my own senior package, senior trip, spending money, and all kinds of stuff."

"She got a point dere, Adele," Earl said, pushing back in his recliner. "Whatcha think?"

Adele shook her head. "If y'all like it, I love it. I done tol' her though dat ain't no job gonna interfere with school and church."

"I agree," Earl said.

"I assure you both that it won't," Twylite said, holding her right hand up as if making an oath in court.

"I know you do, but dat's easy ta say now when you ain't got no job," Earl said. "You 'bout to see how da real world work."

"Whatcha mean?" Twylite asked, walking into the living room. Getting a job couldn't be all that bad, could it?

"I'm saying you think you gon' make all dis money 'cause you workin'," he explained. "You will make some, but when you see how much you spendin' on bus fare, how much the state and federal gov'ment gon' take out in taxes, and how much stuff really costs, you gon' wanna work more hours to make up for what you think you lost. Next thing you know, you gon' be askin' us can you skip choir rehearsal to put in overtime, you gon' stop studyin' 'cause you gon' be so tired from workin' extra hours, and you gon' get mad at us for makin' you quit."

"Dang, Daddy, you ain't got no faith in me," the teenager protested, although in the back of her mind she knew her father had a point. She hadn't even considered taxes. How much would they really take from her? How could she get that money back?

"I got faith in you, baby girl, but you gotta be realistic."

"So you don't want me to get a job?"

"Baby, I think you gettin' a job will teach you a lotta responsibility, so I support you. Just know dis ain't gon' be no full-time thing."

"Of course not," Twylite assured him. "It's only after school and on weekends."

"You ain't gettin' me," Earl said. "When I was your age I worked at Burger King. It was just like you said, after school and on weekends. But you better bet we tried to get as close to forty hours as we could. We went to work right after school, and usually got home after eleven, and still had to do homework. We tried to work a full eight hours on Saturdays and Sundays, so we always missed out on social stuff with our friends. We had some money, but ain't had no fun and our grades dropped."

Twylite nodded. "Did you work too, Mommy?"

"Yeah, and it was the same as your daddy," she replied. "But now I just enjoy being home to take care of you two. Speaking of which, y'all come eat."

Earl and Twylite did as they were told. Earl took a seat at the table, while Twylite helped her mother fill the dinner plates with baked chicken, collard greens, white rice, and cornbread. She hadn't even realized how hungry she was until she beheld her mother's delicious cooking all on one plate.

Twylite didn't always appreciate living in such a traditional household, but other times she could see that she had what many of her friends didn't. A lot of the people she knew at school lived with only their mothers. Their mothers worked, so many of them were either responsible for cooking for their brothers and sisters or they just fended for themselves. The girls who attended Saint Francis Academy weren't all poor, but they weren't rich either. Their parents sacrificed for them to get such a prestigious education. When Twylite heard the stories of how some of their friends' moms worked two jobs just to be able to afford the tuition, she gained a better appreciation for having two parents who could afford to send her to private school.

She realized that not everyone had it like she did. She was the daughter of devout Christians who were very active in their church and ensured they began and ended every day with a hot meal. Her father ran his own auto garage that was just successful enough that his wife didn't have to work and his daughter attended one of the best schools in the city. She went to a private doctor instead of the county. She had good friends and trusting adults around her who actually cared. No, not everyone could claim that.

Her time with Peanut was her time of rebellion. She was convinced that having such involved parents was suffocating her, making her feel more like a baby than a junior in high school. Always being home, never letting her eat fast food, always wanting her to call home when she went out, having a curfew, and going to church for choir rehearsal, Bible Study, Sunday School, and regular service was just too much sometimes.

Peanut would add to the problem by telling her that she was practically a grown woman and needed to start thinking for herself. When she said she needed to call home and be home at a certain time, he would laugh at her and tell her to stop acting like a baby. Once she got bold and agreed to spend the night with him. She paid dearly with a behind whipping she would never forget and a sentence of being restricted to school, church, and work for the next month.

"I saw da damned Cooper boy today," Earl said suddenly, as if reading his daughter's mind.

"You did?" Twylite asked. "Where?"

"Never mind where," he snapped. "Dat boy ain't no damn good at all. He tried to bother you since all dat happened?"

Twylite shook her head and shoved a forkful of greens in her mouth.

"Dat boy better know betta than to come 'round my child," Adele proclaimed. "Did you say something to him?"

"No, I just watched him," Earl said. "Believe me, I wanted to kill dat boy dead, though."

Twylite knew he meant every word. He expressed it on more than one occasion. She thanked God that his faith was strong because if it had been any other father, Peanut would have been dead weeks ago. She was sure her father prayed hard every night that he wouldn't make that happen.

"I wish dat boy could be behind bars where he belong," Adele said.

"Yeah, me too, but ain't nothin' we can do about dat," Earl said. "I talked to a police friend of mine on da way home, and he told me dey get rape cases like dis all the time, but dey don't pursue 'em because it's hard to prove he say/she say. You ain't gonna believe this, but he said less than half of rape cases even get prosecuted, and half of those end in conviction. On toppa dat, a lot of dese women get raped by people dey know. Ain't dat some shit? She woulda had a better chance of pressin' charges if she had been attacked by some nigga on the street."

"Dat's ridiculous!" Adele exclaimed.

"Yeah, well, in these cases, the responsibility is usually on the victim," Earl continued. "It's her responsibility to scream and kick. It's her responsibility to tell her story over and over. It's her responsibility to act like a victim."

"I didn't act like a victim?" Twylite asked.

Earl shrugged. "I guess you did. I'm just tellin' you what Keith told me."

"So he may never go to jail for what he did?" Twylite asked.

"There might be something we can do, but it would require you to have to go through relivin' what happened again," Earl said. "And frankly, I don't know if I want you to go through dat. You just startin' to get over dat situation."

"Whatcha mean, Earl?" Adele asked.

"I mean, Keith told me dat since she reported the incident the night it happened, the evidence in dat kit Dr. Duplessis took is credible," he explained. "Luckily, Ms. Kay is qualified to do the exam or else all dat woulda been a wasta time. We could ask the doctor if the results are back and use dat to press charges. If the results are back, do we really wanna put Twylite through retellin' her story? It's been awhile since she talked about it. What if somethin' she say don't match up to what she said dat night? Dem damn police would have a field day on her."

"Could you handle dat, baby?" Adele asked, looking into her daughter's eyes.

Twylite thoughtfully chewed a piece of chicken and washed it down with a gulp of Kool-Aid. Did she want to relive that night? Could she handle all of the questions and judgments? And what if she went through all of that and nothing came of it? He'd still be walking the streets and the situation could get worse for her. Would it be worth all of that?

"Can I have some time to think about it?"


Her parents had changed the subject after her request, but truthfully, she really didn't want to think about Peanut or rape cases. She had become excited about entering the world of the Internet and the possibility of making her own money. She'd save the gloom and doom talk for another day. And as long as Peanut and that bitch

Yasmine left her alone, she could live life carefree for the first time in a long time.

After her parents went to bed, she went back on Facebook to see what her friends had posted. Some had gone to parties, while others lamented about completing a project that was due Monday. She felt their pain. She had a test on Monday that she hadn't even started to study for.

"I'll take care of it tomorrow after church," she mumbled.

She commented on a few statuses and updated her own to say she was chilling for the evening. Almost immediately, Pamela commented: What else is new?

Twylite laughed and responded: You must be doing the same thing if you answered that quick.

Yeah, you right, was the response.

We're too young to not have a life.
Let's catch a movie tomorrow.

Twylite frowned. Can't. Gotta study for this test. We'll catch up Monday.

Cool.

After commenting on a few more statuses, Twylite logged off and began surfing YouTube. She ran across a channel that featured a very pretty lady giving makeup tutorials. Twylite all of a sudden felt plain. Outside of lip gloss and mascara, the Knights had never allowed her to wear makeup. At least she didn't think so, although she never bothered to ask. She figured they were strict on everything else, so why not be strict on makeup too?

She continued watching the lady, marveling at how plain she looked at the beginning of the video. Without makeup, she was cute. However, after her transformation, she looked like a supermodel. And her makeup didn't look caked on or clownish. Maybe if Twylite could learn to apply makeup like that, her parents would be willing to let her buy some.

After watching a few more tutorials, she closed out of YouTube and began surfing the Web for more job opportunities. School wouldn't end for quite some time, but she wanted to begin saving money. If what her dad said was true, she wanted to have a few hundred in the bank before the summer so she could afford to be self-sufficient. *Thank God for school uniforms.*

She ran across a few department stores that were hiring, but decided against them since it would take too long to get to that side of town after school. She needed something that would be easily accessible by bus, and not so far that her parents would complain about coming to get her at night.

Well, it was obvious that she wouldn't find a job that night. It was getting late, and eight a.m. would come early. She logged off and headed to her room, stretching and yawning as she walked. An image of Peanut flashed in her mind as she changed into her pajamas. *Later for him. His punishment will be that he didn't keep me down.*

# Chapter Twenty

"You feel like going out tonight?" Isis asked Cain as they lay on her couch.

"You not enjoying my company?" he asked with a smile.

"You know it's not like that. I just haven't been any-where since the night I met you, and I feel like working off some steam."

Cain shot her a mischievous grin. "Oh, I can help you do that."

She playfully kicked him in the shin. "Not like that. Slow your roll."

"Hey, never hurts to ask. You might change your mind one day."

"You've got to be less mysterious with me for that to happen," Isis replied, rising from the couch. She walked into the kitchen area and refreshed her drink. "You want something?"

"Naw, I'm good." He sat up and watched her from the couch. "Whatcha mean about me being mysterious?"

"Sweetie, I like you a lot, but I don't know anything about you," she said, sitting next to him. "I don't know what you do, I don't know anything about how you grew up, hell I don't even know if you're really from New Orleans. Come to think of it, have you told me your last name yet?"

Cain chuckled. "I thought we were doing pretty good getting to know each other."

"Maybe in your eyes. You know almost everything about me. I, on the other hand, have to guess about you."

"We talk a lot."

"Yeah, but when the conversation gets personal, you either change the subject or shut down."

"I do that?"

"Um, yes," Isis said, rolling her neck slightly.

"My bad, baby," he replied, giving her a kiss. "I'm not tryin'a make you play guessing games with me. I'm just not used to talkin' about myself. Besides, you're a special lady, and I just enjoy hearing you talk."

"That's sweet, Cain, but I want to know about you too."

Cain sighed, still maintaining his easy smile. "How about we go have a good time tonight? I'll show you how I party, and then we can talk about me all you want."

He had deflected the subject, but Isis chose to overlook it because at least she was getting a night on the town. However, she was determined to keep Cain at his word. It would be awhile before she fell in love with him, but she refused to waste her time with a stranger.


The night turned out nicer than expected. Cain had a lot more class than Isis had given him credit for. What she thought would be a night stuck in some bar had actually turned out to be a tour of the mini-mansions on the Lakefront, followed by a late dessert and drinks at the Cheesecake Factory. He then took her to listen to jazz at a really nice cafe in a part of town she would have never thought to visit.

"Cain, is this place safe?" Isis asked, looking at the dark houses and shady-looking characters who walked past.

"Don't tell me you ain't never been to the hood before," he replied with a laugh.

"It's not that," she said with a nervous chuckle. "I mean, the music coming out of the place sounds good, but why does it have to be in such an . . . um . . . interesting place?"

"It's gonna be all right. Wait 'til you get inside before you start judgin'.'"

"Okay, but if they start shooting, I'm the first one out of here."

"I have no doubt that you speak the truth."

Isis wasn't sure if that was a compliment or an insult, but she was here now, so why not make the best of the situation? As she exited Cain's Lexus SUV, she was pleasantly surprised to see so many luxury vehicles in the parking area. There were a few average cars in the mix, but nothing that made her think twice.

When they walked into the place, she noticed right away that the decor was nothing to write home about, but the ambiance was off the charts. A live band performed a Temptations classic in front of a well-dressed audience. The crowd swayed back and forth in their seats, while a few waved their hands and shouted back their appreciation to the band. Although the decor was plain, the place was clean and the atmosphere seemed peaceful.

"You gonna trust me now?" Cain whispered in her ear as he seated her at a table set for two.

"You did all right."

"One of these days you gon' believe me that I would not ever knowingly put you in danger."

"I believe you."

"You sure about that?"

"I told you I believe you," Isis replied. She smiled, but worried inside about the ominous tone Cain took. It was obvious even over the loud music.

"Hello, how y'all doin' tonight?" asked a waitress who looked way too young to be working in a place like this. She looked at the couple and her face lit up when she recognized her male customer. "Oh, hey, Cain! I didn't even notice that was you comin' in. You want the usual?"

"Hey, Lawanda, I forgot you was workin' tonight," Cain greeted. "How ya momma and 'em doin'?"

"They cool under the circumstances."

"Well, tell 'em I said hey. And yeah, the usual is cool, and whatever my girl wants."

Isis stared at the scene under eyebrows raised so high they looked like the McDonald's arches. Was Cain that well known that the waitresses knew him, or was this an ex he'd failed to tell her about?

"Hey, sweetie, what would you like?" the waitress asked her, finally noticing that Isis was there.

"Oh, um, a Sea Breeze will be good." She really didn't want a vodka cranberry, but it was the first thing that entered her shocked little mind.

The waitress laughed. "That's cool. You two like the same drink."

"Yeah, funny how that worked out," Isis said.

"Y'all want anything else?"

"No, we're good for now," Cain replied.

"Well, aren't you Mr. Popularity," Isis remarked once the girl waitress walked away.

Cain laughed as if smelling Isis's jealousy. "Girl, I been comin' to this spot for the longest. I got Lawanda this job for her twenty-first birthday. I went to high school with her daddy."

Isis pursed her lips, not sure whether to believe him. She'd experienced her share of lying men, and she hoped that Cain wasn't one of them. Despite the mystery, he'd seemed honest up to this point. With any luck, tonight wouldn't be the night that he would prove himself differently.

She decided to leave the situation alone for the moment so she could enjoy the show. The lead singer had just started singing an Anita Baker classic, and the song was just starting to get good. Just as Isis had begun to sway back and forth to the rhythm, she caught of a glimpse of Cain shooting a cheese-eating grin.

"What?" she asked, scrunching her eyebrows.

Holding his grin, he leaned toward her and said, "You're feeling the shit out me, huh?"

Isis cocked her head back in shock. "Excuse me?"

Cain laughed. "You heard me. You want me, don't you?"

"It sounds to me like you're feeling yourself more than I ever could."

"Yeah, yeah, you ain't gotta admit it. I know you're feeling me. That's why you keep askin' questions about where I'm from, and you were 'bout to lose your mind when ol' girl spoke to me."

Isis sucked her teeth, fighting the urge to admit he was right. She did like him, but there was no way she would tell him that now. Not after he'd called her out. She had more pride than that, and no sweet-talking stranger would change that.

Instead, Isis rolled her eyes and pursed her lips, and then turned her attention back to the band. Once the song ended, she excused herself to go to the restroom. Cain nodded, his smile turning into a knowing smirk.

*That man sure is full of himself,* she thought as she waded through the tables. *I love that!*


"I'm givin' dis thirty minutes, and I'm out, playboy," Peanut announced as they walked up to the restaurant. "I tol' you I don't like that bougie-ass places."

"Man, chill," Boe said, wincing at his friend. "This ain't even about you right now. Just lemme hear my cousin sing like I promised her, and we'll be out."

"She betta be good," Peanut mumbled.

"You really need to open ya mind to some new shit," Boe said as they pushed their way through the crowd.

"Life ain't about playin' bones in a hole in da wall all the fuckin' time."

"So now you classy and shit?"

"I ain't said dat. I'm just sayin' I like doin' some different shit every once in a while."

They found a table near the bar and sat down just in time to hear the band begin playing Michael Jackson's 1987 hit "I Just Can't Stop Loving You."

"That's my cousin right there," Boe said, pointing to a woman standing to the left of the guy singing Michael's part.

Peanut appraised the young girl as she showered the audience with her melody. Her voice was on point, but her overly thick frame would never allow him to think of her as potential street material. He knew some men liked thick women, but he wanted to establish the reputation of having every man's fantasy, women with bodies that wouldn't quit. Boe's cousin looked all right, but she didn't measure up to his other women.

He looked over at Boe, knowing his boy was waiting for him to voice his approval. There was no way he could comment on how fine she was, so he decided to keep it on the talent level. "She got a good voice. How long she been singin'?"

A proud smile stretched across Boe's face, telling Peanut he'd said the right thing. "That girl been singin' since she was four. Started singin' in the choir at church and it took off from there."

"That's cool," Peanut replied, visibly uninterested. To him, there was nothing exciting about Boe's cousin's story. Every little girl with half a voice started out in the church choir. So the hell what? It wasn't like she made any money. Singing groups were a dime a dozen in New Orleans. Now if she had been getting dollars as a child like the chick from that TV show *The Parkers,* then he might be impressed.

"She use'ta sing every chance she got," Boe rattled on, obviously unaware of his friend's boredom.

*Maybe if he shut the hell up, we might be able to hear the girl sing,* Peanut thought. He scanned the restaurant in search of a waitress. A shot of Hennessy had been calling his name all night. A cute, young-looking waitress with a long, curly brown weave walked toward him. *Now, this girl is more like it. I could charge double for her cute ass.* He reached for her as she walked past.

"Hey, boo," he called out.

The waitress turned toward them and shot a friendly smile. She walked toward them, her pen already primed to write down their orders. "How y'all doin'? What can I getcha?"

"Gimme a Hennessy and Coke with an extra shot on the side," Peanut said.

She wrote the order and then looked at Boe. "And you?"

"Gimme a double Crown and Coke, not too much ice," he said.

"Y'all want anything else?" she asked, not looking up from her notepad.

"You can write your number down so I can get up with you later," Peanut suggested with a wink.

The waitress merely responded with a roll of the eyes. "Really?"

Boe let out a belly laugh once the young waitress left the table. "I guess those tired-ass lines only work on the high school chicks, huh, playboy?"

Peanut sucked his teeth. "Shut yo' ass up. If I wanted the bitch, I could have her. I got bigger fish ta fry."

"Yeah, okay," Boe said, leaning back in his seat to finish listening to his cousin croon. "I'ma introduce you to her when she finish this set."

Peanut nodded and began scanning the room again, a habit he'd taken on since his early teens. In his business he always needed to be aware of his surroundings. He had to admit the place was kind of nice. Not exactly his style, but it wasn't bad. If he gave it a try, he could probably learn to appreciate this spot. Good music. If the drinks were just as good, he might even consider making a return appearance, an admission he never expected to make out loud.

Another quick sweep of the place uncovered another unexpected but welcome sight. A familiar-looking clean-cut man wearing a royal blue button-down shirt sat a few tables down. A woman had just walked away from his table. He couldn't see her face, but if she was with Cain, she had to be hot. Peanut couldn't picture Cain with anyone but a fine-ass woman.

Peanut looked over at Boe and nudged his upper arm. "Looka dis shit here."

"What?" Boe asked, looking around.

"Calm down, nigga. Don't be so obvious. Just look to your left, a few tables down. And be cool about it."

Boe did as he was told, and then turned back to Peanut. "Ain't dat dat nigga Cain?"

"Hell, yeah! This li'l bougie-ass place done paid off big time."

"Whatcha gon' do?"

"His girl just walked off. I'ma go holla at him before she get back."

"Your drink all right?" Lawanda asked Cain.

"Like always."

"Where ya girl at?" she asked, looking around.

"She just went to the bathroom," he replied after taking another sip from his drink.

"Oh, okay. Well, I'ma get back to work. But you need to keep her. She look a li'l mean, but she cute. Probably smart as hell."

Cain laughed. "Yeah, she all dem thangs."

Lawanda smiled and patted him on the shoulder, but before she could say anything, she felt masculine hands on her own shoulders.

"Excuse me, sweetness."

She looked up and frowned. Looking back at Cain, she said, "Lemme know if you need anything else."

Without waiting for an invite, the man sat at Cain's table. Cain scrunched his eyebrows in confusion, but his uninvited guest didn't seem to notice. "What's up?"

"Aw, bruh, you don't remember me from da otha day when we played bones?"

"Yeah, I remember you, but I don't think I got your name."

The man cocked his head back, seemingly taken aback by Cain's demeanor. "It's Peanut."

"Yeah, Peanut," he said with a slow nod. "You come here much?"

"Naw, man. First time. Chill li'l spot, though."

"Yeah, it is."

"Well, look," Peanut said, leaning forward. "I ain't gonna take too mucha ya time."

"Yeah, 'cause my girl's gonna be back in a few."

Peanut looked around and, satisfied that no one was coming, leaned in again. "I'm sayin', let's do some business together. I got some contacts dat can put dis game on lock if we work together."

Cain responded with a glare and lips pursed so hard that Peanut contemplated whether he would need to grab his gun out of the car. He was sure Cain wasn't the type to cause a scene, but he wasn't sure what the look in his eyes meant. What he did know was that this was no time to show weakness or indecision. Instead, he kept his eyes transfixed on Cain and showed him that he expected an answer to his proposal.

"You serious?" Cain finally asked, straightening in his seat.

"Fuckin' right, playboy," he replied with a confident smile. "I know you big time and shit, but I know dese streets. We could work together and stack even more chips."

Cain rolled his eyes, an unimpressed aura circling about him as he shook his head. "Bruh, it don't even work like that. I'ma make this quick because, like I said, my girl'll be back in a few. I didn't get where I am bringin' just anybody who asks into my business. What you make, about six hundred dollars or so a week? Nigga, I make that shit in a hour! I'm sittin' here with you right now and I'm makin' money. You talkin' about contacts? Get the fuck outta here wit' that bullshit! I'm not about to mess my shit up over a couple bags of weed and some underage hookers."

Peanut stared back at him, awestruck. He had no idea how Cain knew about the side prostitution ring, but this wasn't the time to show weakness. He had to come back strong or this whole thing would blow up. He looked around, grateful for the band still performing onstage. They drowned out what could have been epic embarrassment. "Nigga, you ain't even had to come at me like dat. I came to you wit' a business proposition. We can discuss this like men."

"Then step to me like a damn man and don't try to corner me in the fuckin' club," Cain shot back, showing genuine anger for the first time. "I don't fuckin' discuss my shit in public anyway, and if you was really about business, you would know that. Now as far as I'm concerned, this conversation is over because my girl is coming back."

Peanut knocked his knuckles softly on the table, and then stood up. This definitely didn't go as planned. "All right, playboy. We'll see each other again."

Before Cain could respond, Peanut returned to the table where Boe sat nursing a new drink. He looked up once Peanut sat down.

"What happened?" he asked.

Peanut shook his head. "We gon' hafta approach dis shit from a different angle."

Isis would have to be blind not to notice that Cain's demeanor had changed while she was gone. *I know I wasn't gone that long,* she thought. *What's going on in his head?* Her wonder remained a thought because he definitely wasn't in the mood to talk. He barely said anything to her when she sat down.

She'd seen someone leaving the table as she made her way from the restroom. It was difficult to tell who the person was, but it was obvious that Cain wasn't happy when he left. What kind of argument could they have had in such a short amount of time? Hopefully he would calm down so she could ask later.

They sat in silence, listening to the rest of the band's set. The band was good. Very good. And when they hit the audience with Carlos Santana and Rob Thomas's "Smooth," Isis thought she would lose her mind. She began bouncing in her seat until she could no longer take it.

"You going to dance with me, or what?" she asked, leaning close to his ear.

Cain shot her a half smile and held back a chuckle. "Whatcha know about dancin' to this type of music?"

"Baby, I moved here from Texas," she announced, rising from her seat. "I learned a salsa and merengue or two."

He laughed and shook his head, but followed her on the dance floor. A few other couples had beaten them there, and were already giving poor merengue demonstrations. Cain, himself, wasn't very good either, but he moved so fluidly that Isis found him to be an easy student.

"Damn, girl," he mumbled in her ear after pulling her close. "You are one sexy-ass woman. I didn't know you could move like this."

Isis laughed. "You met me in a club."

"You were mean as hell that night. I was too busy watching my back."

She laughed again. "You're silly."

"You gonna let my silly ass spend the night with you tonight?"

"I might."

Cain smiled and continued dancing. Isis smiled back and continued dancing. It hadn't gone unnoticed that he'd again offered to spend the night with her. In the short time they'd been seeing one another, Cain had never once asked her to spend the night with him, nor had he even taken her to his home. She doubted that he was married, but it bothered her that he continued to be so mysterious. His earlier anger only added to the intrigue.

Yet, she had fun with Cain. He was a much-needed stress relief from the mental boxing match she had with herself whenever she met with Twylite. She wasn't sure how long she could put up with the mystery, but until then, she vowed to enjoy the moment.

Peanut watched the happy couple as they twirled around the dance floor like a couple of jackasses. How could Cain have the nerve to dance like that after he'd acted the ass earlier?

"Fake ass," he mumbled.

"Whatcha say?" Boe asked.

Peanut sucked his teeth and winced at his friend. "Nothin', nigga." He was too embarrassed to tell Boe what had really happened. How do you say that one man who could get you on the map cursed you out in the middle of an uppity club he had no business being in in the first place? On top of that, the man knew more of his business than he should have. Instead, he told him that Cain had suggested they talk later since his girl was around. That was kind of the truth, wasn't it?

Truth was he could see why Cain was so worried about his lady friend. She was cute. A bit old for his taste, but her long braids and classy but sexy dress gave her a mature beauty his young girls could only hope for. Yes, they looked good now, but it took effort to still look like that after they turned twenty-five. Cain's girl seemed to have that feat on lock.

There was something familiar about Cain's woman. He knew he said that a lot. He wasn't blessed with much, but what he did have was a knack for remembering faces. Cain's woman was definitely one he'd seen before. But where? They definitely didn't run in the same circles.

But for now he had bigger problems. If Cain knew about his operation, how many other people did? All this time he kept a low profile, but apparently someone had been watching and reporting on him. Cain might be a power player in the city, but he didn't know Peanut from a hole in the wall. Something was up.

Yet, he still wanted to work with Cain. Anybody who made money while dancing in the club was definitely someone he needed to know. And the fact that Cain knew about Peanut's side businesses was even more intriguing. Peanut had some play, but nothing on Cain's level. He could only imagine the money he could make with that type of power.

But how could he do it? Cain had already made it clear that he definitely didn't want to work with him. And he would look like an ass running back up to Cain to ask for another chance. Another option was needed, and soon.

"You ready to go?" Cain asked, snaking his arm around Isis's waist.

The band's last set had ended more than forty-five minutes ago, but the DJ had taken over and had the crowd dancing like a new party had started. Cain and Isis had been on the dance floor for nearly twenty minutes, and their skin had begun glistening with sweat. Cain could tell that Isis was growing exhausted, but she refused to say anything.

"Come on, babe, this place is getting tired," he coaxed, tugging her away from the floor.

"You okay?" Isis asked as she followed him off of the floor.

"I'm cool. It was just getting hot in there."

That was only a miniature part of the truth. The biggest part of it was Peanut. He was still irked by the way he had approached him earlier, and the fact that Peanut had been staring him down all night only added to his anger. Cain had really been ready to leave an hour ago, but he refused to let that wannabe Nino Brown–ass drug dealer see that he had gotten to him.

The rumors floating around New Orleans about Cain were only partially true. While it was true that he sold cocaine and had been very successful, the real drug king of New Orleans had been arrested last year. No one had even heard of Cain until after the arrest, opening the door for Cain to expand his business. Even then, he moved carefully, doing more listening than talking, more watching than doing. He made it his business to know who the dealers in the city were, whether big or small.

It wasn't an easy task since the drug dealers were returning to New Orleans in droves since Katrina in 2005. The job market had forced even those with jobs to become pharmaceutical representatives to make a few extra dollars. Those who showed potential and demonstrated that they could take care of business were invited into his empire. Shaky people like Peanut remained on the outside looking in.

There was just something about Peanut that Cain hated. Well, two. He couldn't stand the juvenile nickname Peanut chose to call himself. Why couldn't he just let people call him Calvin? Or at least something that fit a grown man.

Cain again snaked his arm around Isis's waist. She had yet to give him any, but he had really started feeling this woman. She always carried herself with class. He could tell she was different from the first time he laid eyes on her. Yet, he wasn't sure how much longer he'd be willing to wait. No woman had ever made him wait, but then again, most women knew about his business and saw him as an opportunity to get some money and status. He'd be damned if he let any woman come up on his power. She would need to work for what she wanted, and she wouldn't do it on her back.

He would try tonight, but he knew he wouldn't leave her if she turned him down. And he wouldn't force the issue. She'd give herself to him in her own time, and when she did, he would make sure it was the best experience she ever had. She'd beg him to forgive her for making him wait so long.

The thought made him smile. There was no way in hell any of that would happen if he didn't start talking to her. She wasn't wrong when she accused him of being mysterious. He just wasn't sure if he was ready to tell her his secrets. On the real, it had only been a couple of weeks. Could he really tell his business to a woman he'd only known for a couple of weeks? It wasn't like they were getting married anytime soon. He didn't even want to be married.

But if he did, Isis would definitely be the type of woman who would make a good wife. He knew he had a bit of a temper, and he knew he was rough around the edges. But Isis seemed to smooth him out. Maybe what the Alkaline Trio and Ja Rule said was true: every thug did need a lady.

Maybe if he took one or two more associates on, he might be able to set himself up to remove himself from the game altogether. That could put him in the position that if he did decide to make it official with Isis, she would never have to know his business. Maybe he would take a closer look at Calvin. At least he knew how to make money, albeit in a dumb way. He guessed that was where mentorship came in.

"You gone?" Lawanda asked as they passed her. She sat at the bar, taking a quick break.

"Yeah, we out," Cain said. "It was good seeing you though. Tell ya daddy I asked about him."

"I sure will," she replied. She looked over at Isis. "It was nice meeting you."

Isis gave her a genuine smile. "Nice meeting you as well. Don't work too hard tonight."

"Girl, I'm good," Lawanda said, waving her off. "I can do this all night. The tips ain't too bad. It's just when people like his friend start actin' the ass, I be wantin' to go off."

"What friend?" Cain asked, confused. He hadn't seen anyone he normally did business with at the club. And there were very few people he called friends.

"You know, ol' boy you was talkin' to earlier. He was tryin' to get his holla on with dese corny-ass lines. He sounded crazy."

"I wasn't talkin' to nobody."

"Yeah, you was," Lawanda pressed. "Dude dat was sittin' at your table."

It didn't take long for Cain to realize that Lawanda was talking about Calvin. Knowing what Cain knew about him, he would never let his young friend anywhere near a wannabe pimp like Calvin. "That mutha—"

"Chill, Cain," Lawanda said, recognizing the anger in his eyes. "You know I handled myself."

He shook his head and tried to calm himself. "Yeah, I know you did. Good work, baby girl."

"You taught me right."

"I did see you talking to somebody when I came from the bathroom," Isis interjected. "He wasn't a friend of yours?"

"Not in this lifetime," Cain mumbled. He turned back to Lawanda. "You sure you good? I don't mind rockin' his ass to sleep if I need to."

"I promise you I'm good," she assured him. She turned to Isis. "Boo, take this man home and give him some so he can calm da hell down."

Cain noted the nervousness in Isis's laughter. It wasn't a hard laugh like he definitely wouldn't get her sex. Instead, it told him that she still wasn't sure whether she wanted to. This would be a night he would have to play by ear. It was fine, though. Calvin was so hard on his mind now that he wasn't even sure he'd be able to concentrate if the moment did happen.

"I'll see you later, Wanda," he said, guiding Isis to the door.

The scent of barbecue mingled with the warm air as they stepped outside. A small crowd had gathered next to a food truck parked half a block away from the club. The food smelled good, but he wasn't hungry.

Fate was really messing with him tonight. Cain could see Calvin and his friend leaning against a green car, directly in the direction of Cain's truck. There was no way he could avoid him, so he hoped he could ignore him. No such luck.

Isis froze, a look of horror etched on her face.

"What's wrong?" Cain asked. "I know you're not still scared of this neighborhood."

His joke hadn't made her smile. She didn't even look at him. Cain followed her gaze to Calvin, who stood less than ten feet away from them.

"Da hell wrong wit' ya woman?" Calvin asked. He threw the cigarette he was holding into the street. "Y'all all right?"

"You dirty, rapist motherfucker," Isis mumbled, her eyes never leaving Calvin's. "You stand on these streets free as a fuckin' bird while the teenage girl you raped and left on the side of the road like a piece of garbage sits home with burns and scars. What the hell are you doing here?"

"Rape?" Cain asked, confused. "Whatcha sayin'?"

"Yeah, bitch," Calvin snapped. "What the fuck you sayin'? You don't know me, and I don't know what the fuck you talkin' 'bout."

"You know what the hell I'm talking about, Peanut!" Isis shouted. "And call me a bitch again. I got ya bitch!"

Calvin looked momentarily stunned, but gathered his bearings in an instant. "Awww, you Twylite's friend. You still believe dat shit she tellin' you?"

Cain watched as Isis went crazy and Calvin antagonized her. Calvin's friend watched, not saying a word. Cain wanted to step in, but he was so shocked at this new personality that he wasn't sure what to do. Yet, he knew he had to do something. Calvin, Peanut, or whatever his name was wasn't going to keep calling his lady out of her name.

"Baby, baby, baby," he said, wrapping his arms around her waist and spinning her away.

"No, Cain, that rapist motherfucker needs to know what he put that girl through," she cried. "He needs to be under the damned jail for what he did."

It all began making sense. Isis was a rape counselor. He remembered her mentioning a Twylite a time or two, but she never gave him any details. Calvin was the one who raped her? This city was just too damned small.

"Babe, let's go," he ordered. "This ain't the way to handle this."

"Yeah, you need to listen to ya man because you can get hurt in dese streets," Calvin called after her.

Cain pointed his remote at his truck and ushered Isis toward it. A small crowd had started to form, and a few people had wandered from the food truck to check out the commotion. This type of publicity was the last thing Cain needed. It took some effort, but he managed to force Isis into the passenger side.

"Let me at him!" Isis cried. "That bastard needs to pay for what he did."

"Shhhhh." He wiped her tears and kissed her forehead. "Baby, I don't need you on the street causing a scene. Lemme handle this."

"You just don't know what he did."

"I can imagine, but you ain't gonna put him in jail by yourself. Calm down. I got dis." With that, he closed the passenger door and walked to where Calvin and his friend stood.

"Ay, man, sorry 'bout dat," Calvin said. He chuckled. "Ya girl got some issues, though."

"Sound like she got reason to," Cain said.

"Man, it ain't whatcha think. Just a li'l high school girl tryin'a be grown."

"Whatever, man," Cain replied. His face suddenly contorted with a violent anger. "But I'ma tell botha y'all like dis. You fuckin' threatin' my woman, call her anything but her name, or even muthafuckin' breathe too hard her way, I will whip your bitch ass. And dat shit goes for any female who claims she knows me. If she say my name, you better take that shit like it's da gospel."

"Hold on, na, playboy," Boe interjected. "I know you tryin'a do right by ya girl, but you ain't gon' roll up on us like dat, ya heard me? It ain't dat kinda party."

"You two insignificant-ass niggas don't know who da fuck I am, do you?" Cain seethed. "Don't make me hafta prove what the fuck I mean."

"Look, we havin' a whole damn misunderstandin' over some shit ya girl said," Calvin said. "It ain't even gotta go down like dis."

"I'ma find out what the fuck she talkin' 'bout," Cain said, backing toward his truck. "As long as the shit ain't gotta nothin' to do with my woman, we ain't got no problems. We got a understandin'?"

Neither Boe nor Calvin replied. They just stared at him as he returned to his truck. Cain could still see them staring as he looked into his rearview mirror. *Later for them.* He needed to get Isis out of there before the situation got ugly. It almost did. The steel from the Glock he snuck into his pants as he comforted Isis pressed hard into his back.

# Chapter Twenty-one

It was a typical day in New Orleans. The sun blazed, with only a slight breeze to provide a respite from the heat. Yet, Alexis didn't mind the morning heat. Living in New Orleans all her life, she'd grown used to the humidity. Spring would be there in a few short months, and it would only get hotter.

She pulled into the parking lot of her medical practice a little early, so she decided to sit back and listen to a few more minutes of the *Tom Joyner Morning Show*. The Wednesday Morning Christmas Wish caught her interest.

As she listened to Tom read the letter, her mind drifted back to a few years ago when she blessed the family of one of her patients with a home. They had been living in a FEMA trailer for nearly a year, and it had drastically affected the boy's health. The home allowed them to improve the boy's health, as well as give them a new lease on life. She still checked on them from time to time, and the boy was still her patient, although thankfully his visits had become infrequent.

"That's what it's all about," she thought, smiling. "If I could do something like that again, I'd jump at the chance."

The health fair she'd started that year still happened annually, with many repeat sponsors, including the New Orleans Saints and Zeta Phi Beta Sorority. She'd even developed such a relationship with the Zetas that she considered their invitation for membership. Unfortunately, the private practice claimed much of her time, but she vowed to talk with some members if the opportunity ever rose again. Their initiatives with prenatal care and young girls' self-esteem and education were right up her alley.

"But before I can do anything, I've got to start clearing my schedule," she said aloud, as if speaking the words would make them more true.

Jamar had told her she was doing too much. That she had become nearly worse than her cousin Brenda in taking on people's problems as her own. Yet, every time she pulled away, something else pulled her back.

Like last night's phone call from Adele Knight. She had called Alexis to ask her to look into the results from Twylite's SAFE kit. Alexis didn't know what to think about that. On one hand, she was glad that the Knight family had decided to go forward with pressing charges against Peanut. However, the other part of her wished they would just leave things alone and go on with their lives. She knew that was easy for her to say since she wasn't in the situation. Hell, she didn't know how she would react if it were her niece Elizabeth in such a situation. Actually, she did. She'd do her best to kill the bastard.

Yet, that was also easy to say because she wasn't in the situation. She'd been with her share of men, but she'd never been raped. She'd just started going to church, but her faith in no way measured up to the Knights'. She had no child, and she would never have one.

But what she did know was kids. She treated them every day, and many of them thought of her as a big sister or second mom. She knew what many of them thought before they even said anything, because of the amount of time she spent listening to them.

Twylite was no different. She had always been some-what fragile. The girl wore her emotions on her shoulder, and wasn't afraid to show it. If she was mad, she'd tell you. If she was sad, she cried. Excited? She'd become as giddy as a schoolgirl. The latter was what made Twylite most special. She was always happy, even when she was with Peanut. Although his control had dimmed her light, she still managed to spread positivity in a way not often seen in sixteen-year-olds.

Alexis could see that most when Twylite used to help around the office. She'd play with the babies while their mothers took their older siblings in to see the doctor. She'd stick around after her own appointment to clean up the toys the children had strewn around the waiting room. And when she sang, Lord! That girl could bring goose bumps with just one note.

Alexis wasn't so sure that going after Peanut would bring that joy back to her patient's life. It was painful watching her go through this ordeal to begin with. Could anyone involved handle watching her go through it again?

"It's not my decision to make," Alexis mumbled as she exited her BMW.

She strolled up to her office and unlocked the door. The darkness greeted her. Once she turned on the light, a bright, empty waiting room gave its own greeting. Ms. Kay and Lakeisha would be there in about ten minutes, just enough time to start the coffee brewing and log on to her computer.

She used to require Lakeisha to start the coffee, but soon realized her cousin didn't know a coffee bean from a lima bean. Since then, Alexis found it more cost-effective to make the coffee herself. Besides, she enjoyed the peaceful solace of having the office to herself for a few minutes. The waiting room would be jumping with kids and impatient parents soon enough.

The sound of the hot water percolating broke the silence, but added to the solace. It reminded her of how quiet the office truly was. Yet, the peace was quickly broken by the sound of a ringing bell, followed by high-pitched chatter. Her nurse and receptionist had arrived.

As if confirming Alexis's assumption, Lakeisha poked her head into Alexis's office. "Hey, cuz, just lettin' you know we're here."

"Okay, cool," Alexis said, clicking her e-mail. "That was Ms. Kay who came in with you?"

"Yeah, she pulled up about the same time I did."

Alexis nodded, an e-mail capturing her attention. "Keisha, you mind checking to see what time my first patient is coming?"

"I already know," she replied, pride emanating from her voice. "You got Hassan Young comin' in at nine, so you got a little time."

"A whole hour," Alexis said. She smiled when she noticed Ms. Kay had joined them. "That doesn't happen often. This might turn out to be a good day after all."

"Don't say that," Ms. Kay said. "Every time you do, we get three or four walk-ins."

Alexis laughed. "You're right. Let me be quiet and enjoy the moment."

She turned back to the e-mail and bit her lip. "Ms. Kay, Twylite's results are back."

"I'll let y'all talk," Lakeisha said. "You want me to pour your coffee? I see you made it already."

Alexis cocked her head back and scrunched her eyebrows in surprise.

"Don't look at me like that," the receptionist said with a laugh. "I can be nice sometimes."

Ms. Kay smiled and shook her head at the young woman. "Doctor, your cousin is a trip."

"I know," Alexis agreed. She then got serious and turned back to her computer. After clicking on the e-mail, she scanned the words in search of the important information.

"It looks like they found a good bit of Calvin's DNA," Ms. Kay said.

"Yeah, but that's not enough to prove there was a rape. It just means the sex got out of hand, like he said."

"Yeah, but looka here." Ms. Kay pointed to a line that read "genital injury." Another line read "sperm-semen-positive."

The two women looked at each other and then looked back at the screen.

"I guess it's true what they say about a rape victim being a walking, talking crime scene," Alexis said.

"I'd better call Officer Mosley," Ms. Kay said, reaching for the phone. "It looks like this rape case is back on."

Alexis could barely contain herself. She wanted so badly to call Isis right away to let her know about the development, but Ms. Kay's prophecy held true. Not only did all of her scheduled patients show up, but three walk-ins added to her caseload. By the time she was able to get into her car, it was already approaching seven in the evening.

Alexis slid into the driver's seat and set up her cell phone to speaker. She was glad Jamar had convinced her to upgrade her BMW, because talking through the car speaker was so much easier than struggling to keep her earpiece from falling out. The line rang twice as she rolled out of the parking lot.

"Hello?"

"Hey, Isis," Alexis greeted her. "How you doing today?"

"Okay, I guess."

"You guess?"

"I just had a long night and an even longer day, is all."

"Well, hopefully I can cheer you up. Are you home yet? You mind if I come over? I have some news I'd like to tell you in person."

Isis sighed. "Yeah, I'm home. You remember how to get here?"

"Girl, yes," Alexis replied with a laugh. "I've been living in this city all my life. I know New Orleans like the back of my hand. They oughta be paying me for tours."

Isis grunted. "If you say so."

Alexis scrunched her eyebrows, finally noticing the gloom in her friend's voice. "You okay?"

"Yeah, why you ask?"

"The hell you are. Just tell me about it when I get there."

Isis sucked her teeth as she threw her cell phone on the sofa. Normally she would have welcomed a visit from Alexis, but today was not the day. Her head still spun from her confrontation with Peanut two nights ago. The scene was still so fresh in her mind that she couldn't bear to go to work. Instead, she called Mrs. Delachaise and requested permission to work from home. Permission was granted, but Isis only took the time to sleep until one and then drink half a bottle of vodka. It was nearing seven, and the bottle was now empty.

She didn't know whether to be hurt, angry, frustrated, humiliated, or confused. Why was Peanut walking the street without a care in the world? When would the Knight family pursue charges against this asshole? And why did she act like a common thug in the streets when she saw him?

Was it possible that she had committed an advocate's worst possible mistake and taken Twylite's case too personally? She'd seen the videos, and Mrs. Delachaise had preached it over and over again. Advocates were not to get so involved to where they get emotionally invested in the case. Those who did could wind up taking on the stress of themselves and the survivor. They stopped thinking rationally. They couldn't sleep because their heads were filled with thoughts of how they could help their survivor and punish the offender at the same time. They wouldn't rest until the perpetrator was behind bars.

A tear stung the corner of her eye as she downed the last swallow of alcohol in her glass. She felt like a fool. Screaming in the middle of the street like a common hood rat. Cain had been supportive and had taken care of her, but she couldn't help wondering what he thought of her at this moment. She had prided herself all this time for always being so self-assured and strong around him. Now the one time she showed a moment of weakness, she went full force. She hadn't shown that type of a lack of self-control since her miscarriage years ago.

Isis didn't want Alexis to be the person on her way over. She needed it to be Cain. She needed to apologize for losing her temper the way she did, and for putting him in such a position. She needed to ask him how he even knew a person like Peanut. He didn't strike her as someone who would know such people. But then again, there were still so many secrets swirling about Cain that nothing should have surprised her.

Alas, however, she hadn't seen or heard from Cain since early Sunday morning. He'd taken her back to her apartment, helped her get into bed, and wrapped his arms around her until they both dozed off. The next morning, Isis woke up alone. She tried calling his cell, but it had gone straight to voice mail. She tried again a few times throughout the day, but received the same result. Finally, she'd given up and began seeking comfort in her liquor cabinet.

She knew she had begun drinking too much. The cabinet over the stove rivaled her grandfather's liquor cabinet, displaying a variety of champagnes, vodkas, rums, and mixers. She had some form of alcohol with every meal. She resorted to a cocktail every time she felt she couldn't think straight, yet the buzz she gained did nothing to help her thought process.

It was easy to blame moving to a city known for strong drinks and excessive partying as the reason for her increased drinking, but she honestly couldn't do that. Moving to New Orleans was only part of the problem, and it had nothing to do with drinking or partying. She'd always had a drink here or there, but the drinking got heavier and the beverages stronger shortly after Kendra was killed. It only increased once her divorce was finalized.

Little by little, alcohol became her vehicle of choice for escaping all the bad that had happened in her life. She'd grown used to the buzz, although she credited herself for never getting overly intoxicated. Unfortunately, that changed once she began seeing a younger version of herself in Twylite.

Now she drank to rid her mind of the images that caused her to be seen as the town whore. The alcohol helped her escape the mental feeling of lying with a man who she knew was only using her. Getting buzzed was the only way she could convince herself that Twylite wouldn't one day turn out like she did. Although her sober self knew how much of a stretch her thought process had taken, the high she received at least gave her temporary relief. But it wasn't just Twylite. Isis was just sad. And lonely. And scared. The only familiar friend she had was alcohol, and since the one human whom she'd grown close to had disappeared, alcohol would have to do. Either that, or go crazy as her wild thoughts consumed her.

A knock at the door startled Isis back into reality. She glanced at her watch and was surprised to see that nearly a half hour had passed since she'd spoken to Alexis. It could be no one else but her. She stood up to answer the door, but the alcohol-induced steel weight on her head nearly knocked her back down. She grabbed her head and froze, waiting for the pain to pass.

The doorbell rang, followed by another knock.

"I'm coming, Alexis," Isis called out, feeling every syllable in her head.

She knew she looked like a bad crime scene at the moment, but it was too late to fix herself up. Instead, she tried smoothing back her braids as she walked to the door. Before opening it, she straightened her clothes and tried her best to smile.

Alexis wasn't fooled. Her face scrunched as soon as she looked at her friend. "I knew your ass wasn't okay."

Isis responded with a shoulder shrug and invited her friend into the apartment. "I'm about to make some coffee. You want some?"

"Not at this time of day," Alexis replied, settling herself on the sofa. "A couple sips of that and I'll be up all night."

Isis nodded and walked into the kitchen. She really didn't want any coffee, but she didn't want Alexis to see her drinking. It was obvious that she'd already had a good bit to drink, so she didn't want to add any more fuel to the fire.

"So what did you want to tell me?" Isis asked after the coffee began brewing. The process seemed to take forever. Maybe she'd stop at Macy's and grab that Keurig that she'd seen on sale. At least she wouldn't waste any more coffee.

"Later for that," Alexis said. "I'm more concerned about you right now. Sit down and talk to me."

Isis wanted to smile, but the muscles would make her head hurt even more. Alexis's genuine concern touched her. God always seemed to bless her with good people everywhere she'd ever moved. She thanked Him that New Orleans wasn't an exception. Although she and Alexis had not grown especially close, she could see that the doctor was a good person. Maybe having her as a friend would deter Isis from drinking as much, but who knew?

She took a deep breath and explained the events that took place two nights ago. She tried downplaying the level of emotion she displayed as she tore into Peanut, but she was sure Alexis could imagine it.

"Wow," Alexis said. "I can't stand that li'l bastard."

"That's what I'm saying," Isis agreed. "He was just chillin' out as if he had no care in the world. I just don't understand what's taking the police so long to arrest his little ass."

"Well, that's the reason I came over," Alexis said, some of the excitement returning to her eyes. "The results from her SAFE kit are back."

Isis nodded. This was the news she'd hoped to hear one day. "I know you can't go into details, but does it look like there's enough evidence to get his ass?"

"Definitely," Alexis replied, balling up her fist in victory. "And they couldn't have come at a better time. Adele Knight called me yesterday and said they were ready to move forward, and wanted to know if they could use the kit as evidence. It just so happened that the results came in the day after she called me. It's like divine intervention."

Isis immediately felt guilty. Twylite had crowded her thoughts, but Isis hadn't called her client in days. The last time they'd spoken, Twylite had asked for advice, but Isis had never called to check on her. She just took for granted that since the girl was in better spirits she was doing okay. She reasoned that if Twylite hadn't called everything was going okay. It never even occurred to her to make sure that this was actually the case. Some advocate she'd turned out to be.

"How is she doing?" she asked.

"According to Adele, she's fine, although I didn't talk to her myself. She mostly concentrated on what she needed to do to press charges against Calvin."

"I should check on her," Isis said, reaching for her phone.

Alexis stopped her and laughed. "Yeah, that'll do a lot of good. Call her while you're drunk off your ass."

Even through her brown skin, Isis was sure her friend could see the blood rush to her face. "Huh?"

"Come on, Isis. I have been in this medical game for a good minute. You don't think I can tell when a person has had too much to drink? And why else would you want coffee this time of evening?"

"Lots of people drink coffee at night."

"Yeah, people at restaurants, and old people. You're neither one."

Isis hid her face with her hands and grunted. "All of this is just becoming so much. I'm still trying to adjust to this city, this case with Twylite just won't end, and now Cain has disappeared without a word."

"What do you mean, Cain's disappeared?"

"I haven't seen him since Saturday night," Isis explained. The tears streamed full force now. "He fell asleep in my bed, but when I woke up, he was gone. His phone has been off ever since."

"Has that ever happened before?"

"No. He's never gone more than a day without calling me."

Alexis pursed her lips and rubbed her friend's back. "Are you two getting serious? You've only known him a couple of weeks, and you're already this distraught over him?"

Isis rolled her eyes and shook her head. "It might seem crazy to you, but we've done a lot of talking over the past couple of weeks, and have gotten pretty close. It's still a little early say we're serious, but we do like each other. We spend a lot of time together."

"What does he do?"

Isis turned away, embarrassed. "He hasn't told me yet."

"Huh? How old is he?"

"I don't know, I guess thirty-five, thirty-six."

"Isis. Do you at least know where he lives?"

"Near the lakefront, but I don't go there because he always comes here."

"I don't give a good goddamn if he lives here, but baby girl, you are letting a virtual stranger spend all his time here," Alexis said, taking Isis's hands. "You say you've been doing all this talking, but you don't know shit about this man. How do you know he's not married with kids, or into something illegal and is using you as a hideout?"

Isis chuckled, but she knew her friend's words could have some truth to them. "How could a man spend all day and night with me if he had a family somewhere else?"

"He's not here now, is he?"

Isis looked away and bit her lip. Damn, she felt stupid right now.

"Girl, don't worry about me," Alexis said, obviously noting Isis's discomfort. "I always think the worst of people. I guess I've been with my lawyer husband for too long."

A ringing came from Alexis's purse. "Excuse me," she said, relinquishing Isis's hands to retrieve her phone. "I know that's my husband wondering where I am. I forgot to tell him I would be stopping here."

She found the phone and hit TALK. "Hey, baby."

Isis watched the easy smile that spread across Alexis's face as she spoke to her husband. She'd never met the man face to face, but she admired the glow that seemed to overtake Alexis whenever she spoke to or about her husband. Any man who could make his wife that happy without even being in the same room had to be a good man. Ashford & Simpson's "Solid" popped into her mind.

"Aw, hell no!" Alexis exclaimed. "You know I don't like him. Why does he have to come over tonight?"

Isis rose from the sofa and went into the kitchen. She'd nearly forgotten about the coffee she'd brewed. She fixed herself a cup more out of a desire to give her friend privacy than for a craving for caffeine. However, her ears perked up once she heard her name.

"Yeah, I won't be too much longer," Alexis said. "We're just sitting here talking about men."

Isis suppressed a chuckle, thankful that Alexis hadn't gone into much detail about their conversation.

"Now, if you want to invite some decent folks over for dinner, we should invite her and her friend Cain over. I don't know," she continued, her face dropping a bit. "I haven't seen him in a while, but he's tall, kind of dark skinned, dresses really nice." She looked up at Isis, and then diverted her eyes. "You think so?"

Concern crept up Isis's spine. What could Alexis's husband be telling her? She carried her coffee back into the living room and reclaimed her seat on the sofa. This was the moment she needed her own phone to ring. A call from Cain would silence the doubts that had begun forming inside her head.

"Okay, Jamar," Alexis said, her tone signaling to Isis that she was ending the call. "I'll be home in about forty-five minutes. Just tell Vernon not to drink up all our damned alcohol."

Alexis dropped her phone into her purse and looked directly at her friend. Isis took a sip of her coffee, bracing herself for what she was sure would be an unpleasant conversation. Isis looked over at her friend, who remained quiet, as if searching for the right words to say.

"Your husband okay?" Isis asked, hoping to stimulate some kind of conversation. The silence was killing her.

"He's fine," Alexis replied. "He just told me his cheatin'-ass friend is bringing his wife over for drinks tonight, so I have to pretend I didn't see him at the Perfect Fit with some ho a couple weeks ago."

"That's a tough one," Isis said. "You can't just come out and tell a woman her man is messing around on her. The messenger always loses out in that situation."

"I know, right? I like his wife, too. She's a cool lady."

"I'm sure you'll handle it well."

Alexis gave her a grateful nod and became silent once again.

"Now, it's my turn to ask what's wrong."

Alexis looked up at her friend. "Does Cain drive a black Lexus SUV?"

Isis swallowed. Her eyes grew into circles. "Yes, why?"

"Does it have spinners?"

Her mouth dried. Was the mystery about to be solved? "Yes."

"Jamar thinks he may know who he is. And now that I'm thinking of it, I may have heard his name a time or two, myself."

"Why do I get the feeling that if your husband knows who he is, this can be nothing nice?"

Alexis shook her head and stood up. "You need to get out of this apartment for a while. Why don't you freshen up and come to my place for a few? You know, watch somebody else's drama for a while?"

"I don't think so," Isis said, rubbing her eyes. "I feel better than earlier, but I'm in no shape to drive."

"Then leave your car here and ride with me. Jamar and I will bring you back home."

Isis winced. "You must really want to change the subject if you're trying that hard to convince me to be a fifth wheel."

"It's not like that. I just don't feel good leaving you by yourself. And sitting in here worrying about Cain isn't going to do any good."

Isis nodded. Under any other circumstance, she would have loved to get out and socialize. Especially with Alexis. She and her husband seemed to be well connected. However, the alcohol in her system and Alexis's haunting questions wouldn't allow her to be very good company. "Not tonight, Alexis. Now, please tell me why you're asking all these questions about Cain. I know there's more than what you're telling me."

Alexis sighed, looking back and forth as if trying to find an escape route. "Damn, why did he have to put me in this position? Okay, here it is, straight, no chaser. Cain's real name is Mathias Jackson. His nickname is short for Cocaine. He's one of the biggest dealers in New Orleans."

Isis scrunched her eyebrows and looked at her friend sideways. She couldn't possibly have heard her correctly. "Come again?"

"It's true, Isis. I used to have a couple of patients who could never pay their bills on time. Come to find out my money was going to him. I wish I had put two and two together earlier, but I never pictured anyone I know to get involved with him."

Isis dismissed her words with a wave of her hand. "That's ridiculous. You've got the wrong person. You should get your facts straight before you put people out there like that."

"Isis, Jamar is one of the top lawyers in New Orleans. He's paid to have his facts straight. If he said this, you can best believe he knows what he's talking about."

The headache made its return. Isis leaned on the kitchen counter. Her stomach felt queasy. "You need to leave now. I don't feel so well."

"I'm sorry, Isis. This wasn't easy for me either. I guess the messenger loses no matter what kind of news it is."

Isis didn't bother to acknowledge her friend. After a few tense moments, she heard the door slam.

Just like that, she was alone again.

# Chapter Twenty-two

"Disheartened" would have been putting it mildly. Twylite had been on the job search since Sunday after church. Who knew looking for an afterschool job could be so difficult?

This just wasn't the way she'd pictured it. She'd left applications at every store on Canal Street that was open on a Sunday, and had even applied as a cashier at the grocery store down the street from her house, but no one seemed even remotely interested.

After school, it seemed more of the same. She'd taken the bus directly to Metairie and combed the Lakeside Mall, filling out applications at all of the retail stores. Not even the promise of a bite.

Reality should have told her that managers rarely hired people on sight. It hadn't even occurred to Twylite that it could be days before she heard from anyone. All she knew was that she wanted a job now. It was time to make her own money, make her own decisions, and just be her own woman. Yeah, her parents would have something to say like they always did, but if she had her own money, she figured she would have a little more power over the decisions they made about her life.

But none of that would happen if no one offered her a job. She glanced at her watch as she filled out what seemed like her tenth job application. Almost seven-thirty. She'd called her mother for a ride nearly half an hour ago. This would be the last application of the night, because Adele would be there any minute.

She slurped her smoothie before signing her name to the form. Was it possible to actually be sick of writing your own name? After tonight, Twylite would have to vote yes.

After downing the last of her strawberry drink that people claimed was good for her, she rose from the small table and walked to the nearby jewelry store to return the application. The saleslady who had given her the application was busy helping a young-looking couple. They were huddled over a set of gold rings. Not the marrying kind, but the showy kind. The ones with crazy shapes like apples, music notes, and fraternity symbols.

The lady in the couple held up a ring with an indistinguishable shape. Yet, it wasn't the shape that caught Twylite's attention. It was that she was with Peanut. Twylite's stomach dropped. Maybe if she turned and left, no one would notice her.

But no such luck. The saleslady noticed just as she turned away.

"Sweetie, don't go," she called after her. "Hold tight, and I'ma be right wit' you."

Predictably, Peanut and Yasmine looked up to see who had captured their saleslady's attention. Peanut made eye contact with her, but instead of saying anything, he sucked his teeth and whispered something in Yasmine's ear. Yasmine then glared at her and backed away from the counter as if preparing to approach Twylite.

Twylite felt like a deer that had been trapped in the woods. She wanted to turn and run, but the moment held her prisoner. Should she say something? Should she ignore them? Should she stare right back?

It then hit her. This was her chance to show them both that she wasn't broken. He may have stolen her spirit, but this was the moment that she could show Peanut that he hadn't kept it. This was a new day.

Twylite returned their evil looks, and then rolled her eyes and turned away. She pretended that a set of gold necklaces had stolen her attention. Her stomach continued performing acrobatic flips, but she refused to reveal it. Instead, she said a silent prayer and allowed herself to deal with the conflicting emotions going to war inside her mind. On the outside, she displayed a pillar of strength, but on the inside, she shook like a leaf caught in the wind.

She wished like hell that Pamela had come along with her. She'd asked, but her friend had declined because she needed to get ready for a science test the next day. Twylite understood because she, herself, had a history paper she still needed to turn in. Yet, she knew she wouldn't be able to concentrate on the paper if she had put off the job search. In her mind, the two hours of sleep she'd sacrifice later would be well worth it.

At least, that was before she ran into Cruella de Vil and Jack the Ripper. Why was this woman taking so long?

"Ma'am," Twylite said to the saleslady. She held up the application. "I'm sorry to interrupt you, but I gotta meet my momma in a couple minutes. Is it okay if I just leave this by the register?"

"Yes, that's fine, baby," the lady said. "I promise you I'll give it to my manager when she gets back. She just stepped away for a few."

"Damn, bitch," Yasmine snapped, cutting her eyes at Twylite. "Just stand ya ass there and be patient. Or you wanna get outta here and spread some mora my man's business through the streets?"

"Sweetie, you gonna hafta watch ya language in here," the saleslady admonished her.

Twylite raised her eyebrows, but she didn't bother responding. She had no idea what Yasmine was talking about. She looked at Peanut for clarification, but his face only held amusement. *Both of their silly asses need mental help,* she thought as she placed the application near the register. She left the store without looking back.

Twylite had only gotten a few feet from the store when she heard a female voice call after her. She took a deep breath and threw her head up in exasperation. Her mother was sure to be outside the food court having a fit because she wasn't waiting outside. But before she could deal with her mother, she would have to deal with Yasmine.

"What, Yasmine?" she asked, turning around to face her enemy.

"First of all, you can put that fuckin' attitude in ya pocket, 'cause I ain't the one!" Yasmine said, punctuating each word with a roll of the neck.

Twylite cocked her head back in shock. What was wrong with this girl? "You talkin' to me about attitude when you just walked up on me? I didn't say shit to you a minute ago, but you keep comin' at me. What do you want?"

Yasmine glared at her and pointed directly into her face. "I'm getting' real fuckin' tired of hearing about you lyin' to everybody, tellin' folks that Peanut raped you. The shit needs to stop now."

Was she serious? The rape happened weeks ago. Why was she bringing it up now? And why would Yasmine think she had lied about it? "Why would I lie about something like that? You saw my face. I still have scars from that shit."

Yasmine sucked her teeth, visibly unmoved. "He told me about that. Just because a man beats your ass doesn't mean he raped you. Learn the difference before somebody gets hurt."

"Excuse me?"

"Yeah, he told how you shot your mouth off like I be seeing you do at school," she replied, folding her arms.

"I bet that ass beatin' shut ya ass up that time. And you gonna get another one if you keep talkin' shit."

She punctuated her last statement by stabbing the air just in front of Twylite's nose. That did it. There was no way she would continue to let this girl disrespect her in the middle of this mall. People had already begun to stare, slowing their walking pace to get a whiff of the drama. A couple of guys were even bold enough to stop and lean against the wall in anticipation of a cat fight. Yasmine looked like she was poised to not disappoint, but Twylite refused to give them the satisfaction.

"Yasmine, you've got one more time to put your boney-ass finger in my face," she said. "You might wanna shut up while you're ahead, because it's obvious you don't know what you're talking about."

"And neither does that bitch you gassed up to get all stupid with my man the other night, so you better watch yourself."

"What are you talking about? Who came up on who?"

Yasmine blinked and shifted her eyes, but refused to back down. Twylite could tell that the girl didn't have the full story. Neither did she, for that matter.

"Just watch yourself," Yasmine snapped. She walked away.

Twylite could see Peanut coming out of a clothing store. He smirked, but she couldn't tell if it was for her or Yasmine. She could picture him setting up Yasmine to look stupid. He'd nearly placed Twylite into that position before. He probably hoped they'd get into a fight. That way, she'd get beaten up, and Yasmine would look like a fool. Two for one.

Twylite turned and looked at the two guys who had stopped to watch. "Whatchall lookin' at? The show is over."

The two guys laughed. "Don't get mad at me 'cause you got handled," one of them said as they walked away.

She sucked her teeth and shook her head as she walked toward the food court. *This just isn't my day,* she thought.

Just as she thought, she could see her mother's car waiting near the curb as she exited the mall. And just as she thought, she met an angry face once she settled into the passenger seat.

"What the hell took you so long?" Adele asked. "Got me out here waitin' wit' all dese people lookin' at me crazy. Probably thought I was casin' the place."

"Ain't nobody thought that," Twylite mumbled.

"What's wrong wit' you?" Adele asked, pulling away from the curb.

"This girl from school just walked up on me talkin' about some crazy stuff," Twylite explained. "She's messin' wit' Peanut now and she doesn't believe he did what he did."

Adele's face softened, but she shook her head. "Another damn fool for love."

"Dag, Ma, I guess I was a fool too."

"Hell, you were. You just finally got sense enough to get outta that situation. She'll learn. I just hope it'll be before it's too late."

Twylite shrugged. Whether her mother's words would prove prophetic remained to be seen, but she'd been right in the past. As for right now, Twylite thought it best to avoid Yasmine. She wasn't afraid of her, but she wasn't sure how many times she could restrain herself from reaching out and touching that girl. The only thing going through her mind when Yasmine kept pointing in her face was whether the saleslady at the jewelry store could see the confrontation. The lady might think twice about talking to her manager about hiring a teenager who would bring nothing but trouble to the store.

Who was she kidding, anyway? Twylite had never seen a teenager working at a jewelry store. What did she even know about selling diamonds? What did she know about selling anything, for that matter? Maybe she would have more luck applying for a cashier job at Burger King or McDonald's. At least those places were closer to home.

Save for a random curse at a slow driver, her mother remained silent during the drive home. The silence caused Twylite's mind to drift away from the job search and back to Yasmine's rants. What was she really talking about? Who was she talking about? What bitch did she gas up? She knew she couldn't have been talking about Pamela, and no one from church even knew Yasmine or knew what Peanut looked like. He once said the church would burn down if he ever set foot in one, so she'd never had a chance to introduce him to her friends from church. Besides, even if she had, they would never approach him like that.

She pulled her phone from her jacket pocket and sent Pamela a quick text. She then scrolled through her address book, glad for the distraction from her thoughts. Isis's number came up. *There's somebody I haven't talked to in a few days,* she thought.

"Ma, you mind if I call Isis? I haven't talked to her in a while and I wanted to tell her how the job search is going."

Adele shrugged. "Go ahead."

Twylite hit SEND and held the phone to her ear. She was eager to tell her how much of an epic fail her job search at been. Maybe Isis would have some ideas for her.

After four rings Twylite frowned and settled for leaving a message. Would *anything* go right tonight?


Isis stared at the phone as it rang. It was strange how things worked. A couple of hours ago, she would have sprinted to the phone, hoping it was Cain on the other line. But after hearing Alexis's words, Cain being on the other end of the line was what she feared most.

She wanted to believe that Alexis was wrong, but what if she wasn't? In her mind, she knew that leaving him would be the only option. How could she, a sexual assault advocate who worked with the police on a daily basis, carry on a relationship—albeit platonic so far—with a drug dealer? A man who would forever duck the law? The entire idea seemed stupid.

But she couldn't help but admit that she'd grown attached to Cain. She hated that he was so mysterious, but that was part of what excited her most about him. He seemed to be able to read her mind, which made him even sexier. And when they had conversations, it was as if she'd known him forever. His easy smile and natural good looks didn't hurt, either.

Once the ringing stopped, she picked up the phone and checked the caller ID. Another wave of guilt ran through her when she saw Twylite's name appear on the screen, but it didn't overpower the disappointment she felt that it wasn't Cain.

What was wrong with her? How could she be disappointed, and not relieved, that Cain hadn't called? Hadn't she just convinced herself to avoid his call?

She sighed as the real reason for her disappointment settled in her head. She really did want Cain to call, but not so she could talk to him. If Cain had called, it would have told her that he actually cared. That he hadn't just left her high and dry in the middle of the night without a trace. That he might try to convince her that he was more than just some drug dealer.

"I guess that's not going to happen anytime soon," Isis mumbled.

She trudged to her bedroom and crawled under the covers. It occurred to her that she hadn't given much thought to ignoring Twylite's call, but she reasoned that Alexis was right about one thing—she didn't need to call her client with this much alcohol in her system. Her inebriation was wearing off, but the headache had just begun. This would be one call that she'd willingly push off until tomorrow.

# Chapter Twenty-three

Twylite waved once she saw Pamela board the bus for school. The bus was already crowded, so Pamela elbowed her way toward Twylite and stood over her. She didn't look happy.

"What's wrong?" Twylite asked.

"You ain't see the news this morning?" Pamela asked, setting her backpack at her feet.

"Girl, no. I barely got outta the house on time. What happened?"

"They found two people dead not far from my house late last night."

"What?"

"I heard about dat too," interjected the girl sitting next to Twylite. She wore a checkered skirt similar to Twylite's, but the red color indicated that she attended a different school. Probably public school. In New Orleans, all kids, whether in public or private school, were required to wear uniforms since so many kids were killed or robbed over their clothes back in the early nineties. Twylite, herself, had an older cousin who attended his graduation in a wheelchair after being shot in the process of having his Starter jacket stolen. Pamela's older brother walked home in his socks after having his Air Jordans stolen from his feet.

"What happened?" Twylite asked, looking back and forth at both girls for clarification.

"They ain't say much on the news," the girl said. "No names or nothin'. Dey just said dat the two dudes was found in Gentilly on Elysian Fields."

Twylite's stomach did a flip. Peanut lived in Gentilly, close to Elysian Fields. What if she had gotten caught up in whatever happened last night?

"One of 'em was shot in the head," Pamela added.

"Damn, that's scary," Twylite said, rubbing the nervous chill from her arms.

"This damn city," remarked the girl. "Seems like everybody went damned crazy after Katrina. I thought it would get better after Gustav blew through, but it just keeps gettin' worse. I'm moving my ass outta here as soon as I graduate."

"And do what?" Twylite challenged. She'd heard enough of this pointless preaching from her family. Why did everybody think the answer to the city's problems was to move away? All it did was make the economy tougher, keep the crooked politicians in office, and make the crime problem worse. The way she saw it, if more people did something about the problem instead of running away from it, maybe things could get better.

"I don't know but anything is better than staying in this raggedy-ass city," the girl said.

A couple of other passengers shot the girl dirty looks. Even Pamela rolled her eyes and shook her head. It made Twylite glad that everyone didn't share the girl's evil opinion of her city.

"I'm glad not everybody thinks that way," Twylite said. "My doctor came back to New Orleans after Katrina and she's done a lot to help the city."

"Well, congratulations to her, but ain't everybody like dat," the girl said. "Folks too busy trying to milk the city, and they ain't doin' nothin' to rise us up. My momma been lookin' for a job for the last year, and can't find nothin'.'"

"Maybe you could do somethin' about it," Pamela suggested.

The girl laughed as she reached for the cord to signal for her stop. "Yeah, I'll think about that."

Pamela slid in next to her friend once the girl left. "That girl was a trip."

"Yeah, but she ain't the only one who thinks like that," Twylite said.

"I know, right?"

"Makes me wanna do more. I read about people not much older than us running for political office. If they can do that, I know I could do a little something."

Pamela giggled. "You thinkin' about runnin' for office now?"

"Girl, no," Twylite replied with a laugh. "I can't even get Macy's to hire me, so how I'ma get a whole city to vote for me?"

The girls laughed again.

"But on the real, this job search thing ain't no joke," Twylite said. She reached up and pulled the cord for their stop. A few other girls dressed in similar outfits also began gathering their things to get off the bus.

"No luck last night, huh?"

"Not so far," Twylite replied, following her friend off of the bus. They trudged up the sidewalk toward Saint Francis. "You would think they'd be happy to hire some people, but I guess not."

"Hang in there. It's probably gonna take a couple days before they call you. They probably hafta check schedules, review other applications, stuff like that. I'm sure you're not the only person applying for a job."

Twylite shrugged. "I guess, but that's not the only thing I needed to tell you."

"What else is going on?"

"Yasmine," Twylite said, but it wasn't in response to her friend's question. Once they reached the school, she saw Yasmine standing near the entrance. She watched them approach and straightened as they got closer.

"What's up with her?" Pamela whispered.

"I'll tell you later."

Yasmine waited until they reached the doorway. "Twylite, can I talk to you for a minute?"

Twylite and Pamela looked at each other, both unsure where this would lead.

"Yasmine, I don't feel like fightin' with you today," Twylite said. "You said enough last night."

"Last night?" Pamela interjected. "She tried to front on you last night? Where?"

"Chill, Pam, I got this," Twylite said.

Yasmine sighed and rolled her eyes. "Look, it ain't even about all that. I just need to talk to you in private."

"Ain't first period about to start?"

Yasmine pursed her lips in frustration. "This is important. We both make straight As, so I think we can afford to miss one class."

Twylite looked into her enemy's eyes for the first time. She didn't see malice. Yasmine looked as if she really needed to talk. Maybe she wouldn't learn about Peanut the hard way after all.

"Go 'head, Pam," she told her friend. "Can you cover for me?"

"You sure?"

She nodded. The bell rang just as Pamela walked into the building.

"Let's go before somebody notices we're not going to class," Yasmine said, pulling Twylite inside. She led Twylite to the auditorium. She looked both ways to ensure none of the nuns had seen them, and then pulled her inside. They walked through the auditorium and into a nook that Twylite had never seen before.

"Yasmine, what's up? Why you actin' so crazy?" Twylite asked, her eyes darting every which way. She wasn't sure if she was about to be jumped or cursed out. Either way, she was nervous.

"Shhh!" Yasmine hissed. She took another look around and, satisfied that they were alone, faced Twylite and looked her in the eyes.

"Did Peanut really rape you?"

Twylite's face dropped, already tired of the conversation. "Come on, Yasmine. I told you I didn't wanna fight with you. Yeah, he raped me. Damn near put me in the hospital. Why would I lie about that?"

Yasmine blew out a mouthful of air and looked down. Her fists tightened, making Twylite think the girl really did want to fight. She immediately began looking for an escape route.

"I guess if he's capable of murder, he can be capable of rape," Yasmine mumbled.

"Excuse me? Murder? Yasmine, what are you talking about?"

She took another look around and leaned in close to Twylite. "I don't know why I'm tellin' you this shit, but it better not leave this fuckin' room."

"Tell me what?"

"I heard him say he did some shit last night. My ass might be next if he finds out I heard him."

Twylite's stomach did another flip as she thought about the news report Pamela had told her about earlier. Didn't she say it had happened on Elysian Fields? "Yasmine, you're scaring the shit outta me right now. I promise I won't tell anybody anything, but what are you talking about?"

Yasmine's face hardened. "Never mind. How I know I can even trust you? Your ass don't like me no way. You might be happy to see me gone."

"Because, I'm not that kind of person. I don't even like to fight. I just act like that with you because you're always startin' shit with me."

"You don't have to worry about that anymore," Yasmine mumbled, sliding down the wall until she sat on the floor. Her book bag remained on her shoulder. "I got my own problems these days."

"Yasmine, I promise I won't say anything," Twylite pleaded. "Just tell me what got you so shook."

Yasmine sighed and looked up at the girl in school whom she would have to trust to be her confidante. It was amazing how one evil man could bring two people together.

"I heard him say he killed somebody last night," she whispered.

"What?" Twylite exclaimed. "Did he see you?"

"Shut up! Shit!" Yasmine looked around again. No one seemed to have heard them, and the auditorium remained empty.

"What happened?" Twylite asked, lowering her voice. "You sure you heard him right? I ain't never seen him kill nobody."

"Well I don't think he does it in front of an audience, Twylite."

"Yeah, okay. Now what happened?"

"Well, after we saw you last night, he was supposed to take me home," Yasmine explained. She punched her book bag as she spoke. "He got a call on the way there. He pulled over and told me to step out the car so he could talk."

Twylite wasn't surprised. He'd done that to her a couple of times. He explained that he couldn't talk about his business where people could hear. It was easier for him to talk in the car with the music playing, while she waited out in the cold. She knew Yasmine was embarrassed to admit that she had complied with such an outrageous request, so she nodded in encouragement, although part of her was glad that she wasn't the only fool who went through that.

"How did you hear him if he had the music turned up?" Twylite asked.

Yasmine offered a half smile, and Twylite patted herself on the back for her moment of empathy. It was her way of saying, "I've been there."

"I guess he was really pissed off this time because he was louder than the music," she explained. "I kept my back turned to him and pretended I didn't hear anything. I didn't even look halfway at him. Just stood in the middle of the sidewalk like an asshole, but close enough to the car where I could hear without him suspectin' anything."

"I used to try to listen, but he never said anything I wanted to hear."

"I used to feel like that too, but lately he been actin' so crazy that I wanted to listen just so I could see what was up with him," Yasmine said. She punched her bag a little harder. "I hate when he be actin' like that."

Twylite nodded, but she needed to get back to the point. "What did you hear him say?"

Yasmine cut her eyes and winced. "Something about 'put his ass to sleep.' And I clearly heard him tell somebody that he needed to make a move quick before people figured out what he did."

Twylite frowned. "That doesn't mean he killed anybody."

"It does when he says, 'I can put a bullet in your ass just as easy as I did that nigga, Wayne,'" Yasmine snapped.

"Who is Wayne?"

"I don't know. I never heard him say that name before," Yasmine replied with a shrug. "But then again, the only name I ever heard him say was his friend, Boe."

Twylite nodded. "I remember him. That clown licks the ground Peanut walks on."

The girls shared a chuckle. Yasmine checked her watch. "Look, we only have about twenty minutes before the bell rings for second period, so I'm gonna make this quick."

"What?"

"I already told you this stays between us. I'm not trying to be the next one shot up. But I just wanted to say I was sorry about last night. When you left the jewelry store, Peanut told me you was goin' around talkin' all kinda shit about him, and that you bucked some woman up to front him at the club."

Twylite scrunched her eyebrows. She was just as confused as she had been the night before. What woman was he talking about? She didn't know anyone who would even think about doing something like that. "I don't know what he's talking about. I'm trying to get on with my life. Why would I want to keep bringing that night up?"

"That's what I thought," Yasmine said. "He told me he whipped your ass for gettin' smart with him, so you've been tryin'a get back at him by tellin' everybody he raped you."

"That's bullshit, Yasmine. I broke up with him two weeks before the incident happened. He came and picked me up from school one day talkin' about he wanted me back. When I told him no, I guess he figured he would take what he wanted."

Yasmine shook her head and looked away. "I don't know why I even believed him. He never forced himself on me, but he did put his hands on me a couple of times. Damn, why am I so stupid?"

"You're not stupid," Twylite assured her. "I know how Peanut is. I hated myself for a long time after what he did to me. You gonna leave him alone?"

Yasmine shook her head. "I can't. At least not right now. What if he figures out that I heard him? I was all crazy about him before, and now all of a sudden I start trippin' on him? That man's not stupid."

"I know what you're saying, but you can't keep puttin' yourself in danger. I know you didn't believe me before, but now you know he's a rapist and maybe even a murderer. You gotta get away from his ass."

"How am I supposed to do that, Twylite? I shouldn't even be talkin' to you right now. He would really whip my ass if he saw us right now. And yours too!"

"I don't know. We'll think of something. Haven't you ever gotten mad at him before? Cursed at him? Something?"

"A few times, but not since Saturday. And even then, it wasn't all that."

"Well, maybe the next time you two get into it, you can say you're done," Twylite suggested. "Or maybe tell him your momma's mad at you because you stayed out too late and now you have to leave him alone."

"I don't know if that last one will work. He'll just tell me to sneak out. He's done that before."

"Damn, that boy's MO don't change at all."

"He did the same thing to you?"

"Yep."

Yasmine grunted. "Goes to show you how special I am. I can't stand that motherfucker right now."

A few moments of uncomfortable silence settled over the girls, neither knowing what else to say. Finally, the bell rang, giving them both a respite from the tension. They each stood up, gathered their book bags, and left the auditorium, blending with the crowd. Twylite looked back before Yasmine got too far, and found that she was looking right back at her. They nodded, each vowing to pretend their life-altering conversation had never happened.

Yasmine's secret was hardest to keep from Pamela, who was relentless in her pursuit to find out what the private conversation was all about. No matter how times Twylite said it was nothing, Pamela kept at her. Finally, as they walked to the bus stop after school, she broke down and lied with as much of the truth as she possibly could.

"That silly-ass girl fronted me in front of everybody at Lakeside Mall last night," Twylite explained. "Peanut pushed her up to do it. I guess she wasn't finished tellin' me about myself today."

Pamela jumped up and down in excitement, looking around as if she was ready to fight right on the street. "Girl, why you ain't tell me? I woulda took care of her ass for you."

"Pam, girl, I told you it wasn't that serious," Twylite nearly shouted. "Leave it alone!"

The shout stopped everyone within earshot in their tracks.

"Y'all all right?" asked a classmate who had been leaning against the stop sign, reading a book.

"Apparently not if my girl is loud-talkin' me like that," Pamela replied, her eyes glued on her friend.

"I'm sorry, Pam," Twylite said. A green BMW passed. She could see Yasmine in the passenger seat with her head against the window. "I didn't even need to come at you like that. It's just been a long day dealing with my classes, the job search, and Yasmine's shit. My bad."

Pamela nodded. "It's all good."

The bus pulled in front of them, and they boarded without another word. As they rode, Twylite pulled out her cell phone. She powered it on and checked her voice messages. Most people knew she was in school, but her mother often left messages during the day if she needed to tell her something important. Sure enough, her mother had called.

"Twy, when you get out of school, meet us at Dr. Duplessis's office. She got some news for us."

Twylite looked up to see how many more stops she needed before transferring to the streetcar that would take her to Dr. Alexis Duplessis's office. It would be another few stops before she got to Canal Street. As much as she loved Alexis, she was nervous about the news she would receive. She was sure it had nothing to do with a sexually transmitted disease. Wouldn't she have received treatment for that by then? It couldn't have been pregnancy, because that test came up negative weeks ago.

*Stop thinking crazy, Twylite.* Maybe Dr. Duplessis wanted to offer her a job. Or maybe she had news on how they could put Peanut in jail for what he did. That would be good. He would be out of her and Yasmine's lives for good.

"My momma called and told me to meet her at Dr. Duplessis's office," Twylite mumbled. "Don't know what that's about."

"You want me to go with you?" Pamela offered.

Twylite smiled on the inside, but refused her friend's offer. Even when she was crabby and moody, Pamela never failed to be a friend. She wondered if Yasmine had friends like Pamela. She had cronies, but Twylite doubted how many of them could be thought of as any more than associates. And with Peanut in the picture, she knew Yasmine didn't even talk with her associates very much. Peanut had a way of demanding all of a girl's time.

The bus reached Twylite's transfer stop about ten minutes after Pamela disembarked. Twylite felt like a cow being herded to pasture, being caught in the crowd that left the bus at the popular stop. She crossed the street into the median and was happy to walk right onto her streetcar, which had pulled up stop just as she arrived.

She sat near the back of the streetcar and texted her mother that she was on the way. The rocking of the half-full streetcar was soothing. Normally it would have put her to sleep, but her worry about what Dr. Duplessis would tell her kept her awake. To calm her nerves, she began scrolling through her address book. Sue's number appeared. *That lady must think I'm crazy,* she thought as she remembered the night Isis dragged her and Pamela out of the poetry night at Loyola. *I never did call her to apologize.*

She hit TALK, expecting not to reach Sue since she was probably still in class. Twylite wasn't sure how long a school day was for a college student, but she figured at had to be longer than a high school schedule.

"Hello, whatcha got?" a woman greeted.

Twylite giggled. She loved Sue's Asian soul. "Sue?"

"Yeah, who dis?"

"It's Twylite, the girl you invited to the poetry thing awhile back?"

"Yeah, Twylite, I remember you. You doin' all right?"

"I'm fine. I was just calling to apologize for having to leave so early. I shoulda called you sooner, but I had a lot goin' on."

"I'm sure," Sue replied, her smile apparent even through the phone. "And ain't no need to apologize. I was sixteen once too. Just don't get me in no trouble while you tryin'a do your dirt."

"Dirt? But I told you we had to leave because it was an emergency."

Sue cackled with laughter. "Yeah, okay. You don't think I saw that look of fear on both y'all faces when that lady came and got you? And she wasn't lookin' too happy either."

Twylite smiled. "Yeah, you got me. But it's all cool now. You don't have to worry about me doing that again."

"That's good. So what else you been up to?"

"Just looking for a job. I told my mom I wanted to start making my own money."

"That's good. All kids should have some responsibility. I babysat when I was thirteen, and my mommy got me a regular job for my sixteenth birthday!"

"Wow, really?" Twylite asked with a laugh.

"Don't laugh," Sue said. "Because of that, I never had to worry about money. I learned how to make my money work for me at a young age. You have any luck finding something?"

"Not so far."

"I'll tell you what—I'll ask around here and see if anyone is willing to hire a sixteen-year-old girl who has no experience except for how to sneak out of the house. How's that?"

Twylite cackled in laughter. "Sue, you are crazy! But are you serious about helping me?"

"I wouldn't have said it if I wasn't serious. I got your back."

"I really appreciate that," Twylite said, a genuine smile crossing her face for the first time that day. She looked up and noticed that the streetcar was approaching her stop. "My stop's coming up, but thanks again for everything."

"You're welcome," Sue replied. "Stay in touch, and I'll let you know if anything turns up."

Things were finally starting to look up. Twylite was so happy that she almost skipped to Touro Infirmary. The elevator seemed like it took forever to come, but she wasn't bothered. Her mind was still on her conversation. She knew Sue hadn't promised her a job, but it meant something that a woman she barely knew had offered to help. That bit of good news would carry her, no matter what Dr. Duplessis told her later.

As she exited the elevator, she could already hear her mother's animated voice coming from the doctor's office. She didn't sound angry, but she wasn't happy, either. Her father's voice could also be heard, but as usual, it wasn't as loud as her mother's.

Twylite pushed the door open and peeked in. "Hey, I'm here."

"Hey, baby," Earl Knight greeted her. "I didn't think you would get here for another few minutes."

"I lucked out and didn't have to wait for the streetcar," she explained. "Why y'all didn't just come get me from school?"

"Because we were already in the area when Isis called me and asked us to meet her here," Adele Knight said.

"Isis is here? Where is she?"

"In the back with Dr. Duplessis," Earl said.

"Well, what's the news?" Twylite asked, taking a seat next to her mother.

"The results are back from the kit you took that night," Adele replied. "Dr. Duplessis already told us the details, but basically we have enough evidence to put that li'l bastard behind bars where he belongs."

"So what do we do now?" Twylite asked.

"I done already called Officer Mosley," Earl Knight announced. "He's on the way. With any luck, they'll pick him up tonight."

That was good news, but Twylite wondered if she should say anything about what Yasmine had told her. Maybe that would be extra weight for Peanut to stay in jail, and not come after either of them later.

"I'm sorry we took so long," Alexis announced, interrupting Twylite's thoughts. Isis followed close behind her, but remained silent. They each took a seat across from the Knight family. "We had to go over a few extra things."

She looked up and smiled when she saw Twylite. "Twylite. Hi! I'm glad you got here. I know your mom and daddy already filled you in."

"Yeah, they did. You really think he's gonna go to jail?"

"I sure in the hell hope so," Isis murmured.

"Whatcha say, Isis?" Twylite asked.

"Nothing."

Adele looked at Isis, scrunching her eyebrows in concern. "You okay, baby? You don't look so good."

"I'm fine, Mrs. Knight," she replied, her lie etched into her forehead. Even Twylite could see that something was wrong, but felt it wasn't her place to call her out on it. "This has just been a hell of a week."

"Tell me about it," Adele said, apparently taking Isis's words at face value. "I'm just so glad that this thing is just about over."

"We hope so," Alexis said," but if this thing goes to trial, it could last a little longer. But you know Isis will be there for you, right?"

Twylite thought the question was for her, but couldn't help wondering if it was really meant for Isis. Dr. Duplessis's eyes seemed to peer into her advocate's mind, as if they shared a secret no one else would be privy to. She nodded her head and gave the doctor a halfhearted smile so as not to seem disrespectful.

Isis knew she needed to get it together. It was obvious to everyone in the room that she would break out in tears any minute. It took every bit of strength she had to put on such a strong front, but the truth was that she really needed a drink. No one in there could understand what she went through, because no one in there had just found out that her man had been murdered.

When Alexis had called her earlier to say she needed to talk, she assumed it had to do with Twylite's case. She realized she was only half right as soon as she walked into

Alexis's office and saw her sitting with a handsome man whom she'd never seen before.

"Isis, this is my husband, Jamar," she introduced.

He stood up and shook her hand, and then offered her his seat. Isis was confused, but couldn't help noticing that the attorney was also a gentleman.

"What's going on?" she asked.

"I, um, asked Jamar to come because he has some more news about Cain that I think you should hear from him," Alexis explained. She began wringing her hands, only stopping when her husband grabbed one of them.

"It can't be any worse than him telling me the man I've been seeing for the few weeks is a drug dealer," Isis said, forcing a chuckle. It came out sounding more like a dry cough.

"I'm afraid it is," Jamar said. His voice sounded like satin to Isis, but she had a feeling that it wouldn't make whatever he had to say any easier to hear.

"Say what you have to say."

Alexis and Jamar looked at each, and then Alexis let go of her husband's hand and caressed his back. He cleared his throat and then spoke. "I got another call late this morning about Cain. You said when you woke up Saturday night, he was gone?"

"More like in the wee hours of Sunday morning, but yeah, that's right. Did you catch him in a drug bust or something?"

"It's a little worse than that," Alexis said, leaning forward. She didn't reach out to touch Isis, which she appreciated. Instead, Alexis rested her elbows on her knees and looked down, as if bearing the load she carried had exhausted her.

"I wish you two would stop beating around the bush and just tell me what's up," Isis said. "Whatever it is, y'all are taking it a whole lot worse than I will."

"Isis. Cain was killed Sunday morning," Jamar said. "He was found on Elysian Fields with two bullet wounds. My contact says he was DOA."

DOA? Isis knew it meant dead on arrival, but she never thought she would say those words again. Her friend Kendra had been DOA after being stabbed to death. Her ex-husband had been DOA after being hit by a sniper's bullet in Afghanistan. There had been no love lost between them, but still, it was someone she knew. And now, a man she'd actually begun having feelings for had been killed. Over some bullshit like drugs? What kind of world was this?

"Isis?"

Hearing Alexis's voice made Isis realize she'd been sitting there frozen with her mouth wide open. She shook herself back into reality, feeling like a fool. "What happened?"

"That's the messed-up part of it," Jamar said. "No one knows what he was doing over there because he lives in Lakeview. They just know he was found with another man, Bilal Gardner, also known as Boe. Have you ever heard that name before?"

"Never in my life," Isis replied, shaking her head.

They continued talking for a few more minutes, Isis still in shock over the news she'd heard. Everything she thought she knew about Mr. Cocaine had been a lie. Well, maybe not a lie, but a well-constructed ruse. She thought her days of choosing the wrong man had finally come to an end, but apparently they hadn't.

All those years, she chose men who only used her for her body. She thought she'd overcome that when she married Vincent, but he wound up taking his frustrations out on her, to the point where she'd lost her baby. She'd stayed single for years, only dating here and there, trying to avoid making the mistakes of her past. And now, when she thought she was ready to open herself up again, she nearly fell for a drug dealer? She sure could pick 'em!

Jamar eventually excused himself so the ladies could talk. On his way out, he kissed his wife and patted Isis on the shoulder, apologizing for having to tell her such terrible news. She kind of felt for him. Who wanted to report anything like that?

Almost immediately, Jamar stuck his head back in into the office and told the ladies that the Knight family had arrived. Alexis stood up.

"I'm going to talk to them about the SAFE results," she told her. "You just stay in here and get yourself together."

Without awaiting a response, she picked up her clipboard and walked out, shutting the door behind her. A half hour later, Alexis returned, letting her know that the Knights had decided to call the police. They'd also called Twylite and told her to come.

"Baby, you're about to have a whole office full of people asking you what's wrong if you don't straighten up your face," she had told Isis. "I know this wasn't the best news to tell you, and it's messed up that you had to find out today, but I just couldn't see letting you beat yourself up wondering where he was like you've been doing the past few days."

Isis nodded. "This whole situation is messed up. I can't even blame anybody but myself for even being involved with all this."

"How so?" Alexis asked. "How were you supposed to know what Cain was doing?"

"I should have known something," Isis retorted, trying not to raise her voice so the Knights could hear. "How can I be a help to anyone when my own judgment lacks so much? I should have seen something was up with Cain from the very beginning. Even if it wasn't illegal, he had to be married, strange, a womanizer, or something. No one who has nothing to hide could be that secretive."

"You're being a little hard on yourself, huh? It's easy to say all of that after the fact, but that's how life goes. He was a nice-looking man, you were new in town. It's not like he had been lying to you for years."

"True, but I could have held back a bit, but instead, I continued telling this man all of my business while he told me none of his."

"You think you're the only one who's ever made bad choices when it comes to men?" Alexis said, sitting next to her friend. "My bad choices are what made me barren today. I had an abortion after fuckin' around with a married man. I used to play men like I played chess, but it backfired on me. Hell, I almost ran Jamar off, but he was too damned hardheaded to get the message."

A tear finally found its way out of Isis's tear duct. "I lost a baby once too. I didn't have an abortion, but a fight with my husband caused me to lose it. I guess we both suffer from the 'what if things were different' syndrome."

"Yep, but only we have the power to change that," Alexis said. "You can either continue letting the past rule your present, or you can learn from your mistakes and move on. I got my good man by accident, but I almost let my past run him off."

"Yeah, but you got him."

"And even if I didn't, I would still be a successful doctor with her own practice, I would still be working in my community, I would still have a great family, and I would still be a good friend," Alexis corrected her. "My man didn't make me. Now, you have a girl out there right now who needs you, so you need to get it together and go there for her. Cain is dead, but he was not your man. Don't let him take your energy away from the people who need it."

The doctor's words hit home. They weren't the cure-all, but they did give Isis the strength to go out and face the Knights. Now, as she sat facing them, all she wanted was a drink. A cranberry vodka wouldn't bring Cain back, nor would it change this really messed-up situation, but it sure would make her feel better for the moment.

It was time to change her focus. Dwelling on Cain didn't solve anything. Besides, she was more than weary of the curious looks everyone kept giving her.

"Twylite, Dr. Duplessis told me you've been looking for a job," she said, forcing a smile.

"Yeah, that's what I was gonna tell y'all," Twylite said. "Y'all remember Sue, the Asian girl who went to Loyola?"

"You mean . . . uh, yeah, I remember her," Isis stammered, stopping herself from opening another can of worms. "What about her?"

"I talked to her on the phone earlier today, and she said she would ask around for me," Twylite announced. "This job search thing is harder than I thought."

"That's life, baby girl," Earl Knight remarked. "There's grown folks out here who can't find work, so I can imagine it being even harder for a teenager."

"Well, something will come up," Isis assured her. "You seem like you have the tenacity to keep trying."

"Yep," Twylite agreed.

The door opened, capturing everyone's attention.

"Well, we meet again," Officer Mosley said, walking into the office, his partner, Officer Yarbrough, right behind him.

"Yes, and this time I hope it results in an arrest, because I'm tired of seein' dat li'l boy runnin' the streets," Earl Knight said, rising from his seat. He shook hands with the officers. Alexis pulled up two folding chairs so they could all be seated.

As Alexis filled them in on the details of the SAFE kit findings, Isis's mind rolled back to the last time she'd seen Cain alive: the night she'd exploded on Peanut. There was another man there. When Cain had walked her back to the truck, he'd gone back to talk to both of them. She couldn't hear what they said, but the conversation looked like it had gotten ugly.

She wondered. It was a really big coincidence that Cain would end up dead the same night he'd gotten into an argument with a man already known to be violent. Was it possible that Peanut had killed Cain?

"Officer, do you know much about Calvin?" she asked.

"Not as much as we'd like, ma'am," Officer Yarbrough replied. "He's a two-bit drug dealer, but he doesn't deal enough for us to be concerned about him. When it comes to drugs, we try to concentrate on the big fish like one we caught a couple months ago, and the one we found dead Sunday."

Isis's stomach jumped because she knew they were talking about Cain. Should she say something? Would it matter? Were they even looking for Cain's killer?

"The one Sunday," Twylite repeated. "My friend Pamela told me she had heard about that on the news. Two guys found dead on Elysian Fields Avenue?"

"My God," Adele said, shaking her head. "What is this world coming to? I drive down Elysian Fields every day."

"Yeah, that's the one," the officer confirmed.

"I saw dat report," Earl said. "I thought they found them boys Monday night?"

"They did, but the time of death was determined to be about twenty-four hours or so before," Mosley explained.

"Shit," Isis hissed. This just kept getting worse. "Are they even looking for the killer?"

"It's not our case, so I can't really tell you what they're doing with it," Yarbrough said. "I can say that all cases are investigated to some extent."

"But they ain't gonna put too much into this one because it's just a coupl'a black thugs, right?" Earl surmised.

He hissed, but Isis could have sworn it sounded like a curse word. She could see the tension form throughout his body. He'd gotten angry all over again, and the officers' silence only confirmed his thoughts. *How tough it is to be a black man in the South,* she thought.

As Twylite listened to the grownups around her talk, her mind went back to Yasmine. She was probably with him right now. What if she couldn't keep her act up for long? What if he figured out she had overheard him? What if he really did try to kill her? Maybe if she could just speak up, they would arrest him before something bad happened.

But then again, what if she caused Yasmine to get hurt? What if Yasmine was doing just fine, and wound up getting killed because of Twylite's big mouth?

"You know," Adele said, cutting off Twylite's thoughts, "we need ta get back at da case at hand, which is puttin' dat rapist in jail. We gonna make dis happen tonight, or what?"

"Ma'am, based on the evidence we got from Dr. Duplessis, I think we have enough to get a conviction," Officer Mosley assured her. "I'm not a doctor or any kinda specialist, but what she showed me was enough to prove forcible intercourse. And personally, I don't care how rough he claim they got, the scratches and lesions she got and the amount of skin the doctor found under her nails don't come when folks are enjoying themselves. He better get him a good lawyer."

"You sho?" she asked. "'Cause dat boy done already put his new girlfriend up to confrontin' my child da otha night. I ain't about havin' all dese problems."

"What happened?" Isis asked.

"You okay?" Dr. Duplessis chimed in.

Twylite pursed her lips and shrugged. "It wasn't nothin'. I saw Peanut and Yasmine at the mall Monday when I was filling out applications. Yasmine started yellin' at me in the middle of the mall, talkin' 'bout I bucked some woman up to confront him at the club, and that I needed to stop tellin' everybody he raped me before somebody got hurt."

She caught a glimpse of Isis putting her head down and cradling it in her hands.

"Shit," Isis mumbled.

"What's wrong, ma'am?" Yarbrough asked. "You all right? You need something?"

"How small is this damned city?" she yelled in frustration.

"What happened?" Earl asked.

Dr. Duplessis sighed and shook her head. "You're not going to believe this, but the woman your little friend was talking about was Isis."

"You're the woman she was talkin' about?" Twylite asked. She wanted to laugh just picturing Isis going off at the club. That was a sight she would have paid to see. "Wow, Isis, I guess you really do care about me."

"Shut up, Twy," Adele admonished. She turned to Isis. "You tried to fight Peanut at a club? What in the world?"

Isis looked up, but kept her head in her hand. "I didn't try to fight him. My friend and I were leaving a jazz spot and I happened to see Calvin as we were leaving. I guess I let my temper get the best of me."

"When was this, ma'am?" Yarbrough asked. He tried to hide his smirk, but Twylite caught it. It made her want to laugh some more.

"Saturday," she replied.

"You might as well tell them the rest of it," Dr. Duplessis said. "This is all starting to make sense now."

"What is?" Earl asked.

"The friend Isis was with was Cain," Dr. Duplessis replied before Isis could even open her mouth.

"Damn, Alexis, can I tell my own story?" Isis snapped.

"Do your thing," Dr. Duplessis said, holding up her hands in surrender.

"Cain?" Yarbrough asked. "Mathias Jackson?"

"That's one of the subjects we found on Elysian Fields," Mosley exclaimed. "When did you last see him alive?"

"Isis, you were hangin' with a drug dealer?" Twylite asked with a bit too much excitement.

Isis sucked her teeth. "I guess we have more in common than you think."

"You ain't gotta talk to my child like dat," Adele snapped. "It ain't her fault you can't choose ya company better. She's a child. What's your damned excuse?"

"I didn't know he was a drug dealer!" Isis shouted. "And I damned sure didn't know he knew Calvin. I only met him a few weeks ago."

"But, ma'am, when did you last see him alive?" Mosley asked again.

"You think I killed him?" Isis asked, whipping her head toward the officer.

"No, ma'am, but you're the only one in this room right now who knows him, and you're the only one in here who saw him that night."

She sighed. "I yelled at Calvin, Cain dragged me to his truck, closed the door, and went back to talk to him and his friend. They looked like they got into another argument, and then Cain took me home. He stayed at my place until I fell asleep, and sometime in the middle of the night, he left. I haven't seen him since."

"That's scary," Twylite said. She scooted closer to her father, who sat still, taking in the entire situation.

Isis turned and faced them. "Mr. and Mrs. Knight, I assure you that I would never knowingly involve myself with anyone who deals drugs or does any type of illegal activity. I only recently found out what he did, and had already planned not to see him anymore, but unfortunately, he died before I could tell him that."

"It's true," Dr. Duplessis added. "My husband is an attorney, and he's the one who let us both know what Cain was into."

Earl nodded. "I believe you. I been in dis city all my life. I know how these fellas can be."

Earl's words jolted Twylite's mind back to Yasmine. In all the commotion, she'd nearly forgotten her worries about Yasmine. She might actually be in danger. She said Peanut had said something about killing somebody named Wayne. Could it have been Cain?

"Oh, my God!" Twylite exclaimed.

"What is it now?" Adele asked, throwing up her hands in exhaustion.

"Yasmine pulled me to the side this morning at school," Twylite said.

"That girl again!" Earl shouted. "Do I need to go to dat damned school?"

"She ain't even important right now," Adele said. "Let dese men go pick up dat boy."

"Listen, y'all, this is important!" Twylite pleaded. "She told me she overheard Peanut say he had killed somebody named Wayne, but I think she may have gotten the name wrong."

"Wayne?" Isis asked. "You think she said Cain? You think Calvin killed Cain?"

# Chapter Twenty-four

Peanut watched Yasmine through slit, inebriated eyes as she fixed him another Hennessy on ice. She had been mighty quiet since he picked her up from school. The sex was still on point, but the Chatty Cathy she usually was after sex had been replaced by a mute.

The attitude, now that was definitely still there. He almost welcomed her eye rolls because they at least showed some life. The more he thought of it, she had been acting different for the last couple of nights. He guessed she was still pissed off about him making her stand outside the car the other night.

He didn't know why she acted all new about the situation. She knew good and well that she was not to be in his presence while he spoke business. He kept his business to himself, and his business didn't include his girls.

Yasmine especially didn't need to hear this business. If experience served him correctly, he had less than a day before somebody figured out that he had killed Cain. Whether it was the police or some of Cain's crew, he knew his ass would be grass if he didn't move quickly.

He wished his boy Boe were still around. Boe could work a nerve like a piece of dough, but he could always help Peanut think. But no chance of that. Cain had blown his ass away without a thought.

Thinking back, nothing had gone right that weekend. Yasmine's attitude, going to that bougie-ass restaurant, that woman going crazy on him, and then Cain coming out of nowhere and causing a shootout.

What had happened anyway? He was still trying to understand. He wasn't even sure how Cain had found him. But then again, if Cain knew as much as he said about him, he guessed it wasn't hard. If he knew what he did, he knew how to find him at his favorite after-hours spot. However he found him, Cain showed up and wasted no time getting to business.

"Look, I couldn't say what I wanted to say in front my woman, but I'm tellin' you," Cain said, "I'm not tryin'a do business wit' y'all asses. I got a million-dollar operation goin' on right now, and I don't need a coupla two-bit-ass weed dealers tryin'a fuck it all up. Especially seeing how you talked to my girl. That shit ain't hap'nin', so I'ma tell you like this—stay away from me, stay away from her, and stay away from any woman who claims to be associated with me."

"Bruh, you said dat shit at the club," Boe told him. "You had to come searching us out to repeat it?"

"Look, before this shit gets outta hand, let's step outside," Peanut suggested.

The other two men obliged, and they walked outside, away from any houses and crowds so they could speak freely.

"First off, watch who you talkin' to," Cain told him once they'd walked a respectable distance. "Y'all been comin' at me wrong all night. That ain't the way you handle business, ya heard?"

"I apologized to ya at da club, playboy," Peanut said. "You ain't gotta gimme no lessons on business. And you damn sure ain't gon' stand dere and disrespect me in my own house. You lucky I let ya ass in. Now, I been doin' dis shit for a long fuckin' time, and I don't need help, potna!"

"You coulda fuckin' fooled me," Cain sneered. "You came to me beggin' to do some business wit' you."

"Mothafucka, get the fuck outta here!" Peanut shouted. "I wanted to give us both an opportunity to make some *paper in this fucked-up-ass city, but I don't need you, playboy. I can get shit done wit' or wit'outcha ass."*

*That was where everything went wrong. One thing led to another, and that thing led to all three men pulling out their guns. They all could have walked away with an understanding, but Boe, the least experienced of the three, just had to pull the damned trigger. Problem was, he missed and only succeeded in pissing off Cain, who dropped him faster than Peanut could exclaim, "Oh, shit!"*

*The shooting left the two men at a standoff with Peanut knowing that it was only a matter of seconds before he would be next. It was kill or be killed, and Cain was no joke with a gun. It must have been divine intervention that allowed Peanut to get Cain before he got him. They shot at each other at the same time, but Peanut got Cain in the chest, while Cain's bullet only grazed Peanut's arm. Another shot to the head secured Peanut's safety for the night, but how long would his luck hold out? Why couldn't Cain leave well enough alone? He must have really cared about his girl.*

That was why Peanut vowed to keep feelings out of his dealings. Business was business, but love was something separate. He didn't need love getting in the way of business. He would never put a woman he loved out on the streets, but he had no problem putting Yasmine out there. As long as she loved him and believed he loved her, she would move the world if he gave her the word.

Ever since the shooting, Peanut had been forced to keep a low profile. He shouldn't have been out Monday, but Yasmine kept yapping about him taking her shopping, so he took her to Lakeside just to shut her up. The trip actually turned out to be pretty nice until they ran into Twylite.

He knew it was stupid, but knowing the bad blood between his new girl and his old girl gave him the idea to start a little drama. He had hoped Yasmine would drop her right in the middle of the mall. It would be a small payback for all the shit Twylite had brought to his life. He'd have to settle for a little embarrassment, but the look on Twylite's face was enough to give him a good chuckle for the night.

That chuckle was only a brief respite from his problems, though. That reminder came that same night when Rick called to tell him that the police had found Boe's and Cain's bodies. Peanut was incensed. He'd asked Rick to do one thing—to get rid of the bodies, and he put them where every Tom, Dick, and Five-O could find them. He should have made good on his promise to kill his ass.

He took a sip from his drink, half wondering if Yasmine had spit in it. He couldn't put his finger on it, but something just wasn't right with her. Had she overheard his conversation? Had she caught wind of his plan to put her on the street? Whatever it was, this needed to stop now.

"What's up wit' you, girl?" he asked before taking another sip of his drink.

She lay on the bed, propped on her elbows watching 106 & Park. Without looking back at him, she mumbled, "Nothing."

"Look at me when I talk to you."

Her head whipped back, revealing a scowl. "I'ma need you to stop actin' like you my daddy. Why you always gotta talk to me like that?"

"Talk to you like what?" he asked. "Silly-ass girl. You think I don't get tired of your mouth?"

"I don't call you out your name, though."

"And you better not, either."

"Or what?" she spat, turning around fully to face him. "You gonna beat my ass like you did Twylite's? I done told you before, we are two different people."

Peanut sucked his teeth and dismissed her with a flip of his hand. "Both of you bitches are just some plain-ass hoes without me. Go 'head on wit' dat shit."

Yasmine jumped off the bed and gathered her clothes. "See, that's what ya not gon' do. I ain't Twylite, and I ain't havin' you talk to me like you crazy."

What was going on tonight? Had Yasmine lost her mind? He was used to her attitude, but this was on a whole different level. He'd seen this before . . . from Twylite. She'd gone crazy like this the night he had to put her in her place.

It looked like this would be the night he'd have to show his ass. Jay-Z was never lying when he wrote that song "99 Problems" back in the day. He had enough on his mind, and didn't need this little bitch adding to his problems.

"You can take me home, Peanut, because I don't need this," Yasmine proclaimed as she buttoned her top.

"I ain't takin' you no-fuckin'-where," he shot back. "Now sit your ass down and watch TV until I'm ready to drive you somewhere."

"Oh you don't have to drive me, because I know very well how to take the bus. RTA rides all over the city."

"I said, sit your ass down!"

He smiled at the look of indecision and fear on the girl's face. He could tell she felt as if she'd lost this battle and didn't know what to do or say next. This was the type of power he loved. She looked so defeated, sitting on the edge of his bed holding her face in her hands. Tonight, she would get no encouraging, loving words. She didn't deserve it.

"What the fuck is up wit' you tonight, Yaz?"

"I'm tired of this shit, Peanut. I wanna go home."

"You wanna go where they treat you like a baby? When you gonna start actin' like the grown woman you are? You actin' real stupid right now."

"I'm not stupid."

"Then stop actin' like it and come show me how much a woman you are," he said, leaning back. He pulled his manhood from the opening in his boxers. It wasn't hard yet, but he knew that would change in a matter of seconds. Well, minutes, since Yasmine stood there looking at him like she would be sick. "What?"

"I don't want to," she said, backing away from the bed.

"Bitch, you better come over here and suck this dick!"

"No, Peanut."

He sprang from the bed and was in Yasmine's face so quickly, it made her jump. She immediately started to cry.

"The fuck you cryin' for?" he asked. "Why all of a sudden you actin' like you scareda me?"

She replied by backing into a corner and cowering.

"The hell is goin' on? You actin' like I'm 'bout ta do somethin' to you, even though I just might the way you bein' right now," he exclaimed, pacing back and forth. And then it hit him. "You ever know me to do anything to anybody?"

"T . . . Twylite," she stammered.

"What I do to her?"

She shook her head.

"What did I do to her?" he shouted.

She screamed at his rage and covered her ears. "You told me you beat her."

He took a breath, thankful that she hadn't mentioned the rape. He still wasn't ready to admit that he'd raped that girl. For him, it was easier just to say he'd beaten her. Rape was for animals, wasn't it? "I told you why I did dat. You act right and you ain't gotta worry 'bout dat."

"I just wanna go home," she cried.

Before he could answer, a booming knock came through the door. "Calvin Cooper, open up! NOPD!"

Peanut couldn't believe his ears. He shot Yasmine an incredulous look. "Is dat why you been actin' crazy? Bitch, did you set me up?"

"No!" she screamed. "I told you to take me home. You did that, you wouldn't even be home right now."

"Naw, fuck dat," he said, punching her across the cheek.

She fell to the floor and again cowered in the corner.

"You knew I wasn't takin' you nowhere. You wanted me ta be here. I guess ya ass did hear me on da phone."

"Hear what?"

The pounding at the door continued. Peanut knew he didn't have much time before they tried to break down the door. He'd have to take care of Yasmine later. He pulled on a pair of jeans and a T-shirt.

"Get yo' ass away from da door," he ordered as he grabbed his gun from his dresser drawer. He turned toward the door. "Hold up!"

"Open the door, Cooper!" a policeman shouted.

"I oughta shoot yo' mothafuckin' ass right now for dis," he told Yasmine.

"I promise I didn't do anything," she pleaded.

He held the gun toward her, but before he could pull the trigger, the door came crashing in. There was no time, or nowhere to run. Peanut had been caught. All he could do was drop his gun as the officer had ordered and put his hands on his head. As Yasmine ran out of the house crying, the officer placed him in handcuffs.

"Calvin Cooper, you are under arrest for the rape of Twylite Knight," the officer informed him. "You have the right to remain silent—"

"Rape? I thought y'all told me y'all ain't have nothin' on me fa dat?" Peanut asked, interrupting his Miranda rights.

"Things change," the officer said as he led him out of the house. "Oh, and congratulations. You're also a suspect in the murder case of the month. You about to be a damned celebrity."

# Epilogue

It might have seemed strange, but the last sprint was usually the easiest for Isis. She was always exhausted at the end, but she loved the burst of energy she felt as she closed in on the last mile. She'd give it all she had because she knew the end was near.

Her run with Alexis and Shalonda Sunday morning reminded her a lot of the past few weeks. After Peanut's arrest, Isis spent a lot of time finding herself again. Twylite's case had taken more out of her than she'd thought, but it also helped her to learn some things about herself. She still hadn't learned to keep her emotions in check, and she might have had a drinking problem. Until she could get a handle on both issues, she requested a leave of absence from her job, which Mrs. Delachaise understood and accepted.

She spent her free time exercising and getting reacquainted with God. She'd finally taken Twylite up on her offer to visit her church, and she had to admit that it was just what she needed. The congregation knew she had been the one to help the Knights through the rape ordeal, and welcomed her with open arms.

"Dang, girl," Alexis remarked, catching up with Isis at the finish mark. "You really turned it on with that last leg. I liked that, though. There aren't too many ladies who can hang with me running."

"I can tell," Isis said, watching Shalonda bring up the rear as usual.

"Shut up, both of you, I don't want to hear it," Shalonda said, walking right past them. She stopped a few feet ahead and bent down as if out of breath.

"Don't even try it, Shalonda!" Alexis shouted, laughing at her friend.

"You two are just too funny," Isis said. "Y'all still coming to church today?"

"Of course," Alexis replied. "I wouldn't miss my girl Twylite's solo for anything."

"I'm looking forward to it, myself," Shalonda added, stretching out her calves. "The way I heard she sings, she could be a new Jennifer Hudson."

"You never know," Isis said. "I only heard her hum a couple of tunes, but I could tell she has talent. I just hope she sticks with it."

"I'm sure she will," Alexis said. "But it's almost nine-thirty, so we'd better get going if we're going to get there on time."

Isis made it to the church just before eleven. When she entered the building, she found Shalonda and her family standing in the foyer.

"Hi, you made it," Shalonda greeted her. "I wish I could say the same for my girl."

"She's not coming?"

"Oh, she's coming, but she just texted me and asked me to save her and Jamar a seat because they're running behind," Shalonda explained. "If I know my girl, I know why they're late."

Realization hit before Isis could ask why. She chuckled a little at the thought of the couple getting in a quickie before church. "I guess I can't be mad at her when she has a husband who looks like that."

An older sister overheard her statement and frowned at her.

"Oops," Isis whispered, shrugging her shoulders in embarrassment.

"Um, can we sit down before you two get us kicked out of here?" Shalonda's husband asked, placing his hands on Shalonda's shoulders.

"You heard the man," she said, smiling. Shalonda made quick introductions as they searched for a pew that would accommodate Isis as well as Shalonda, her husband, and their daughter, in addition to Alexis and Jamar.

No sooner had they gotten seated than the chords from the organ signaled for the congregation to stand as the choir marched into the sanctuary. Isis found Twylite in the procession and waved. The girl smiled and waved back, and then mouthed the words, "Where's Dr. Duplessis?"

"Late," Isis mouthed back. Once the choir passed, she took in the rest of the church. Although she'd been there a couple of times before, she still hadn't gotten over how beautiful the sanctuary was. It was complete with stained-glass windows, flowers adorning the pulpit, and a choir stand that spanned the entire width of the church. It almost reminded Isis of her old church back in Radcliff, Kentucky, where she, herself, sang in the choir. Those were the days.

She made eye contact with Earl and Adele Knight, who sat with the deacon and deaconess boards. They each gave her a friendly nod and continued clapping and singing along with the choir.

Alexis and Jamar finally slid next to her.

"Sorry we're late," she whispered. "I see we didn't miss anything yet."

"No, they just marched up on the stand," Isis replied.

The service was anything but boring. Even the announcements were interesting since the lady who read them stayed animated throughout her presentation. She even made Isis want to volunteer for a couple of projects, but she had yet to officially join the church.

Just before the sermon, the choir stood for a final selection. Both Alexis and Isis perked up when they saw Twylite walk up to the microphone.

"Praise the Lord, church," she announced.

"Praise the Lord," the congregation replied in unison.

"I know a lot of you know what I've been through the past weeks," she said. A few nodding heads and a low rumble confirmed that they had. "It wasn't easy, but I thank God for my momma and daddy, and some special friends who helped me to get through it. I asked my doctor and my advocate to be here today, and I thank them both for coming."

The congregation applauded, many members shouting, "Amen." Isis could see Adele Knight dabbing her tears as her sisters rubbed her back and shoulders.

"I'm glad she didn't ask us to stand," Alexis murmured.

"You ain't never lied," Isis whispered back. "It was bad enough standing during the welcome."

"One thing I learned through all of this was that even though it was a bad situation, God is helping me to use my story to help other girls," Twylite continued. "Nobody deserves to go through what happened to me, so I'm asking every young girl in here to learn from my mistakes. Listen to your parents. Listen to God. And trust Him when He sends someone in your life to help you."

By this time, the entire congregation was on its feet. Some applauded. Others jumped around. A few shouted, while many cried. Earl Knight paced back and forth, shouting, "Glory." It was an emotional sight, and Isis couldn't help getting teary, herself. Listening to Twylite's speech made her realize that the teenager had helped her just as much as Isis had helped her. Twylite had actually listened to her speeches, and it looked like she was applying them to her life. Now, it was time for Isis to take some of her own advice.

She glanced at Alexis and was surprised to see that she also had gotten teary-eyed. It was nice to see the strong doctor showing a bit of weakness. She'd always admired Alexis for seeming to always have it together, but their talk a few weeks ago had revealed a few cracks in the surface. Alexis was human after all, which made her more touchable in Isis's eyes. She needed that.

Once the congregation had calmed down, Twylite continued. "I'm happy to announce that the man who raped me is in jail for a very long time on rape, drug, and murder charges, and I am a stronger person. Thank you all for the support and love you gave my family. This song I'm about to sing is my testimony, and I ask you to pray with me as I lead my first song in months."

The congregation applauded and sat down once the organist began playing. The director guided the choir as they swayed back and forth, some still dabbing tears.

"'They said I wouldn't make it,'" Twylite sang, drawing many in the congregation to pop back to their feet. "'They said I wouldn't be here today. They said I'd never amount to anything.'"

Isis stood up as she heard the familiar Walter Hawkins song. It was a song she'd sung herself once upon a time.

"'Though the road has been rough, and the going's been mighty tough, I ain't goin' nowhere, I'm out here to stay,'" Twylite continued singing. As she sang the words, she grabbed the microphone and stepped away from the podium. Her hand waved as she sang, "'And I'm still holding on to His hand.'"

More of the congregation stood to their feet as the choir joined in with Twylite. To Isis, they sounded like angels on high. She felt something brush her arm, and noticed that Shalonda had also stood. Her arms waved as high as she could get them as she swayed back and forth. Once Twylite hit her final note, it was over. Women walked the aisles. Men shouted. Even the children stood and clapped.

Isis looked around as the Spirit moved throughout the sanctuary. She saw a young lady who looked to be around Twylite's age standing near the door. She wasn't shouting or moving around, but her face looked to be wet with tears. Something told Isis to go to her, although she didn't know why, or even who the girl was.

"Excuse me," Isis whispered as she squeezed past Alexis and Jamar. Once she cleared the pew, she walked straight to the young girl and hugged her. "You okay?"

"I will be," she replied, wiping her tears.

"You know, prayer works." Isis shocked herself with her words because her knees had only starting touching the ground again in the last couple of weeks. At one time, she'd felt close to God, but since her move, she'd let life get in the way. She wondered if that may have been the root of her drinking problem.

"Yeah, I know," she said.

Once she looked up, Isis saw how pretty the girl was. Much prettier than Isis had thought herself to be at that age. The girl looked like she could have the world in her hands if she wanted to.

"Are you Isis?" the girl asked.

"Uh, yes. Have we met?"

"No, but Twylite mentioned you before, and when she pointed you out earlier, I figured it was you," the girl explained. "I'm Yasmine. We go to school together."

"You're Yasmine," Isis replied with a gasp. "How are you?"

"Getting better," she said. "I wasn't hurt that bad. More scared than anything."

"I can imagine."

"My momma didn't even want me to leave the house today, but I didn't want to miss Twylite singing," Yasmine explained. "And I was also kinda hoping I could meet you."

"Me? Why?" Isis was shocked. Why would anyone want to meet her?

"Twylite told me how much a help you had been to her," she replied. "I was hoping I might be able to call you sometime to talk. It's just me and my momma, and she works a lot. I know I wasn't raped, but I could use somebody to talk to from time to time."

Isis could feel the tears returning, but willed them not to fall. She hadn't worked as an advocate in weeks. She wasn't even sure how she had helped Twylite since they didn't talk as much as they should have, but she guessed she must have done right by Twylite if she was referring her to people.

She smiled. "Do you have a cell phone with you?"

Yasmine smiled back and pulled her phone from her pocket. Once she stored Isis's number, she turned and walked out of the church. Isis stood and beheld the closed door, a new peace washing over her.

"Father, you do work in mysterious ways," she prayed. "You've saved me in so many ways these past few weeks. Thank you."

"Everything okay?" asked a voice from behind.

Isis turned and was surprised to see Alexis standing there. "I'm fine. Believe it or not, that was the famous Yasmine I was just talking to."

"Really?"

"Yep, and I believe she's going to be okay," she said. "And as for Twylite, we both already know she'll be fine. Let's sit and finish service."

The ladies crept back to their seats, and Shalonda showed them the scripture the pastor spoke from. As he spoke, Alexis leaned toward Isis and whispered, "I think we're all going to be okay."

# Author Bio

Rhonda M. Lawson is the award-winning author of five novels. She is also a master sergeant in the US Army, stationed in Belgium, where she works as an Army journalist. During her twenty-year career in the Army, she has earned awards for both commentary and feature writing, as well as Journalist of the Year and Noncommissioned Officer of the Quarter. Her career as a soldier journalist has taken her to various parts of the world, including Japan, Hawaii, Korea, Afghanistan, Iraq, and Egypt. This summer, she will embark on a new journey when the Army reassigns her to Belgium. Her work has appeared stateside in various publications, including *Soldiers Magazine,* the *Seattle Times,* and the *Army Times*. An active member of Zeta Phi Beta Sorority, Inc., Mu Theta Zeta Chapter, Rhonda holds a bachelor of arts in communication studies from the University of Maryland University College and a master's in human relations from the University of Oklahoma. Currently she is working on her doctorate in organizational leadership at Northcentral University. She is also a member of Divine Literary Publishing, and the US Army's

# Author Bio

Sergeant Audie Murphy Club. She has contributed to six different anthologies: *Second Chances, Crimes of Passion, Gumbo for the Soul, The Heart of Our Community, Surfacing, Heart of a Military Woman* and the recently released *Color of Strength: Embracing the Passion of Our Culture.* She lives in Belgium with her daughter, Beautiful Lawson.